Praise for *Definitely Thriving*

"Honest, witty, and quietly dazzling, *Definitely Thriving* is a wise, tender, and genuinely funny balm for the soul. Kerry Clare captures the absurdity and grace of everyday life with a depth of insight that makes the smallest moments shimmer. Deeply modern, yet beautifully timeless, this accomplished novel—about finding one's path and one's people—is both a comfort and a revelation."

—Marissa Stapley,
New York Times bestselling author of *Lucky*

"Here it is: the perfect choice for your next book club meeting. *Definitely Thriving* is a story about a woman who blows up her life and starts from scratch, but it's also a story about community and curiosity, about trusting your gut but also knowing when to push past your first assumptions. Kerry Clare writes with such insight, such humour, and such warmth, creating a cast of unforgettable characters who surprise each other and her readers at every turn (even up to the last sentence of the very last page). As I read this book I felt as though I were making real friends—and I laughed, out loud, a lot."

—Suzy Krause, bestselling author of
Sorry I Missed You and *I Think We've Been Here Before*

"Don't let the whimsy and hilarity fool you ... *Definitely Thriving* is a sucker punch of a book that will leave you winded and wanting to pick apart the seams of your life to test how strong they really are."

—Bianca Marais, bestselling author of
A Most Puzzling Murder

"With her signature wit and lovely prose, Kerry Clare's *Definitely Thriving* is a modern-day *Bridget Jones's Diary*. Funny, surprising, real, and impossible to put down. I just loved it!"

—Chantel Guertin, bestselling author of *It Happened One Christmas*

Definitely Thriving

Definitely Thriving

A Novel

Kerry Clare

Published in Canada in 2026 and the USA in 2026 by House of Anansi Press Inc.
houseofanansi.com

House of Anansi Press is committed to protecting our natural environment. This book is made of material from well-managed FSC®-certified forests, recycled materials, and other controlled sources.

House of Anansi Press is an eBound Digital Certified Accessible publisher. The ebook version of this book meets stringent accessibility standards and is available to readers with print disabilities.

30 29 28 27 26   1 2 3 4 5

Library and Archives Canada Cataloguing in Publication

Title: Definitely thriving : a novel / Kerry Clare.
Names: Clare, Kerry, 1979- author
Identifiers: Canadiana (print) 20250278073 | Canadiana (ebook) 20250278081 | ISBN 9781487013936 (softcover) | ISBN 9781487013943 (EPUB)
Subjects: LCGFT: Novels.
Classification: LCC PS8605.L3605 D44 2026 | DDC C813/.6—dc23

Cover and text design: Alysia Shewchuk
Cover illustrations: Melanie Lambrick

House of Anansi Press is grateful for the privilege to work on and create from the Traditional Territory of many Nations, including the Anishinabeg, the Wendat, and the Haudenosaunee, as well as the Treaty Lands of the Mississaugas of the Credit.

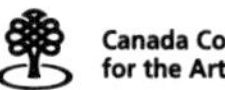

With the participation of the Government of Canada
Avec la participation du gouvernement du Canada | Canada

We acknowledge for their financial support of our publishing program the Canada Council for the Arts, the Ontario Arts Council, and the Government of Canada.

Printed and bound in Canada

This novel is dedicated to the people
in my neighbourhood

One

A nun's cell: this is what Clemence had been expecting. She'd signed the lease on the basis of blurry photos with resolution so low it was hard to make out the details. A studio flat with a meagre kitchen comprising a mini fridge and a hot plate all at the top of a tumbling-down house off Roncesvalles Avenue in a neighbourhood described as "in transition." She'd have her own bathroom, at least, though the bathtub had no shower, but she has visions of washing her hair in that tub, pouring tepid water over her head from a chipped ceramic jug. She even has the jug, one of the few things she has brought with along from her old life, packed in a box in her best friend Jillian's cherry-red Audi SUV.

Jillian's car is parked down on the street, and Clemence can see it from the window, that one small window she'd noted when she'd first seen the ad. Mostly insufficient for natural light, not to mention ventilation. Because why live in an attic that wasn't fusty and stale? It's the spirit of the thing, and Clemence has become intent upon spirit, intent upon making deliberate and meaningful choices, coming—as she is—off the tail end of nearly a decade during which little meant much or was deliberate at all.

But the balcony—Clemence had not been forewarned. The ad had given no hint, and the photos must have been taken at the worst time of day, conveying nothing of how the room would be filled with light filtered through French doors, the white walls adorned with prism rainbows, and how the balcony itself was tucked into the ripe boughs of a maple.

"It feels like a treehouse," says Jillian, who'd been put off by the squalor at first, but is starting to come around. "You'll be living in a treehouse." And Clemence considers this, its precedent, as her heart sinks. The Berenstain Bears, and Swiss Family Robinson. No, a treehouse isn't in keeping with the spirit of the thing at all. This attic is far from the one she had in mind, and perhaps it's not too late to flag the mistake, to turn around and run.

But where would Clemence go? She has been staying in the spare room at her friend Naomi's condo in Liberty Village, but Naomi's parents are flying in from Japan tonight. And Naomi is the only person Clemence knows in the city with a spare room, because most people's apartments and condos are too small for such things, and everyone who owns an actual house has filled their extra rooms with children.

Which is why it had been so hard to find the listing in the first place. A basic furnished room, Clemence had supposed, quite naively, would be easy to come by. She wasn't asking for much, certainly for nothing like luxury or comfort. But it turned out that all these big, old houses—places where, decades before, working men and maiden aunts were able to make their lives in modest rented rooms—were being converted back into single-family dwellings. On this very street, three houses each feature a dumpster out front, evidence of this societal shift occurring before her eyes. And Clemence wonders how long this house will remain a holdout—Mrs. Yeung, the landlady, could easily sell and pocket two million, or maybe less because the place needs work, but the building has good bones. Clemence can feel it. The maple tree outside is swaying in the breeze, but the house is solid, as it has been for well over a century.

"I thought you were a man," Mrs. Yeung had declared upon greeting Clemence on the porch that afternoon. "Your name. It's a man's name." She said, "I don't usually rent rooms to women. Too much drama."

And this is another reason why Clemence has to stay, why she isn't going to flee down the stairs and out the door, away from the balcony and all that gorgeous light, not a ray of which she deserves. Clemence doesn't want to live up to Mrs. Yeung's worst expectations. The spirit of the thing also is to prove—to her landlady, to everyone—that she is not like all those other female characters, that she herself is a sensible person. *Becoming*, finally, is the point of this exercise.

Jillian is walking around now, peering at the nearly right angle where the wall and ceiling meet. "It's really not so bad," she says. The whole way up the stairs, they'd been overwhelmed by the smell of other people's meals, mixed with the cloying scent of lemon cleaner. "It's not bad at all."

"I know," says Clemence, disappointed.

And Jillian hears it in her tone, turns her attention back to her friend, comes over to put an arm around her shoulders. They stare out the French doors together, out to where the tree is lush and verdant in all its June glory. "I don't understand why you're punishing yourself," Jillian tells her. "You have nothing to be sorry for."

Clemence says, "Well, a little bit." She doesn't want to be pandered to. She needs to know that she's strong enough to take it.

"Yeah, okay," Jillian says. "But don't drag it out forever. You don't need to be a martyr, I mean. How does that help anyone?"

"I'm not a martyr," says Clemence. "It's more like a shift, a journey. I'm thinking of it as research."

"For, like, *My Year of Living Grimly?*"

Clemence says, "I'm going to have to think of a better title, but I've certainly got time."

SIX WEEKS HAVE PASSED since Clemence's marriage exploded, or, more accurately, since Clemence exploded her marriage, accidentally on purpose, by being discovered by her husband, Toad, in bed with Larry and Lisa, the couple next door with a fondness for tanning beds and leopard print. And afterward, a normal person, a good person, would have been able to explain to Toad that it had been a mistake, a one-time thing, except it had been happening for months. Clemence had even orchestrated Toad's discovery, timing it right down to the minute she knew she'd hear his key in the door. A good person, afterward, would also have been able to promise her husband, "It's not you, it's me." To tell him she'd just been looking for something different, something to spice up their lukewarm love life ... except Toad was the problem in its entirety. Clemence hadn't even liked being in bed with Larry and Lisa, which in its physicality was basically overwhelming and confusing, like having sex with an octopus, but sex with Toad was so much worse.

And maybe she had always known. This is the part she feels guiltiest about. Clemence still remembers the first time she'd gone out with Toad, walking down the street, arm in arm, listening to his grating voice, and thinking, *At some point I'm going to have to find a way to get out of this.* But she never did, because it was easier not to, because their bodies fit, because Toad was tall enough for her to lay her head against his chest when he wrapped his arms around her, and she'd listen to his heartbeat, her fondness for its solid consistency more than making up for the fact that he never made hers leap at all. Or so she thought. She hoped.

Clemence wrote for wedding magazines, and being one half of a couple had been the goal for as long as she could remember, and maybe this could be enough to build a life upon—certainly others had done more with less—and Clemence crossed her fingers and kept hoping as things progressed, as she moved into his place, and they got married, and bought a house, the years adding up. Through all of this, Clemence feeling as though she was playing a part, and she wondered if maybe everyone felt like this in love, but nobody had the nerve to admit it.

Everything changed on that evening last July, almost a year ago now, when Toad arrived home after work, the slam of the door and slap, one, two, of his shoes hitting the wall as he shook them off, the same sounds he brought home every single day. And Clemence did what she always did, which was brace herself to be in his presence—Toad was petty, boring, and small-minded, but so benignly that she couldn't even be mad about it—and then she realized that she would be listening for these sounds and bracing for the rest of her life. Which could turn out to be a long time, if she was lucky, something she hadn't properly understood when she got married at age twenty-five, a point up to which she'd basically been measuring time in four-year increments. Getting married had simply been the next step, and it would have been unnatural to resist her life unfolding in that direction, to not go with the flow.

But the flow was untenable, she'd finally realized, and now how was she supposed to bring that to Toad's attention? He really had no idea. Toad had spent their marriage quite sure that everybody's wife was periodically reticent and hostile; supposing it went with the territory, which meant he permitted Clemence her space, and she liked it that way, or so she thought—until she started actually fighting with him and he didn't notice.

"Do you realize that I haven't said a word to you in three days?" she asked him one evening, finally cracking under the strain. He didn't see her. He never listened to her. Sometimes she'd look for her reflection in the mirror just to confirm that she existed.

"I thought it seemed quiet," Toad answered, not looking up from his phone.

It was in September, however, after the publishing conglomerate Clemence had worked for her entire career went bust and she was laid off and started hanging around the house all day, that things started getting out of hand. The weather was still warm, and she'd see Larry and Lisa having breakfast on their little back deck just over the railing from hers, kind as ever, their oiled skin like leather. Soon they'd invited her to join them, have their coffees all together, for a soak in their hot tub, one thing leading to another, and Clemence had been so bored and desperate for something to happen, for any excuse not to keep travelling down the same road forever that she'd gone off course, veering straight into Larry and Lisa's jungle.

Those months had been a strange, unreal time, and she'd felt as though she were someone else altogether, watching it all from outside of her body. Like she was a character in a book, and she kept turning the pages to see what happened next, everything leading to the inevitable climax, to the day Toad would come home to find her in their bed with the neighbours, because there would be no going back after that.

But when it finally happened, there had been no relief, because Toad was so devastated, which she'd not anticipated. And it was infuriating, too—that she'd had to go this far to move him, to actually get through to him. He'd started crying, which knocked Larry and Lisa right off their game, though they'd quickly pulled it together, asking him to join them, but Toad had already collapsed into the fetal position—*so* not sexy. They'd gathered their loincloths and tiptoed out around the heap of Toad in the bedroom doorway, still weeping. Wailing that he hadn't seen it coming, that this might possibly destroy him. Though maybe, he supposed—he was moving through all the emotions, and here he'd found hope—they might be able to salvage things. Toad paused to snort, and then suggested they go back to counselling, or take a holiday. Maybe the whole throuple deal, he said, was something Clemence needed to get out of her system, and could be something they'd pursue together. Toad was willing to be adventurous. He could change. Do whatever it took to get them out of this rut. He would do it, he said.

So Toad loved her! He really loved her! And he was even willing to fight for her—but it was so far from enough.

Clemence told him straight. "I think it's *us* that I need to get out of my system." They were over, they should've never even started, and she was most disappointed in herself for dragging Toad into this life in the first place when she'd never been properly invested. Could she learn to trust herself and follow her instincts after having steered her life so wrong?

• • •

"BUT THE PROBLEM," Jillian reminds Clemence now in the treehouse flat with all that golden light, "is that you never followed your instincts in the first place. Instead, you ignored the red flags and your feelings, trying to convince yourself that the story you were living was true."

They are sitting among the boxes they'd just hauled up the stairs, and they're both sweating. Clemence knows she owes Jillian big time because the stairs are steep, and the boxes heavy and awkward—bits and pieces of crockery, piles of shoes, sheets and towels salvaged from her parents' place. The basics, she'd thought, having left almost everything with Toad, but this isn't minimalism because the apartment is cluttered already, and Clemence hasn't started unpacking.

"What I want," she tells Jillian, not for the first time, "is a reset." She gets up for another glass of water, letting the tap run so the water gets cold. There is a partially filled ice cube tray in the freezer compartment of her mini fridge, but the idea of somebody else's ice is disgusting. The apartment is clean enough at first glance, but the fridge needs to be wiped down. "A *tabula rasa*," she says, refilling her glass and then Jillian's. They are parched. She'd offered to take Jillian out for a drink, but Jillian has no time for that. She's helped Clemence move, and now she needs to get back to work, and then go home to her family.

"Kind of makes me feel young again, though," says Jillian, holding the glass against her sweaty forehead. "I can't remember the last time I helped somebody move."

Everybody else their age has the capacity to hire movers, and even packers.

"Too bad we'll feel ninety-seven tomorrow," says Clemence.

"So many stairs," Jillian admits.

Clemence says, "I owe you."

"You really do." Jillian puts down her glass and looks around. "It *is* a cozy flat, you know. A bit like Bridget Jones's. The kind of place where you'd end up running outside to kiss Mark Darcy in your underwear. You better watch out for that."

And Clemence says, "God forbid." No, there would be no such humiliations here in her new life, no snogging in the street. Her intention is to begin a very different kind of story, one that doesn't end with a wedding. She desires to become one of those excellent women that Barbara Pym wrote about in her mid-century novels, helping out at church bazaars, fortified with a nice mug of Ovaltine. A woman of substance, of character, who isn't defined by her relationship to a man. Because Clemence is finished with recklessness, and impulsiveness. *Clemence Lathbury*, she longs to have people start thinking. *She's such a stalwart.* An actual noun. And she's going to start with her new landlady, Mrs. Yeung, and become the kind of woman that people can count on. "My Bridget Jones years," she tells Jillian, "are behind me."

"But isn't that what you said when you got married?" The closest Jillian will come to saying I told you so. Such disloyalty is cancelled out by the boxes she carried up the stairs, so Clemence lets her have it.

She walks Jillian downstairs and they linger on the porch.

Jillian says, "You're really okay?" Everybody is worried about Clemence. Nobody has been convinced by Clemence's act of keeping it together, if all this is just an act. Is it? Clemence can't even convince herself.

But she promises her friend, "I've never been better." And this she means. For the first time in her life, Clemence is free to chart her own course, and she still doesn't know where she's going, but she doesn't have to have it all figured out just yet.

She's about to offer Jillian one more metaphorical bouquet of gratitude for her help this afternoon, with a promise to pay her back with babysitting, or she'll bake her a cake ... until Clemence remembers she no longer has an oven. And then the front door opens behind them, and Clemence and Jillian turn around, taking in an impressive pair of biceps attached to a beautiful dark-haired man who looks surprised to find them there. Until he figures it out. "You're the woman in the attic," he says.

"Um, the *mad*woman," says Clemence, unable to resist, and Jillian punches her in the arm.

"Well, I'm Edward Rochester," says the guy.

Clemence says "Really?"

He looks disappointed. He'd thought they had a rapport. He says, "No. I'm Charles. This is my mom's place, and she's not happy with you."

"There's been a misunderstanding," Clemence tells him.

"And it's too late to do anything about it now," Jillian has her lawyer's voice on. "The lease is signed. She can't discriminate. If your mother was looking for a male tenant, she should have specified."

"She usually doesn't have to," says Charles. "One look at the place, and that's enough. Most women tend toward, um, a different aesthetic."

"Well, I guess I'm not most women, then," says Clemence, determined to stand her ground, to not be dazzled by this Charles just because he happens to be handsome, but Jillian is punching her again—what? "And I signed the lease sight unseen. I was out of town and needed something fast."

"So you're desperate," says Charles.

"No, I'm just not choosy," Clemence corrects him. "When it comes to an apartment, I mean," she adds, speaking too fast, once she realizes how bad this sounds. "Your mother let me use an online signature. She didn't even ask."

"Well, I hope you know what you're getting into," says Charles, pulling the door shut behind him. "This house isn't very fancy." A screen falls off the window behind him, as if for emphasis.

"That part," says Jillian, "is obvious."

"And I'm not looking for fancy, anyway," adds Clemence.

Jillian says, "She really isn't. She's devoting herself to living austerely, to writing her own story. Becoming like a character out of a book."

"But not *Jane Eyre*," says Charles, who is proving more literate than his biceps suggested at first sight.

"More like *Eat, Pray, Love*," says Jillian.

"But without the love," Clemence insists. "Just *Eat and Pray*."

"Pray," Charles repeats, gesturing toward the steeple above the treetops at the end of the block. "So you're a churchgoer. My mom might come around to you after all."

"A churchgoer," says Clemence, trying out the words. She really wants this living arrangement to work. "Well, I mean, it's possible." An awkward silence hangs in the air, especially because what Clemence has just said is a lie.

"Well. I guess I'll be seeing you around..." Charles says, his voice trailing off as he starts walking away, down the steps to the sidewalk.

"Clemence!" Jillian's shrieking after him as they watch him go. "Her name is *Clemence*."

And now Clemence is doing the punching. "What are you doing?" she hiss-pers.

"He totally likes you," says Jillian, way too loud, perhaps the reason that Charles is looking back over his shoulder, offering a smile and a wave.

"He totally doesn't. And even if he did, it wouldn't matter."

"Oh, you're going to be fighting them off," says Jillian. "There is nothing more irresistible than a woman who's unavailable. Just you wait."

UNFORTUNATELY, JILLIAN IS USUALLY correct about most things. For example, Clemence observes, surveying her surroundings once she's back upstairs, her new place really does have a certain charm, in spite of the dinginess, because the light through the doors acts like a filter that softens everything, making it easy to ignore the stains on the wall from where the roof leaked, or to notice that the kitchen is makeshift to the point of depressing. The furnishings, at least, are definitively hideous—one saving grace. The armchair reupholstered with mismatched prints, the particle-board coffee table missing a chunk on one side. The daybed, which would be her bed and sofa at once, was probably pretty once upon a time, a young girl's princess dream, but the spindles are tarnished now, the mattress lumpy, uncomfortable.

"You're sure you're going to be able to sleep on this?" Jillian had asked.

But the effort to do so would be the point. In her new life, Clemence will learn to adapt and make do, and to not succumb to her every urge or desire. She will learn that she is stronger and more resilient than she thinks, more than everybody thinks, proving that she is tough and has grit. That she has *character*, unlike the sort of woman who wimps her way through seven years of marriage and then ends it all in a most craven act of betrayal.

She'd heard it in the sound of his voice. "I just don't understand," Toad kept repeating, unbearably. It took so long for his shock to wear off. He was like a zombie for days. "You knew I would be coming home. I come at the same time every single day."

"But I was just so sick of hiding," said Clemence. And waiting. It had been the only way she could think of to light the fuse.

"You should have said something," said Toad, for the six hundredth time. "We could have found a way to kick things up a notch. *Together.*"

"But you wouldn't have been listening if I did," said Clemence. "And I think that I was . . . already gone." *Maybe I was never here*, but she wasn't so cruel as to say that. And why is it only after she's hurt Toad that she feels any tenderness toward him? No one can build a relationship on that, though certainly, she's tried.

But now it's over. And perhaps what she'd always suspected isn't even true, that everybody in love has those same doubts, that everybody is simply going through the motions. What if "going through the motions" isn't life at all? Because hers hadn't been a life, instead, an illusion. Clemence had created the kind of life you might order out of a catalogue, and it had proved, in the end, as two-dimensional as that.

What will happen now, she wonders, in her new life, one that's less a catalogue than a yard sale, or one of Barbara Pym's jumble sales, constructed of odds and ends, other people's discards? Clemence would never have selected any of these items, or this room in which she finds herself, but this is the point. Mild depravity and lumpy beds—could this be the road to excellent womanhood?

Two

Clemence Lathbury has never lived alone. Born the second of three virtuous daughters, bookended by Prudence and Grace, Clemence grew up comfortable and happy enough in the bosom of family. Her parents had celebrated their fortieth wedding anniversary the summer before, Clemence and Toad flying across the country to be there, posing for gorgeous family photos that are now out of date because Toad no longer belongs to them. Roger and Bonnie Lathbury are the type of people who make a good marriage seem easy, so in sync without even trying. They even look alike, and dress alike, sometimes, mostly for tennis, which is their favourite game, and they're a perfect pair. They met in high school and have never dated anybody else; neither of them have even kissed anybody else, if Bonnie's stories are true. And Clemence had grown up taking for granted that she'd find her way into a similar situation, that she would find her other half, and he'd call her his "better half," and while he'd not altogether be joking, really, they would be equals, partners in every way.

And when she met Toad, it had seemed like the threads of her life were unspooling, just as she'd imagined they would, into the same tapestries her mother had woven, and her mother before her. As they'd been woven for her sister Prudence, mother of four, and as they also would for Grace, who'd come out as a lesbian in high school, creating a bit of a hullabaloo, but everything settled down and she'd been married the summer after Clemence, clearly making a more successful run of it.

So no, independence was not celebrated among the many Lathbury virtues. After completing her media studies degree, Clemence moved straight from the student house she'd shared with Jillian and Naomi into Toad's condo—three years older, he had his own place already—and nobody raised an eyebrow. Not long after, she would follow him across the continent to Seattle, where he'd located for a new job, and settling down this way was as much an accomplishment as landing a dream job of her own, which she had also done about the same time, writing features for one of the more prestigious American bridal magazines. Magazines' online platforms still held some possibility then, and personal narratives were setting the internet on fire, which timed perfectly with Clemence and Toad's engagement, so she'd pitched a blog series—*My Journey to "I Do"*—that readers were wild about, whether they considered Clemence a bridezilla (she learned not to read the comments) or had bought into her fairy-tale fantasy. Clemence was something of a starlet in those corners of the online world obsessed with layer cakes and tulle.

Her marriage at least, Clemence thinks, had been good for her professionally. Toad didn't mind the attention, plus the wedding had cost them nothing, the entire event an advertisement for an array of vendors, from the picturesque vineyard venue near the Niagara Escarpment to the photographer who'd transformed picturesque-ness into actual prints. The whole thing such a deal that they'd been able to blow a small fortune on a honeymoon in Tahiti—and they'd even found an airline to comp their flights.

The honeymoon had been where the comedown began, however. Clemence had supposed that marriage, the fact of the ring on her finger, would have solidified her bond with Toad, creating an effortless connection like her parents', a spark that would enliven them both, but, sitting across from Toad at a bar on the beach, sipping fancy cocktails, and with all the wedding planning over, she realized that they'd run out of conversation and there was nothing between them at all. Toad had never felt so far away, the gulf only stretching wider as the years went by.

And here she is now in a place where Toad doesn't factor. Finally, a room of her own. The sun is beginning to set, the day's radiance retreating, which makes the apartment less charming, but Clemence likes it that way. Because she is tired of charm, and charms, and Prince Charming, or the idea of such a thing, all of which have managed to lead her astray. Clemence wants to see things for what they are, to connect with solidity, with reality, and items that don't disappear at midnight, transformed back into pumpkins and mice.

Although it's still early for that. Late for dinner, though, and Clemence is hungry. Heading out, locking her own door behind her for the very first time, feeling the weight of that key in her pocket as she heads back downstairs, breathing in the curious odours of other people's lives, that blend of lemon cleanser and fried onions. Are the men who live here cooking on their hot plates all day? This seems unlikely from what Clemence knows of men, and hot plates. She pauses halfway down to the ground floor and listens—it's so quiet. Who would her neighbours turn out to be? Did Charles live here with his mother? What a thing to have moved into a house full of men, absolutely an accident, happy or otherwise.

It is a short walk to the main street, with the church on the corner, a small independent grocery store across the road. The neighbourhood has been improving, as the lawn dumpsters would suggest, and now there is also a cheese shop and a boulangerie among the payday loan shops and dollar stores. But Clemence knows if she starts frequenting the more fashionable establishments, she'll be out of money in a matter of weeks. She's been living off her severance, and she has to make it stretch, and so it's the plain old corner grocery store she heads for in search of something simple, the bell on the door jangling pleasantly as she steps inside.

Clemence recognizes immediately that the woman behind the counter is one of the excellent women of her aspirations. The woman is wearing tweed, along with a sour expression, and no doubt she's been sitting behind the counter since midway through the previous century. Surely she lives above the shop with her cat. All the staunch and silent lives, Clemence thinks, of these women living among us unnoticed. And yet without such women, from whom would we buy our tinned fish?

Clemence likes the idea of tinned fish, ever sensible. Economical and rich with protein, a most substantial essence. Everything in this store is dusty, but tinned fish are as such that they're likely still in their prime in such a condition, and Clemence particularly loves the keys on the top of the sardine cans, the satisfying way the lids peel off and curl up on themselves. It's a good choice for a woman who has just moved into her new apartment and is pretty sure she failed to pack a can opener when she fled her marital home.

Clemence and Toad had their groceries delivered. They must have made a list once and then the groceries kept coming, an algorithm making adjustments based on the season and availability so she never had to think about it. They didn't cook much, anyway, both of them busy with their jobs and usually arriving home late for dinner, so there was always too much in the fridge, a veritable bounty. Clemence was perpetually scrambling to find ways to work overripe produce into salads and shakes. Thinking now about the decadence of mangoes and kumquats, all the avocados she'd discarded for being too soft. There were infinite varieties of lettuce these days, but you'd never think so here in this corner grocery store's modest produce section, a head of sad iceberg brown at the edges.

Clemence selects some apples, breaks off a couple of bananas from a bunch, and reflects on all the bananas she'd left behind in the chest freezer, possibly hundreds, gone too brown on the counter and saved for a banana loaf to be baked in a far-off future that would never arrive. What would Toad think when he discovered these? Another mark against her, along with the sexual deviancy. ("There are some husbands who might have been pleased to discover what he did," her friend Naomi had remarked, but Toad wasn't one of them. If he had been, Clemence would have had a different kind of marriage.)

She decides she will venture into the boulangerie for a baguette because the loaves on the grocery shelf are already a week past their best-before. She picks out a carton of milk, a bag of oatmeal, resisting the urge for mixings—brown sugar or even raisins—because Clemence longs to develop an appetite for plain tastes. Adds cans of tuna and chicken, a jar of mayonnaise because she's not as plain as all that, and a brick of cheddar. What more does a woman need? Digestive biscuits, she decides as she spies them, dipped on one side in dark chocolate. She is obsessed with the concept of digestive biscuits, as though they were medicinal somehow. Good for gut health, entirely sensible.

She brings her armful to the counter and drops it before the woman waiting there who hasn't moved since Clemence jangled into the shop. Close up, the hair on the woman's head is sparse and fine, like chicken fluff, which reminds her—

"Just wait," Clemence calls back, speeding to the fridge, grabbing a carton of eggs, returning back to the counter where the woman remains a statue, strange. Clemence sets the eggs down with the rest of her things, and says to the woman, "That's all."

The woman regarding her finally. "But is it really?"

"I think so?" Clemence says, beginning to realize that she's missing something here.

"Because of course," the woman continues, "I'm here all day. Standing here waiting for you to add one more thing, and then another thing. I've got nothing better to do than wait for you to be satisfied, same with everybody who's in the line behind you."

Clemence turns around, but nobody is there.

"Oh, so there *is* something more," says the woman in a cutting tone, making Clemence feel small. She wants to run. She wants to hide, but she is also hungry, with her heart set on a supper of sardines on toast, and if they even sell sardines at the dollar store, they're likely to be off-brand and sold without the key.

So Clemence says, "No, that's all," annoyed at herself for having assumed a kinship with this miserable woman. That she'd felt benevolent supporting a small store stuck in a time warp, and no wonder the store is empty if this is what passes for customer service.

The woman begins packing the groceries in a flimsy plastic bag, ignoring Clemence's protests that she's brought her own cloth sack. And of course, this store doesn't take cards, cash only, but there's an ATM in the back whose withdrawals come with a five-dollar convenience fee. The plastic bag splits at the seams as soon Clemence picks it up off the counter.

She exits in relief when the whole thing is over, the shopkeeper's chimes seeming a sinister tone now as the door slams behind her. And outside on the street there are more chimes, these ones rich and sonorous, as the bells at the church across the road sound in response to the hour. *Six o' clock, but they don't toll for me*, Clemence thinks, the joyous peals lifting her spirits again after the disappointment of the shop as she transfers her bundle of groceries from the tattered plastic bag to her cloth one. A murmuration of butterflies lifts in her stomach, such lightness. She can do this. Because Clemence lives outside the rules now, the rituals and the hours, and there's a freedom in that, to do whatever she likes and whenever it suits her. *Oranges and lemons*, goes the song in her head, the one that people use to sing to her because of her name, a cheerful tune, though it was years before she learned the unfortunate ending: "Here comes a candle to light you to bed / And here comes a chopper to chop off your head."

But now the boulangerie is shut, the sign on the door being flipped to *Closed* as she's standing there. Clemence has no cause to complain—the hour has gone, and she heard the bells to prove it, but here is the thing, and she decides to channel the nerve of the miserable woman in tweed at the grocery store counter, to use it instead of letting it destroy her. Raising her hand to rap on the glass, summoning a tired-looking baker at the end of a very long day.

"All I need is a baguette," explains Clemence. "Could I possibly . . . ?"

"We're closed," says the baker, who no doubt deals with these disturbances every evening. Which would have been the signal for retreat in Clemence's previous life, where she'd adhered to rules and guidelines, deferring to politeness, caring deeply about what other people thought of her, as though such opinions would be what constitutes one's self, instead the actual fibre of her being.

"But you have baguettes left," Clemence points out, peering over the baker's shoulder, catching a glimpse on the rack behind the counter. "I'm not choosy," she says for the second time that day. "And if you're closed, well, wouldn't you be throwing it out anyway?" Edging closer. She's relentless—and now she's got her, Clemence knows, as soon as she hears the baker sigh.

"Hang on," the baker says, and closes the door again. Secures the deadbolt. Clemence taking a step backwards, and inhaling a deep and most satisfying breath. Watching the life on the sidewalk of which she is a part, the couples and the families and the gaggles of friends, and yes, all the other people walking alone, like her, with their own directions and places they need to be.

Turning around again as the door opens a crack, the baker jams the baguette through. "Take it," she says. "No charge," and the door is shut and a deadbolt fastened before Clemence has time to properly thank her.

And now she has all she needs, the groceries and the

shredded plastic bag neatly tucked into that cloth bag, her capacious hold-all, and she nudges the baguette alongside them. Her first dinner in her new home that night would be everything she has been hoping it would be, simple with substance, the bread good and fresh. She would wash out that tin of sardines and save it as a souvenir, a useful vessel for small objects, things like stray buttons or safety pins.

Three

The first few weeks in her apartment are an adjustment to its rhythms, learning to not be disturbed at what sounds like someone thundering up the stairs, because the thunder is actually a downstairs neighbour partaking in some elaborate exercise routine in his room. Clemence is not sure if it's that neighbour's alarm clock she hears every day at 6:55 a.m., an incessant buzz, or somebody else's. She hasn't met anybody in the house, except for Charles, and she hasn't even seen Charles since then, though his mother, Mrs. Yeung, is everywhere and Clemence wonders if she should ask to be called Ms. Lathbury in return, but Mrs. Yeung doesn't call Clemence anything. She doesn't need to, because when Mrs. Yeung speaks, Clemence listens, whether it's about garbage collection and locking the front door, and how there is absolutely zero tolerance when it comes to keeping pets. The last woman she'd rented to, decades ago, had acquired a rabbit that chewed on the wiring.

Clemence does not have a rabbit, but she's been adopted by a cat, a beautiful one-eyed Himalayan who creeps into her apartment when she leaves the balcony door open. The cat waits for her, skulking along the rooflines, perching on chimney tops, going unseen by most of the world below, and now Clemence waits for him, too, no longer attempting to shoo him away because there's no point, he doesn't budge, and also he seems well tempered and well groomed: altogether pleasant company. He seems like a creature that doesn't have fleas or chew on wiring.

And so when she goes out for brunch with Jillian and Naomi, and they're concerned about her being lonely, asking whether she's managed to meet anybody in her neighbourhood, she will be able to tell them that she has indeed.

"I've been so worried about you," says Jillian. "Just with all the upheaval, and you jumping into new things so fast. Coming back here, and renting that place before you've even seen it, and the smell in the stairs."

"The smell in the stairs," says Clemence, "has not improved. But I mean, it's not like I'm hanging out on the stairs."

"Is the smell why you haven't had me over yet?" asks Naomi, and indeed it's part of the reason. Naomi is famously fastidious, and even worse than simply being judgmental, she pretends she isn't. To compensate for her judgment, she'd sit down on the stairs, and remark on the fresh air. She'd breathe in deep and pretend it was fine, which would be awkward for everyone.

But the real reason Clemence hasn't had her friends over yet, or even seen them lately, is that her friends are so busy. This brunch had been rescheduled three times already, and, up until the moment Jillian and Naomi arrived, Clemence wasn't sure the gathering was going to happen this time, either. Jillian has two kids and a demanding law practice, and Naomi owns a boutique marketing firm whose downtown office has a living wall. They both own property and vehicles, and have dependents, if you consider a living wall such a thing, which Clemence does, having recently killed a cactus through lack of affection. She'd purchased the plant from the artisan market in Sorauren Park, which featured no fewer than seven purveyors of succulents, and how does a person even choose between all that? In the end, she'd selected the cactus that was most heavily discounted, and maybe you get what you pay for, because she'd taken it home and watched it wither before her eyes.

"You probably overwatered it," Naomi explains once Clemence has filled them in.

"I didn't water it at all."

"Well then," says Jillian, "there's your problem."

"The thing that gets me, though," says Clemence, because they've been talking about work, about what Clemence might possibly do now that the industry upon which she's built her entire career has ceased to exist, "thinking about the succulents, I mean, is the way that capitalism has backed women into a corner. And I say this as a person who made a living for years writing about wedding dresses. But, I mean how can there be seven different people selling succulents at a single market?"

"It's a side hustle," says Naomi, who explains she'd read a thing about that particular market on *blogTO* the week before. "And the hustle is real. The woman who runs it is a tyrant. She banned a vendor once because her name was too long and wouldn't fit on the promotions."

"But isn't a side hustle worse?" Clemence asks. "Imagine having a full-time job and a cactus biz? That's exhausting. And then there are the skincare coaches and dog therapists, and all those women who sell leggings in a cult. Why doesn't anybody have a real job anymore? It's like women entered the workforce but they ran out of jobs, so they just started making stuff up."

"I have a friend," says Jillian, "who's literally a nail mechanic."

"What is that?" Naomi asks.

Jillian says, "She's certified."

"By who?" Clemence is outraged. There should not be an authoritative body certifying anybody's repair of fingernails. "Fingernails fix themselves. Nope, me, I'm going back to basics," she tells her friends. "I'm going to be an indexer."

She is met with blank faces. "People do that?" asks Jillian. "I assumed it's all automated."

Clemence explains how not all of it is, because they barely give out academic tenure anymore, so most university professors are elderly and fixed in twentieth-century non-technical ways. "They post job listings in the back of poorly circulated magazines," she says, "which cuts down on competition in terms of getting gigs." She was even qualified, having aced an elective indexing course back in university.

"Does it pay any better than the cactus trade, though?" asks Naomi.

Clemence says, "Fortunately, I'm a woman of modest means." Today's brunch is a rare indulgence, and she has ordered the cheapest items on the menu—a fruit bowl and buttered toast. But it feels extravagant enough to be sitting on a restaurant patio on a beautiful day in the company of her two dearest friends, watching the world go by along King Street. After she and Toad had moved to the West Coast, it had been hard to acquire friends who felt like real ones. Plus she had been so consumed by the novelty of coupledom, anyway, and it was hard to meet anybody in the subdivision where they bought their home ... until she met Larry and Lisa, and look where that led.

"You know, I'm happy for you. You're really *doing* it," Naomi tells her, and Clemence glows in her regard. "It's not easy, coming back here, and starting over like this."

Jillian asks if she's seen that guy again, meaning Charles from the porch. She's disappointed when Clemence confesses that she hasn't—"I don't think he even lives there."

"You're not just hiding, trying to avoid spicing up your love life?"

"I don't have a love life. I don't want a love life," says Clemence, "... although there is someone." And this is the part where she explains about the cat, everything except the fact that he's a cat.

"Now, come on," they say. "Tell us all about him."

"Or her," says Naomi, very open-minded.

Jillian says, "Spill it."

So Clemence explains about Bailey, which is the name she's given him. "He's kind of quiet," she says, trying to make it all sound normal. "He likes heights." She is failing. They look confused. "Climbing," she clarifies. "Loves rock climbing," she explains.

"Maybe he'll take you sometime," says Naomi. "A little expedition."

"I mean," Clemence says. "It's just nice to have someone around." But has she caught herself out now? Proving them right, that she's bored and unhappy on her own? Because she isn't—but if she insisted, they'd refuse to believe her. Her friends know her too well, except they don't know that now she's different.

"So, what's he do?" Jillian asks her.

Clemence thinks of his stretches, the way he arches his back with his paws out front. "Yoga. He teaches yoga."

"You should have brought him," says Naomi. "We could have met him."

"Oh, I don't think we're there yet," says Clemence. "Things are still pretty casual."

"Between the yoga and the rock climbing, though," says Jillian. "I mean, he's got to be pretty well built."

"He is," says Clemence. "He is, well, built." Not a word of a lie. Oh, except the teaching the yoga part. Everything else, her friends had inferred.

"So you've slept with him," Jillian follows.

"I knew it!" Naomi says.

"No," says Clemence, closing her eyes. Was everybody obsessed with sex, or just these two? She looks at them again. "We're taking it slow." The server comes around again and adds hot water to her little teapot. "Still getting to know him."

"Have you heard from Toad?" asks Naomi.

"Absolutely nothing," she tells her friends. "Which is fine." It was, and it had even been *true* ... until yesterday, when a letter from their lawyer, now only Toad's lawyer, she guesses, arrived in her parents' mailbox. Clemence had left her cellphone in Seattle—it was on Toad's family plan, anyway—so mail was the only way he could get in touch. She had a new number now, and her mother had called to tell her about the envelope, and Clemence can't get that envelope out of her mind, the image of it stacked atop a pile of bills and takeout flyers on the counter by the phone, nondescript and portentous at once.

"A clean break is the best thing for both of us," she tells her friends firmly. Which is also what Clemence has been telling herself, the chief appeal of a clean break from her point of view being that she won't have to keep atoning for her sins for the rest of her life. Those sins a means to an end, it is true, this end specifically—it feels like she's dug her own tunnel out of jail—but now she doesn't want to pursue this conversation any further, and her friends have intuited as much, moving on from her love life to another fraught topic: Naomi's parents, who'd recently returned to Japan after a four-week stay.

Naomi explains, "My mother set me up three times while she was here—twice with people she'd met in the elevator and another time with a guy who was working at Starbucks."

"And how did that work out?" asks Jillian.

"Not great," Naomi answers. "Especially since neither of the elevator guys knew what was happening. I think they thought she was kidnapping them, but they were way too polite to protest, which is the first sign that they weren't my type."

"What about Starbucks guy?"

Naomi shrugs. "He brought me a muffin. It was even fresh. So that was something. But my mother was disappointed. She'd thought he was at least a student, doing his PhD, but he was just really into coffee, so she dismissed him, and now my parents are gone, and so are the dates, and my life and my place are my own again."

Clemence says, "See? That's exactly it. It's luxurious."

Jillian says, "Nothing about your flat is luxurious."

"It's an existential kind of luxury," says Clemence. "Marriage was my prison, and now I'm free of it." It sounds like she's being melodramatic but she isn't.

Four

In the mornings, Clemence bathes in the tub, taking her time, the water lukewarm because the hot always runs out before it's managed to fill the bottom, let alone become deep enough to soak in. She reaches for the chipped blue jug, which sits on the floor beside a mat whose blue is almost matching, and fills it from the tap, the water cool now, then setting the jug down while she lathers her hair. In her old life, washing her hair was the closest Clemence ever came to meditation, her mind taking her to surprising places in the shower's rush, and, as the cliché goes, she had most of her best ideas there. The shower had been an escape from her life, but now that Clemence's entire life is escape, the bath holds something different, a chance to go deeper into the moment.

Here I am washing my hair in my bathtub, she thinks, working up the lather, a vision fulfilled. So satisfying just to have an idea and then bring it to reality. Picking up the jug again and pouring the water over her head, not so cold after all, her face to the ceiling with her eyes closed, and she's imagining how she looks with her body arched, her wet hair straight and falling halfway down her back. She feels the water like a caress, responding with arousal, slipping down into the tub so that the water touches more of her, and then she touches herself, her breasts loose and full in her hands, her nipples hard, and she squeezes them gently, awed by their abundance.

She likes her body, the way it feels. The softness of her stomach now, its roundness, her delicious flesh, erotically charged, it seems, but perhaps just because her hand is travelling farther down between her legs, and she starts touching herself, using her other hand to hold the weight of her breasts, and then to touch herself all over, because she's feeling really hot and all this could be finished in an instant if she wanted it to be. But she doesn't. She wants to linger here in the tension of in-between, letting the sensations inside her rise and rise, pulling them back from the brink, until she can't anymore, and besides, her hand might cramp, and so she moves her other hand inside her, filling her completely, and she's not in control of the sensations, because her senses have taken over, and it's like ripples, or shock waves, one after the other, and she can feel it on her fingers, her muscles throbbing, as she comes and comes and comes.

Clemence has never masturbated so much in her life, not even when she was a horny teenager reading smutty novels under the covers. The habit had fallen off once she and Toad got together, because she didn't have the time or place for it, and figured that marriage should have supplanted the urge, which it did, for a while. Plus, Toad had said it wasn't fair, that if Clemence was feeling randy then she should be having sex with him, and soon that dried up her sexual desire altogether.

But now it's back, and it's like a thrice-daily thing, part of her routine like brushing her teeth, and yes, washing her hair, and she swears it's improving her skin, though that could be the result of a lot of things, in particular her new propensity for oily fish. Clemence actually has a glow, even in the strange unflattering light of her bathroom. She pauses to admire her face in the mirror once she's drained the tub and risen to wrap a towel around her body. A face she's been learning not to take for granted, or to pick apart for supposed flaws—her nose is a little bit too large, but she has decided it's distinguished, and she has large green eyes whose lack of symmetry is only apparent if you look closely. Impeccable eyebrows—she'd been out of fashion for many years while everybody else was plucking, and now all their brows are sad and sparse while her thick ones are desirable. She's got nice lips, full and pink, and she blows a kiss at her reflection before bending to towel her hair dry one more time, and she knows it will dry tidily, a nice flip only a little wonky on one side.

Clemence had left most of her wardrobe behind when she fled Toad, all the clothes she'd worn to the office and didn't need anymore. What's left, she keeps in a cardboard box under the daybed, which isn't fancy, but does the job, and every time she starts to see the bottom of the box, she knows it's time to do laundry. There is a laundromat around the corner and down the street, though she's going to visit her parents today, so she'll bring the dirty clothes along and do it there, saving a handful of change in the process. It's not difficult to choose what to wear from the few clean items left—she picks a gingham sundress that Toad used to complain looked like a tablecloth you'd bring to a picnic.

Clemence has returned to the city she grew up in after more than a decade away, and there are benefits to this—the extortionate rents here are slightly less extortionate than in Seattle, access to laundry at her parents', and Saturday brunch with her dearest friends like it's no big thing. But it also means that her plans for a fresh start are complicated by all the people who've known her forever, vividly recalling every ridiculous person she's ever been, including the teenager claiming to be vegetarian, the drunk girl falling into a puddle of her own urine on her twentieth birthday, or the earnest young woman signing up for a lifetime with a man named Toad. Who was actually Todd, but nobody called him that, a joke whose punchline you kept waiting for, but it never came. "Toad" was even the name he used professionally, which would make it easy to search for online, just to see what her ex was up to, but Clemence didn't want to. Not yet.

She'd always assumed that her parents had liked Toad, but Clemence realizes now that her marriage had been like her stint with vegetarianism—mostly a power struggle and a way to assert her independence from the family. After they were engaged, Roger and Bonnie spent a lot of time asking if Clemence was really sure, and at the wedding, as she and her father had danced to some saccharine song by Paul Simon (not even "Slip Slidin' Away," although, in retrospect it should have been), he'd whispered in her ear, "Any time you want to come home, you know we're here for you. No questions asked." Which had upset Clemence at the time, leading to a distance that stretched well beyond geography for a while, but maybe her parents had the long view and she'd been too young to realize because, when the time came, it had been the greatest gift to know she'd have a soft place to land.

She'd stayed with her parents for a few weeks after she got back in April, but soon it was too much. Clemence's old room was where Bonnie kept her treadmill now, and she'd be knocking every morning far too early, suited up and earbuds in, raring to go. Plus Clemence's sisters were always coming by with their own kids, and it was like living in the middle of a circus. So when Naomi finally invited her downtown, Clemence accepted the offer with gratitude—moving out would mean her family home could be a retreat rather than a sentence. And now her sister Grace was picking her up within the hour, and they'd all head back up to the suburbs together.

"I'll be waiting outside," Clemence had told Grace, knowing she'd be late, inevitable with three-year-old twins to wrangle, but also that Grace would be determined to check out where Clemence was living—no doubt their parents had charged her with scoping out the scene. And Clemence might have been able to hold her off, except when the car rolls up, Juniper has to pee, and so the whole troop files inside and upstairs, Grace and her wife, Allison, Juniper hopping while clutching her crotch, and her brother Jarvis who decides he has to go, too, just for the heck of it.

"It's actually not bad?" says Grace tentatively, looking around. Clemence had tidied up because she knew her sister would finagle her way inside. She always did. "A bit small, and that's not really a kitchen, but still."

"And the neighbourhood is changing," Allison calls out from the bathroom, where she's been helping the kids. "That new café, and the cheese shop."

"Always a sign that I'll be priced out soon and have to move again," Clemence says, trying to herd everyone back out the door. "But there's still a safe injection site just down the block and plenty of petty crime, so I'm not worried yet."

Grace ignores this. "I'm kind of relieved," she says, following Clemence out onto the landing. "From the outside, you can't tell, but your place is almost nice."

They meet Mrs. Yeung on the way back downstairs—her unit was on the main floor, from which she monitored all comings and goings. "We're just heading out," Clemence tells her. "This is my sister," she says, introducing the family, feeling like her landlady might like her better if she knew Clemence had people who loved her, that she was not simply a sad specimen who had turned up at the door with a couple of hastily packed boxes.

In typical fashion, however, Grace, refuses to play her part, certainly making an impression, but one that's far from excellent, as she spies a parking enforcement officer placing a ticket on her windshield. She takes off out the door, across the porch, and down the steps, shrieking expletives. Grace, as it turns out, has parked in front of a fire hydrant.

"Which was hidden in a fucking bush," she rants, all the way out of the city and up the highway toward the suburban streets where their parents live, where everyone can park anywhere. "I mean, did you see it? I didn't see it."

Clemence listens from the back seat where she's wedged in between the twins who are strapped into their giant car seats, because apparently children require car seats until they're old enough to vote now. The car seats seem more suited to space travel than a trip up the highway, aerodynamic, except for all the plastic and metal edges that are stabbing Clemence on both sides, which would be uncomfortable enough, but also Juniper has already vomited twice.

Nobody else is fazed by the puking, especially Juniper herself, who appears, out of thin air, to produce a yellow beach pail in which to spew. The first time it happens, they are still in the city, and Grace pulls over so Allison can empty the pail's contents by the side of the road. But now that they're on the highway, there's no stopping, and Clemence has the bucket on her lap, trying not to breathe through her nose, her arms extended as long as possible, but there is so little room, and she's terrified that if Grace comes to a sudden stop, the bucket's contents could spill all over her.

Upon arrival, Grace helps yank Clemence from her

confines, once the twins are sprung, and Allison accepts the puke pail with a nod of thanks, but she doesn't have to carry it for long, because Bonnie arrives to greet them, taking the bucket without a word—apparently the puking is routine—and managing to hold it steady while her grandchildren climb her like a tree. Balance has always been Bonnie's forte.

It feels good to be home, Clemence thinks, never more so than now that she doesn't have to stay here, which means she can take in the pleasures of the food, and the comfort, and even her parents' attention without it all becoming too much.

"Grace said your place is pretty terrific," Roger tells her when she goes out to meet him grilling burgers in the backyard.

She kisses him on the cheek and asks how he knows that, since Grace is still out front unloading the car.

"She texted your mother," says Roger. When Allison was emptying the plastic pail? When had she found the chance?

Clemence reminds her father, "I already told you the place was all right."

"It's nice to have it verified."

"My word isn't enough?"

Her dad turns back to the burgers. "We worry about you." And they do, because she's giving them reason to lately. Her parents are having trouble taking her seriously, the way they do with her sisters, and she can't blame them entirely, because she's the one who has messed up and had to come home to them.

Clemence tells her father, "I'm doing okay."

"Any news on the job front?" *Of course.*

So she needs to assure him. "I'm still making plans. Strategizing."

Roger puts down the flipper and closes the barbecue lid. Enveloping her in his arms in a way that had been unchanging for as long as he could remember, he tells her, "It's really good to have you back, kid."

CLEMENCE'S ELDER SISTER PRUDENCE is married to Sandro, who is the same age as Roger and on his second family but this one (fortunately) seems to be sticking. Prudence and Sandro have four children, whose ages fall somewhere between five and twelve—Alessia, Lila, Roberto, and Enzo—and Clemence has never managed to remember any of their birthdays, which she knows is much discussed behind her back. She is a very bad aunt, and this one time she held the vomit pail, she knows, will do nothing to change that perception.

But she has also been so far away for so long that her sister's children are more an abstract idea than actual people, which honestly seems preferable to Clemence since abstract children don't puke, or yell, or grab their sibling's bums to make them scream even louder. There are so many of them, too, nieces and nephews rushing around the house and across the backyard like a blur, so fast that it seems as though every child is actually three children. In theory, Clemence would like to know these kids, to grow to love each one of them as individuals even, but how do you get to know a hurricane?

Perhaps with a drink. Prudence presses one into her sister's hand and sits down beside her at the patio table. "Be careful of Sandro. He thinks you want to sleep with him."

"With *him*?" Clemence has always been surprised that there are two women who married Sandro at all, but perhaps it's made him big-headed enough to suppose that anything is possible.

"Don't say anything to make him uncomfortable, I mean." Prudence sips her drink.

"I haven't even seen him," Clemence says. Not since last summer when she was back for the anniversary, and it was true that it had been the beginning of a peculiar moment in her life, but an attraction to Sandro didn't factor into it. He had ear hair. "Where did he get that idea?"

"Well, he knows," says Prudence. "I told him what happened, with your neighbours." She saw her sister's look. "I told you I wouldn't tell anybody, but Sandro doesn't count. I tell Sandro everything. And he's nervous now."

"I will try to resist him," Clemence solemnly vows. There was a time when Prudence had been the person Clemence most revered in all the universe, the lodestar she would have followed anywhere. Dear Prudence was going to be secretary-general of the United Nations, but then she'd fallen in love with Sandro, her Italian professor, in her second year of university, dropping out of school altogether when she became pregnant with Alessia, and since then she has devoted her life to serving her children and moderating various online communities of home-schooling parents, which means (and Clemence is not being flippant) that Prudence's diplomatic skills are being utilized—but to what end?

Prudence says, "Just don't be weird."

Grace and Allison appear, with one of the twins. "She's being weird again?" asks Grace.

Prudence says, "She's being warned not to be."

Grace says, "You're wasting your breath." Grace, the afterthought, who'd always been a little bit abstract herself when they were growing up, because it was Clemence and Prudence who'd been the pair, Grace so little and foolish, just barely formed, and now that she was grown, Clemence wasn't altogether sure she liked her younger sister, the familiarity with which she delivered barbs like that. She was trying to impress Allison, was Clemence's theory, and Prudence didn't disagree with it. Allison was a badass, in a family of virtuous daughters, with her tattooed arms and battered leather jacket. Allison *smoked*. And if Allison were a man, it might have been different, because she wouldn't have been here at the table, she would have been off somewhere, with Sandro and Toad. But of course, that wasn't fair. It was Clemence, after all, who'd disturbed the family symmetry, because Toad wasn't here, and Allison was lovely. They all said that—"Allison is lovely"—to compensate for all the ways in which she wasn't. Bonnie kept ashtrays for her, bringing one outside now, vessels that had decorated all the end tables and coffee tables in their home decades ago, but these days were more like museum pieces.

Bonnie sits down in the one remaining space at the table, a table that seats five, as though the Lathburys were who they'd always been in their tidy backyard. When everybody sits down to eat, the children and superfluous adults will pile all over the lawn. And there will not be enough food, either, because Bonnie still cooks for five. It's all she knows how to do, and Clemence's sisters know this, too, which is why they've both brought bread rolls and salads and trays of cheese and vegetables. No one has asked Clemence to contribute a single thing.

"We had it covered," says Prudence.

"And you don't have a kitchen," Grace reminds her—but now Bonnie looks aghast.

"I have a kitchen," Clemence says. It's a small kitchen, but it's her kitchen.

Grace says, "She's essentially cooking on a camp stove."

Bonnie's going to lose it. "You can't do that indoors."

"It's not a camp stove," says Clemence.

"Because of carbon monoxide, I mean. Roger, did you hear this? Clemence cooking on a camp stove?"

Roger wanders over from the barbecue. "That's not a good idea, honey," he tells her.

And Prudence says, "Seriously. You could poison yourself."

"Like Sylvia Plath," says Allison helpfully.

"Didn't you and Toad have an electric oven? And induction stove?" Bonnie asks. "I kind of wish you'd stuck with that."

"Bonnie," says Roger, evidently reminding her of a line they've drawn.

"Well, not with Toad, obviously," says Bonnie. "By the way, don't forget to pick up the letter. But I mean, with the electric. You both had such a nice kitchen. It's too bad you couldn't have kept it, but it would have been awkward, I mean. Once you start getting involved with all the neighbours…"

"It wasn't *all* the neighbours," says Clemence. "And how do you even know about that?" Prudence raised her hand while staring at her lap. Allison has got her hands clamped over the twin's ears. Clemence says, "This is appalling."

Bonnie shrugs and smiles. "We don't judge."

"Except for the camp stove," says Roger.

"It's a fucking hot plate," says Clemence. "Hot. Plate."

"Well, hello to you, too, Clemence," says Sandro, coming out of the kitchen. "Welcome back to the fold. A hot plate, indeed," and then he kisses her on the lips, in front of everybody, and she can't tell if he's being inappropriate or just European.

Five

A person can get used to anything, which was a fundamental lesson Clemence had learned—almost to her peril—during her marriage, but now she is determined to apply the same principle to her unfortunate mattress, and to her bed, which is short of a few bottom slats. There have been three different nights now that the mattress has fallen through and Clemence has woken up on the floor folded like origami. She decides there is a lesson here, something about the shifting ground beneath a person and how fate might possibly swallow them whole, and it's going to be part of the story she's living as she attempts to become a person of substance.

Clemence is determined to be the opposite of a princess, that proverbial one who slept on a pea. Clemence has kissed enough Toad that she knows that story already, and now she's happy to be exploring a different one, up in her tiny apartment, where Bailey the cat has appeared once more, and she opens the door to let him in, along with the fresh air and sunshine. He's a beautiful cat, and Clemence wants to take a photo, to post it online, *all that light*—but she resists, because she's aspiring to do less of showcasing her glorious moments, to keep something for herself, and also because she's told her two best friends that the cat is a person and she needs to keep her story straight.

Clemence sits at the table, the unopened letter from Toad's lawyer before her, as the cat traces figure eights around her legs, trailed by his bushy tail, soft on her skin, so she reaches down to pet him. Pushing the letter aside, again. She likes the company. Clemence hasn't had a pet since she was a kid, mostly because with her and Toad at work all day, it never seemed fair and they'd been in agreement about so many things like that that it had been easy to believe their relationship was good. That they were compatible, which is what she told herself, but maybe she'd just been catatonic.

Take books, for example. Toad had been an early enthusiast of digital storage, putting all their music and movies online, and then one year for Clemence's birthday, he'd made her put on a blindfold, leading her into her home office, and removing the blindfold for the big reveal.

"What's this?" she asked. Her bookshelves, completely empty, except for the dust, in stark contrast to the pristine spots on the shelf where the books had been.

Toad had been so proud. This had been hardest to take. He'd been plotting this for weeks, refusing to reveal a single detail, but all the while bursting with such excitement that he couldn't help alluding to a secret plan in the works. Clemence hoping that he'd booked them a trip, or designed a backyard garden, or ordered a bathtub with whirlpool jets—there were so many gifts he might have given that she would have received with pleasure. But no, instead, he'd digitized her entire book collection and gotten rid of the books. Like, he'd thrown them out, and not even in the recycling, and the garbage had been collected that morning. It was a tragedy no matter how you looked at it.

And this was years ago—it hadn't even been the final straw. Clemence had convinced herself that her anger and disappointment were unreasonable. Was it possible—as Toad often suggested—that Clemence would have found fault no matter what he did for her? Which did seem to be the case, so she'd decided this was a problem she could fix by fixing herself, by adjusting her attitude. She'd pretended to be delighted by his gift, to be grateful. She told him, yes indeed, the extra space was great, and almost as good as the minimalist aesthetic, and the e-reader was awesome, even if the battery tended to run down too fast. All this instead of bursting into tears at the disappearing of her books, which were also a museum, her history. Clemence had thrown her arms around her husband and said thank you.

A million years ago, it seems, and now Clemence has found a bookshelf on the curb, sitting outside one of the hollowed-out houses with the dumpsters, and she hauls the bookshelf home, all the way up the stairs, not even pausing to examine the spots where it scrapes the stairwell, because those walls were already a mess. She drags it through the door and finds a space for it against the one wall that's not sloping with the roof, and it fits precisely, as though the placement was meant to be. The cat goes to examine it, leaping right to the top shelf, then stepping along its length with ease and grace, sniffing around at the edges. The shelf is old, dark wood, made by hand back in a time when people had such skills. It's a beautiful piece, a discard like all the rest of her furniture, but she'd chosen it, and if she ever moved out, Clemence would take it with her.

However now her back hurts, between the subpar mattress and carrying the shelf, a dull ache between her shoulder blades, and she's got nobody here to give her a rub. Clemence lies down on the floor—cheap, stained linoleum that she's scrubbed enough times to be so intimate with—and lets the cat walk all over her. There is relief in the pressure of her spine against the ground, and above her the bookshelf is towering, and empty. Clemence knows where she is going today.

THE BOOKSHOP IS ON the main street, just north of the church, the streetcar rumbling by as Clemence approaches. It's not one of the new arrivals on the street, a sign of gentrification, but a mainstay, nothing boutique-ish about it. The sign is ancient, *Crampton's Used Booksellers*, but the *B* has weathered away. Not once since arriving in the neighbourhood has Clemence seen anyone going in or out of this store, just one of the many businesses along the strip she's been wondering about, along with the shop that exclusively sells christening gowns; the shoe repair place that's open the first Wednesday of every month; and the variety store that is surely a front for something because the one time she tried to enter, the owner blocked the entrance, claiming that he didn't have what she was looking for before she'd even told him what it was.

At the booksellers, however, Clemence encounters no such resistance. The sign on the door is flipped to *Open*, the smell inside exactly what she's been expecting—dust, and must, distinctly "old book," and old books are everywhere, piled haphazardly alongside the shelves, which in places are packed with books in front of other books, and Clemence can't decide whether she loves this arrangement (for the chance that in such a book trove, she might find some literary thing she never even knew she wanted) or if she hates it (because even if those books are here, how is she going to find them?).

There is a second floor, a poky staircase leading the way, with piles of books stacked on every step, and an ancient sheet of paper, yellowed, thumbtacked to the wall, faded ink explaining the esoteric categories to be encountered upstairs—books on billiards and badminton, hunting, harpsichords, and heretics. Literature, however, is here on the first floor, toward the back, and on her way through, Clemence passes the desk where the clerk sits, a slight man whose features she can't distinguish because he's got a book stuck in front of them. He doesn't acknowledge her presence.

Clemence has an idea of what she's looking for, books to replace the ones she lost in the purge. She'd brought her e-reader when she left, though she hadn't wanted to. She doesn't like reading on screens, for reasons both practical and aesthetic, and the device is also tainted for being a gift from Toad, but if she'd left it behind, she might have had nothing to read at all, been wholly at the mercy of other people's tastes. Thinking about when she'd been a child visiting her grandmother, hiding out in the bedroom reading Danielle Steel novels on the bookshelf, all of them in large print. She wouldn't have altogether minded reading those again, but her tastes have changed since she was eleven.

Clemence is looking for modern classics—*Sula* by Toni Morrison; Margaret Laurence's Manawaka books; as well as classic classics, all the way back to the Brontës—*Jane Eyre* and *The Tenant of Wildfell Hall*. But not *Wuthering Heights*—there is nothing redeemable about *Wuthering Heights*, Clemence had decided the last time she read it. She was through with romantic brutes. Heathcliff was a monster. No, she wants to populate her library with excellent women now, women who intuitively knew the value of themselves and their stories. But oddly, there isn't a single Brontë on the shelf in this shop. She moves back to the *A*s, because surely she'd find some Austen—handsome old hardbacks, academic editions with highlights and underlines, cheap paperbacks riddled with typos by publishers cashing in on the public domain. But there aren't any of these, either.

Clemence has started to get a bad feeling. Iris Murdoch.

Clemence has never read a book by Iris Murdoch in her life, but she knows they should be here. She has perused enough used bookstores to be familiar with the landscape—Anita Brookner, and Margaret Drabble, and Amy Tan, and multiple copies of all those books championed by Oprah in the 1990s. *The Pilot's Wife*. Clemence had once been to a second-hand bookstore where *The Pilot's Wife* was free with any purchase, but here at Crampton's, there is not a single copy. In fact, there is not a single book by a woman author in the entire literature section. Not even Virginia Woolf, she realizes with dismay, as she makes her way to the alphabet's end.

Clemence returns to the desk where the man there hasn't moved. He's reading a play, *The Way of the World*, by William Congreve, and of course he is. She's standing right there, but he still doesn't look up from the book.

There is a bell, so Clemence rings it, and the bell is so loud it makes her jump, but the man behind the counter doesn't flinch, only lowering his book, oh so slowly, and there he is, that face, pale with delicate features, and there's a piece of tissue stuck to a spot on his cheek where he cut himself shaving, and he's missed some other spots, which might be for the best. He needs sunshine. He needs a haircut. He needs, he needs, he needs, which is the kind of man who once upon a time rendered Clemence completely silly, and she almost forgets that she's furious. But only almost.

The delicate features are like stone, his face devoid of expression. He doesn't even speak, as though lowering his book was enough acknowledgement of her presence, and perhaps even too much. Clemence has no doubt that if they remained staring at each other like this forever that he would never be the first to break.

She says, "Where are the women?" He pretends not to know what she's talking about, still unmoving. She gestures behind her, "On the shelf, the fiction. Why are there no women there?"

He finally speaks, "Literature," but he says it in three syllables, "Lit-trit-chure," so maybe he's English, or just pretentious, the latter option plausible. And then he says nothing more—is it possible he doesn't speak English at all?

"You don't stock women in your bookstore?"

He laughs. "Of course, we do." No accent. He's just a jerk.

"I didn't see them," Clemence tells him.

"Because you were looking in the wrong place," he says.

"Well, where are they?"

And he's deigned to raise his arm so he can gesture down the other aisle, the one with another yellowed sign, this one labelled *Women's Fiction*.

"You're joking!" yells Clemence. This is a set-up. Someone's going to jump out with a camera and the punchline, that this is a statement on the value of women's work and women's words. "The difference of value persists," wrote Virginia Woolf over a hundred years ago—but it's only Clemence and the pale book man, and there's no camera. There is nothing funny about it.

The man shrugs, and seems to injure his shoulder in the process, and it's this way that a person can be so repellent and endearing at once. Clemence wants to slap him, but she'd probably kill him, he's so frail, and so she steps away from his desk and goes to investigate the Women's Fiction aisle.

Even though she should have stormed out of the store, haughtily, in a rage. Imagine the bookstore where women's novels don't get to be literature, although Clemence knows that in many bookstores this is indeed the case, but presented with more subtlety. She has to see it for herself, though, this crime against gender equality. It's probably no accident that the lights are dimmer in this section and the shelves are crooked, as though they're on the verge of falling down.

And there she is, Maeve Binchy, like the sight of a friend in a room full of strangers, and before her Chimamanda Ngozi Adichie, and then Angela Carter, and Brontës on the shelf above, Jane Austens all in a row on the floor so that Clemence needs to crouch down to examine them, inhaling a load of dust in the process, and she sneezes boisterously before she can stop herself from doing so. The sound of her outburst echoes throughout the otherwise silent shop.

Everybody is here, she thinks with relief, and notes that it's kind of nice not having to wade through Norman Mailer to get to Flannery O'Connor and Ann Patchett. And she is altogether stunned to find multiple novels on the shelf by Barbara Pym, whose books are usually so hard to come by second-hand. She'd once found a shoebox stuffed with Pym paperbacks at an estate sale, because it's only upon death that most readers tend to be willing to part with them—and now Clemence has grabbed a few before she's even processed what she's doing. *No Fond Return of Love* and *An Unsuitable Attachment*, clutching them close to her chest, never mind the dust. The dust is essential. And she knows that she too is unwilling to part with these books now, never mind her principles against supporting a shop like this. But maybe she could steal them? Wouldn't that be a kind of liberation in fact, taking these novels away to a place where they'd be valued, and dusted, and actually read?

But Clemence Lathbury is not a thief, and also Clemence Lathbury desires an excuse to return to the pale book man, against her better impulses, and she explains the whole thing to herself as she selects some other books—finds a copy of *Sula*, and a first edition of *The Republic of Love* by Carol Shields. A respectable haul, it is, and of course, all of the books are priced at just a dollar or two, which might be the upside of supporting a bookstore in which women are devalued. At least it's a bargain?

And the pale book man. He's reading again, Clemence sees as she approaches the counter. Perhaps this might be just the thing, she wonders, an inappropriate fixation with which to occupy herself, to keep her from falling into lust or obsession with someone too appealing. This man appears unhealthy, unattractive, is clearly a terrible conversationalist, and most likely a misogynist to boot. He looks asthmatic, and she wonders how he functions here amid all this dust. She could long for him the way that Barbara Pym heroines lust after pale young curates, a perfect arrangement, destined to go nowhere. Such an unsuitable attachment, at this moment in her life, might be precisely the distraction Clemence needs.

She resolves to change her approach. Smiling now, as she clears her throat and calls for his attention less obnoxiously than with the bell. Piling the books on the counter, and he consents to put his own down, although he sighs, evidently bothered that she's once again disturbed his reading.

"So, you found them," he says, beginning an elaborate process of marking the sales into a ledger, nothing automated about it, and Clemence realizes that this is another place that's cash-only. She has some money in her wallet, and she hopes it's enough.

"But I don't understand," Clemence tells him. "Why you catalogue the books the way you do."

"I just work here." He enters the final book on the list with his pencil's dull nub. He pushes the pile of books back toward her and gives Clemence the total. "And it's a system as arbitrary as any other."

"But it's not." Clemence fishes a bill out of her wallet. "It's not arbitrary at all. Has anything ever been less arbitrary than the distinction of women's fiction?"

"I wouldn't know," he says, turned away from her now, making change from a drawer beneath the desk. "I don't read the stuff, myself."

"Well, I mean you only work in a bookstore," says Clemence. "It's not like you're supposed to be any kind of an expert on books."

He nearly flings the change at her. "I'm not an expert on anything."

"Certainly not customer service," says Clemence, holding her new books close.

"Nope," says the pale book man, and she can't tell if he knows that she's mocking him. He takes himself very seriously. He doesn't bother to ask her if she wants a bag.

"You could come back, though," he calls out to her as she's walking away. She stops, turns around. "If you've got a problem with the cataloguing," he explains. "Crampton's here Wednesday mornings. If you want to register an official complaint." He's daring her.

"Maybe I will," says Clemence, something catching in her throat, or thereabouts, and then she rushes out of the shop before she starts sneezing again and makes an even bigger fool of herself than she has already.

Six

Clemence goes home with books clutched to her chest, and a third of the way up her second set of stairs, she's stopped by a pair of denim-clad legs topped with the most terrific rear end she's ever seen. Clemence is not normally a butt-marveller, but this one is right at eye level, though whomever it belongs to is doubled over and struggling to breathe.

"Are you okay?" she calls up. Could this be a heart attack? Clemence feels her own heartbeat speeding up, though whether its due to panic or attraction she cannot discern.

But it's probably the latter, for that butt belongs to Charles, the landlady's son. Charles, whose existence Clemence had been wondering if she'd only imagined, with a derrière she'd taken no note of at all at their first encounter, so focused had she been upon the fineness of his upper body. Where has he been all her life? Or at least lately . . .

Charles, fortunately, does not seem to be having a heart attack at all, has simply been burdened with a heavy load and now he's taking a necessary breather halfway up the stairs. He's practically panting. "I'm fine," he's answered her. "Really. Just needed to put this down for a minute." It's steamy in the stairwell. There's a filthy window at the top letting in dim light, but you'd need a ladder to climb up and open it. Or to clean it.

Clemence asks Charles what he's hauling.

"An A/C," he says. He's caught his breath, and picks it back up again, muscles flexed, now carrying it all the way up to the top.

Clemence hurries up behind him, pulling out her key. "I'll get the door." Angling around him delicately, difficult with an armful of books. His T-shirt is wet, and no doubt she's sweating, too. She unlocks the door and he uses his hip to nudge it open, bringing the air conditioner inside. It's on little wheels, so portable, supposedly, except that it weighs a ton. "Are you okay, *really*?" she asks, dropping her books to the floor. Charles's face is red and he is twisting his remarkable body with a grimace as though his back is strained.

"A lot of stairs," he says.

"I didn't order an air conditioner," says Clemence.

"You didn't?" He gives her a withering look. "Oh, well, I'll carry it all the way back down then. Must have got the wrong address."

"I didn't mean *that*," she says. Charles is touchy. "I mean, thank you. Obviously. I just don't understand..."

"My mom," says Charles.

He's still sweating and now his face has gone a funny colour. "Oh my gosh," Clemence says. "I should get you a glass of water." She has become unaccustomed to hospitality, and the only available drinking vessel is a giant plastic beer stein. On the side is a cartoon of a huge-breasted woman, her words in a speech bubble: *I've got no time for small talk. Your place or mine?* Inappropriate, perhaps, but it had come with the apartment, so Clemence takes no responsibility, telling Charles as much as she hands him the glass.

He gulps the water down. "Thank you," he breathes.

She gestures toward the air conditioner. "You really didn't have to." The appliance is bigger than her fridge.

He shrugs. "My mom insisted. It's hot up here."

"And I'm a girl."

"That's part of it." He smiles. "She means well, my mom. She's a bit hard to take. But I think she thinks that with a girl, you have to worry more."

"We should probably tell her that I'm thirty-three years old."

"It won't make a difference," he says. "I'm almost forty and she still makes me soup."

"And you're not even a girl."

"It's how she shows she cares," says Charles. He puts the glass down on the counter, and then pulls the air conditioner over to the small window in the corner. "And *this* is how she shows she cares." He starts pulling out the tube that will fasten to the window, setting up the entire arrangement. "Good thing, too," he says. "It's sweltering."

"So you grew up here?" Clemence asks him while he works, and he murmurs an affirmative.

"We lived in the basement," he explains as he places the panel in the window frame. "Didn't need an A/C down there—it was always freezing. And my parents rented out the rest of the house."

"Your dad?"

"He died when I was seven," says Charles. "Lung cancer. And my mom's been running the show ever since." He is bending over again, plugging in the air conditioner, and Clemence can't stop staring at his body, and then feeling guilty for objectifying him, because he seems like a nice guy and he has just delivered her an appliance. "There we go," he says. The tube fits into a panel that sits neatly in her window, and they're all set. He presses the On switch, and the machine begins its roar—followed by the blast of an explosion, and then silence. The fridge cuts out. Somebody downstairs is yelling, "What the hell?"

"You blew a fuse," says Clemence, figuring it out.

Charles finds her input unhelpful. "You think?" He disappears downstairs again, presumably into the basement where the fuse box is.

Alone now, Clemence opens the balcony door to let fresh air inside, which is all she needs anyway. She's already made it more than halfway through the summer without air conditioning—she looks at the machine hulking in the corner. And then she regards the rest of the room which is, thankfully, tidy—she hadn't been expecting company. The great benefit of owning so little is that it's easy to keep things in order. Clemence straightens the pillows on her daybed anyway, admiring the effect. She has started to love this space, which was never part of her plan. So is it cheating? And wouldn't an air conditioner, such a modern convenience, a *comfort*, make things even worse? She's supposed to be abstemious.

She remembers the books she'd dropped by the door, and picks them up again, bringing them over to the empty shelf where she arranges them by author. It's not much, doesn't even begin to fill that one shelf, but this is just the start, and she's looking forward to never charging her e-reader again.

Running her finger along the short row of spines, she turns when she hears Charles coming, taking the stairs two at a time. He's no longer panting. The guy's got great stamina, really, when he's not bogged down by a hundred-pound weight. Clemence still has her hand on the books.

"You like to read?" Charles asks when he sees her. She guesses this is a world that's foreign to him. Remembering that he'd known who Mr. Rochester was, but no doubt he'd seen it in a movie, or some old girlfriend had told him the plot of *Jane Eyre*.

She tells him, "I do. I'm kind of rebuilding my library. Starting over."

"And you're a writer?" he asks. No doubt, he remembers her and Jillian blathering on about Clemence living a life like a woman from a book.

"Well, I used to be." Clemence steps away from the shelf now and walks over to the patio door, to put some space between them. "It was my job, but I got laid off last year."

"Anything I might have read?"

Clemence hates that question. "I guess that depends what you read," she says. While it was unlikely that Charles had subscribed to *Wedding Belles*, what did his proximity to her work have to do with anything?

He looks put out by her dismissal. Points at the A/C in the corner. "Listen, you're going to have to hold off on using this for a while. I don't know why, but it's overloading the circuit. The wiring here's a bit wonky."

Clemence says, "I know." The fridge is plugged into an extension cord running to an outlet in the bathroom. "But I mean, thank you. For trying. For dragging this thing all the way up here."

He turns around on his way out the door. "I thought you were writing a book," he tells her. "What your friend said."

Clemence curses Jillian's candour. "It's more an experiential thing."

"So you're just doing a lot of eating and praying?"

"I mean," says Clemence, giving what she hopes is a fey shrug. "What else is there, after all?"

He says, "I guess so." He peels the sleeve of his wet T-shirt away from his biceps. "It's really hot."

"It's not so bad as long as you don't keep running up and down the stairs."

He says, "Thank you for the water, though."

"Any time."

NAOMI SENDS CLEMENCE AN Edible Arrangement, which Mrs. Yeung has to carry all the way up to her door.

"I could have come down to get it," says Clemence. The arrangement is heavy, the stairs are a lot.

Mrs. Yeung follows Clemence into the apartment. "Your friend says she's worried about you. That you're isolated, and not working, and she can't really get involved, because she's too busy with her work." Clemence looks confused. "What?" says Mrs. Yeung. "I read the card. Needed to see who it was for."

"But my name was on the envelope." Clemence pulls it out of the arrangement, her name prominently displayed.

"Okay," Mrs. Yeung admits. "I also wanted to see who it was from. And why she had sent it. My house, my rules." She points to the oversized citrus at the heart of the arrangement. "Are you going to eat the pomelo?"

"You want it?" A pomelo seems an acceptable payment for delivery, even factoring in the violation of privacy.

Mrs. Yeung accepts the fruit, holding it close like a baby, but she isn't ready to go yet, looking around the apartment, peeking behind the bathroom door. "No rabbits," she says, almost surprised.

"Not a single one," Clemence affirms.

Mrs. Yeung rubs the knob at the end of the daybed. "This is a beautiful bed. It's brass, just needs some polish. It's high end. You're lucky to have it." Stopping at the shelf. "But this is new."

"I found it."

"Knock on wood," says Mrs. Yeung, as she does so, humming her approval as she hears the solid sound. "This is nice. You could leave it when you go."

"I guess." Clemence won't, but then one never knows

what's around the corner, where she might end up flying to next.

"You like the air conditioner?" her landlady asks. Useless in the corner.

"Yes, I mean—" She hadn't asked for it, in principle it ran counter to her desires, and it didn't even function.

Mrs. Yeung says, "I bought it for you."

This is oddly moving, though. "Thanks."

Mrs. Yeung says, "You tell your friend that you've got someone looking out for you. Some people who aren't too busy with work. You tell her."

Though what Clemence tells Naomi in the end, via text message, is thank you, and that she's doing okay. Naomi's love language is sending deliveries of outlandish things, and now because of her gift, even without the pomelo, Clemence has another week before she's at risk of getting scurvy. She's still buying tinned meats from the miserable lady in the grocery store, who hasn't warmed to Clemence as much as she's ceased to be so actively hostile, but Clemence counts this as progress.

"And I have a job interview this week for an indexing gig," she reports in a follow-up text to Naomi who, Clemence knows, has been feeling guilty since bailing on a lunch date the week before. Hence the Edible Arrangement. And it feels good to have news to report, just to keep everybody's worries at bay. It's strange that during the years Clemence was miserable, nobody was concerned, but now that she's broken free, everyone seems to be on her case.

. . .

WHEN SHE MEETS JILLIAN by the Christie Pits playground the next day, takeout coffees in hand, Jillian already knows about the job interview. Naomi told her. Her friends are texting behind her back, and Clemence wonders if their messages are generous, but she gets it, she's been on both sides, and Jillian is so generous in all the other ways, such as buying her this giant latte, and that counts.

They sit together on a bench while Jillian's daughters stalk the perimeter of the wading pool. Chloe and Hannah are six and eight, and Clemence feels she knows them better than she knows her own sisters' offspring, mostly because Jillian posts their entire lives on social media and just two kids are easier to keep track of. Jillian is also extremely fastidious, and as a result her children are better behaved than Clemence's nieces and nephews. Jillian is so fastidious that she has white sneakers, and so do her children, and all three pairs are spotless, lined up neatly in a row beneath the bench, Jillian's still on her feet.

"It's for a English professor," Clemence explains about the interview. "His wife had always done his typing and indexing, but then she died."

"You're sure he's not looking for a wife?"

"I mean, only for clerical tasks."

"Well, there's a market for it I guess," says Jillian.

"Less than you'd think," says Clemence, "because women live longer than men, and all the old women professors certainly never counted on their husbands for such things, if they had husbands in the first place."

"So this is part of the spinster project," says Jillian.

Clemence says, "I guess so. And to pay the bills. My severance is almost over, but I've saved a lot, and my rent is cheap."

"I should hope so," Jillian says. "It's working out, though? The house is a little rough around the edges." Jillian lives in a beautiful Victorian house in the upscale Annex neighbourhood just east of the park, and has redone the kitchen three times since moving in.

Clemence says, "It's exactly right. I like it there." A room of her own. Maybe it wouldn't matter where or what it was.

Jillian says, "And how is it? I mean, with leaving Todd." Jillian is one of the few people who refuses to ever call Toad by his nickname. Clemence turns to face her, but Jillian is looking out, not meeting her eyes. "Was it one of those things?" Jillian asks her, "Where you couldn't imagine going through with it, and then one day you finally did?"

Clemence considers what her friend might really be saying. She says, "Actually the opposite. Not going through with it seemed like the most impossible thing, continuing on in perpetuity—but I kept putting it off, over and over. I didn't want to rock the boat." You had to tread carefully with Jillian. If Clemence went in too hard, Jillian would retreat.

"You know, I envied you a bit," Jillian says. "That day I moved you in. Wondering what it would be like to just be absolutely free." Her sunglasses are up on her head, and she flips them back down over her eyes. No one renovates their kitchen three times in a decade if they aren't yearning for something.

But also this is Jillian and Jeremy, who've been together forever, whose own marital arrangement was how Clemence had known her own was so faulty in comparison. Clemence loves Jeremy in a way that none of her friends had ever loved Toad. Clemence couldn't imagine Jillian without him, or vice versa.

"You and Jeremy,"—Clemence stumbles to find the words—"are you okay?" She needs to believe that love is possible. She may be ready for divorce, but not for cynicism. Not yet. One or the other, but she can't do both.

Jillian sips her drink. "Oh yeah." With sunglasses on, her expression is inscrutable. "Just makes you think a bit, about other roads one might have travelled. I think you're brave, that's all, to be so deliberate in your path."

"I don't think I've ever been deliberate in my life," Clemence admits. "This is really just meandering."

"But isn't that deliberate, too?"

And it is. To be so deliberately meandering, and Clemence appreciates that Jillian gets that, and maybe even understands. That someone like Jillian might be envious of her situation right now is something Clemence has never imagined.

Jillian sits up straighter and pushes her sunglasses back on top of her head, waving to a woman who has entered the park with two children. One of Jillian's mom friends. Clemence has been so far away for so long that she's never met one of these friends of her friends before, and she's prepared to be alienated, because else what do you expect when you don't have kids, and you've come to visit the playground?

But Jillian brings her in. Jillian is a connector. She says, "Sarah, this is my friend Clemence Lathbury, the one I told you about. Ditched the marriage and she's moved across the country, and now she's living the new *Eat, Pray, Love*."

"But without the love," the woman, Sarah, says. She's heard all about it. "Tell me though, what are you eating?"

"Mainly sardines, to be honest. Smoked mussels sometimes."

"Sarah's got a newsletter," Jillian explains. "A pretty big profile. She writes about all these women doing incredible things. Maybe she could write about you?"

"Honestly, I'm not really doing anything," says Clemence. Incredible or otherwise.

"But these days, isn't that kind of novel in itself?" Sarah asks.

"It would be good for you though, wouldn't it?" says Jillian. "Help your with the job search? Raise your profile? Create some buzz?"

"It does sound interesting," Sarah says, holding one child under arm, applying sunscreen to the other one before they take off for the pool. "We could set something up for sure. I don't want to overpromise on the big profile thing, but it might be fun."

Clemence says, "Sure." This seems more deliberate than meandering, and therefore outside the framework of her project, and she isn't sure how she feels about that, but it's hard to turn down an opportunity that's fallen in her lap, and who knows what it might lead to. Plus, she doesn't want to let Jillian down.

Seven

Underlining every question Clemence is asked about her situation lately is another one unspoken: *What exactly do you do all day?* Everybody too polite to come out and ask, even her sister Prudence, who usually says whatever she damn well feels like, but Prudence's years of stay-at-home motherhood, where she hears it a lot, have surely made her wary of this approach.

Her father is the one who keeps asking her about a job, because he can't comprehend an adult life in which work is not a central component, though Clemence wonders if Roger's real trouble is how her situation puts a damper on their small talk. If they can't talk about work, what is there to talk about? Besides the weather, or money, which is also work-adjacent. Roger asks Clemence how her funds are holding up. He also wants Toad to buy Clemence out of her half of their townhouse, but Clemence isn't ready for the hassle yet, still hasn't opened the letter from the lawyer. She thinks the cost of half their house is a fair bargain for never having to talk to Toad again, or face what she did to him, but Roger disagrees. He knows her severance is almost over; Roger would not remember Clemence's birthday without Bonnie to remind him, but he's keeping track of how long she's been unemployed.

It's not only money matters that are bothering people, Clemence knows. The money is what they can ask about under the guise of concern, but their real concern is with her idleness. For the first time in her life, Clemence doesn't have a morning alarm set on her phone, and she wakes up when she feel like it, her body's natural rhythms finally reset. And most days, she has no real commitments, except to sit at her table, maybe open up a new document if she feels like it and just stare at that empty page. And then to think, which is an integral part of the creative process, not a waste of time, until she closes her laptop and goes to make a cup of tea, the tiny electric kettle that came with her place perhaps the hardest-working appliance in the whole apartment. Clemence measures out her day in tea bags, the unfancy brand she buys from the grumpy woman's grocery store. Tea is tea.

She takes walks up and down the avenues, visiting the library on the corner, borrowing book after book. She opens the door to the deck and she closes it when the sky becomes foreboding. The cat stops by, and they spend time together, Clemence rubbing deeply into the thick fur around his neck. Someone brushes this cat; he is well cared for. Sometimes she meets friends, but not often, and it's as though she hasn't really moved back to town in some ways, or at least to the same town, because her schedule is so different from her friends', everybody else's particularly demanding and structured, so it's as though they inhabit separate universes. Sometimes Jillian and Naomi will make plans and suggest Clemence pick a date, which is tricky, because she can't just say, "All of them?"

Instead, she gets to know the people in her new universe, or at least to recognize them, some of them friendly enough that they smile and say hi. She loves the librarians. She's a regular at the boulangerie now, Mila behind the counter having forgotten or forgiven that first time when she was forced to open up after closing. Clemence knows now to get there on time, usually in the mornings when the bread is fresh, and sometimes if she's feeling extravagant, she'll stop at the cheese shop for Gorgonzola.

Because it's summer, the neighbourhood is quiet. Some of the older shops on the street have stuck a sign in their windows informing customers that they've shut down for two weeks in August in the old European tradition. There is a truck parked on the corner that sells ice cream, and right now it's the only business booming, a line usually stretching halfway down the street, and sometimes Clemence joins it, because ice cream from a truck is a delicacy that never disappoints. But other times she doesn't care to stand around waiting, and heads back to her nest. So high up in the trees, she gets a breeze even when the air down below seems immovable, and it's a good house, however rundown. The smells in the stairwell linger, but Mrs. Yeung vacuums the hallway, and most problems are seen to, Charles turning up in a tight T-shirt with a bag of tools. He's figured out a way for her to plug in the air conditioner by running an extension cord through a vent to the unit downstairs, and Clemence has used it a couple of times, though the roar is overwhelming and she's worried the circuits will blow again. Plus, she really doesn't mind the heat, forcing her body into a cool bath on the most sweltering evenings before she goes to bed, sleeping with the French doors open to let the night air inside.

What Clemence's days are giving her now is space, existential space, which means she doesn't even mind that her room is so tiny. Her only confines, really, with everything else wide open—her hours, her streetscapes, her possibilities. When she does manage to make plans with her friends or her family, there's a part of her that resents the obligation that any part of her day, of herself, should be spoken for. She much prefers to move through the hours to see how they unfold.

Walking by the bookshop one morning and realizing it's a Wednesday, when the pale book man had said the owner would be in, Clemence wonders, what if she walked right in there now and confronted the owner, demanding an explanation for the store's sexist cataloguing system? And because there is nothing else on her agenda, Clemence is free to partake in such an experiment.

As usual, the store is quiet, tinkling bells the only sound when she enters. At first glance, it doesn't appear that anyone else has been in the shop since her last visit, the dusty piles of paperbacks undisturbed. How does a person make a living in a place like this? How does the pale book man manage to get paid? She's been imagining Crampton, an old white-bearded fisherman, someone grizzled and grandfatherly, but the grumpy kind, the sort whose true heart of gold is not made evident until the end of the novel, and even then, he doesn't want anyone to know about it. Clemence will ask him about the cataloguing, and he'll say he never actually knew that any woman has written a book. For the past forty years, he's been rereading infinite *Moby Dick*.

But it's a different face that Clemence finds at the counter, a familiar one. Tweed-clad, grey-haired, but here with a tiny pair of spectacles perched on the bridge of her nose, which she never wears at the grocery store. The stern expression is the same, though, she and the pale book man apparently having been similarly schooled in customer service.

The woman says, "You. You're everywhere. It's like you're haunting me."

Clemence is caught off guard. "I mean—"

"I don't see many customers. And then, suddenly, you start turning up all the time for groceries, and now you're here. A little uncanny, that's all I'm saying."

"I just moved into the neighbourhood," says Clemence. "It's really not that strange. And I need groceries. I like books."

The woman is unmoved. "Most people order online these days. You can do that, you know. Get your books delivered right to your door. Even food—they've got refrigerated vans. Don't you know about that?"

"Of course," says Clemence. "But I like picking out my own stuff, I guess. Getting out in the world, talking to people."

"Well," says the woman. "I'm not much of a people person."

"Really," says Clemence. She knows this might sound sarcastic, but she's actually trying to be polite. She really does want to speak to the owner of the shop, imagining how this might all fit into her larger project, the denegation of women's stories. "I'm looking for Crampton."

"You're looking *at* Crampton," says the woman, meeting her eyes.

"*You're* Crampton?" She doesn't have a beard, only the trace of a bristly moustache. What kind of a name for a woman is Crampton? "Like the shop?"

"The shop was named for my grandfather," the woman explains. Evidently this is a story she likes telling because she's just getting started. "Thomas Crampton, developed the entire block. We had a shoe store, too. Things were different then. Nobody had to go far to get what they needed. The grocers took up three storefronts, but then once the big supermarkets opened up, people stopped coming. The bookstore never brought in much of a profit, anyway; more of a hobby project. My mother inherited it all, and ran it with my father, and then it was my turn, and I've not made such a bad job of it, considering what I had to work with."

And there she'd been, Clemence, walking around in the world, observing, imagining her instincts were good enough that she was getting the basic sense of things, that a tweed suit and a bad haircut might tell her everything she needed to know about this woman. It took a certain kind of nerve to suppose understanding of anything at all.

"You still own the buildings?" Clemence asks. An entire block, with retail and two floors of apartments above, gorgeous century-old buildings with tin ceilings and huge windows. This woman was sitting on millions of dollars.

"As long as I can keep paying the taxes, yes," she answers. "And I'm not selling. Don't you start with that. I've heard the spiels before, and I'm wise to you."

"But I'm not starting," says Clemence. "I wouldn't be even if I could, but I can't. I really can't." She looks around again, at the dust and disorganization. "You run both stores yourself?"

The woman shrugs. "At this point, they run themselves." Only because customers rarely came in, but she was fine with that.

"I'm Clemence Lathbury," says Clemence, putting out her hand. "And I swear that I'm not haunting you."

Her offer accepted. "Crampton Goldberg," is the answer. "*Miss* Crampton Goldberg."

"Miss Goldberg."

"Crampton's fine."

"I've come about the books," says Clemence.

"Oh, the books," says Crampton, as though they were an afterthought.

"You're not a big reader?"

"I read some," says Crampton, indignant. "Or at least I used to. It's hard to find the time."

Clemence isn't sure she believes this. This woman

spends hours and hours in shops that nobody goes into—but Clemence also knows she is in no position to judge anybody for how they spend their days. The store's cataloguing, though, there's no excuse for that.

"I was confused," says Clemence. "About the distinction —'Women's Fiction.'"

Crampton Goldberg actually rolls her eyes. "You're one of those women's libbers, I guess."

Clemence says, "I guess, but isn't that from, like, fifty years ago?"

"The books are written by women, aren't they?" asks Crampton. "And it's fiction. I don't see what the problem is. I've been in places where books are filed under 'Fiction Novels,' and I don't see you out there complaining about that."

"Actually," says Clemence, "I complain about that a lot. 'Fiction Novels' is an egregious crime, but this isn't any better. Why don't you have a 'Men's Fiction' section, then?"

"We do," says Crampton. "We call it 'Literature.'"

"But why?" demands Clemence. "And don't you see?"

"Why it matters?" asks Crampton. "No. I don't. There are problems enough to deal with in this world without people like you going around inventing things to be offended by."

"I'm not offended," says Clemence. "I just think it's wrong."

"And what are you going to do about it?" asks Crampton. "Boycott? Because no one shops here, anyway. Believe me, I wouldn't know the difference if you boycotted me or not."

"But doesn't it bother you?" asks Clemence. "To see women as somehow second tier?"

"Why would it?" Crampton Goldberg is as unmovable as her city block. "I know who I am. What anybody else thinks or where a novel happens to land on the shelf—that doesn't have anything to do with me. And it's got even less to do with you. You don't like it? You can leave any time." She waits. "You're not going."

But Clemence Lathbury is unmovable, too, until she hears a sound behind her, the pale book man clambering down the staircase, presumably after a shift among the books on billiards and badminton. His footfall is heavier than his slight figure might suggest.

"Toby, one of these days you're going to bring the building down," Crampton is saying, her voice far away now that he's locked eyes with Clemence, who now realizes this could become very bad. Clemence had only seen Toby behind the counter before, but now she's examining him head to toe and determining how likely it is that he will die of something tragic like tuberculosis or scarlet fever. So pale, his forehead high and vulnerable, full pink lips, and he's wearing a cardigan, which Clemence has always imagined on a man is a public acknowledgement of one's desire to be enveloped, and what if she is up for the job?

"You're back," he's saying.

Crampton behind the counter. "I gather the two of you have met?"

"I was in the other week," says Clemence. "We spoke."

"Toby, well done," Crampton calls across the shop, and then says to Clemence, "He usually has a hard time talking to girls." At this, the pale book man turns bright red and knocks down a tower of mass-market paperbacks—and then Crampton has an idea. Her face enlivened, and she's standing up taller, and Clemence can almost see the wheels in her head turning.

Crampton says to Toby, "She's come about the books, Clemence. Miss Lathbury—it *is* 'miss'?" she asks, checking. Clemence nods. "She doesn't like the way we put them in order, and I've got to tell you, Clemence, Miss Lathbury, I have neither the time nor inclination to do anything about it. The books are books, and there are books behind the books, plus upstairs, and changing everything around would give me a lot more trouble than the status quo has ever provided, if you know what I'm saying.

"But I'm wondering, seeing as you seem pretty free and easy, shopping at all hours when everybody else is working, and seeing as the notion of women's fiction bothers you so much, if you might be want to be one to take on dealing with the problem. Sorting, organizing, you know. Putting our shelves more in alignment with your politics. Could you spare the time? I'd pay you. Not much, but a fair wage. For you to come in here a couple of hours a week and move the books around. To talk to Toby?"

"Are you offering me a job?" Clemence asks.

"If you'd consider."

"I would. I did."

"And I'd say that Toby could help, but he's got a bad back, and shoulders. He can't lift much, but you appear to be a remarkably sturdy young woman—and no, don't make that face. There's nothing wrong with sturdy. Poor Toby, here, he gets knocked over when the wind blows. We can't have that. You're robust. I like robust. I admire your gumption. I don't understand why you think women's books ought to be stuck among all those others, books about spies and soldiers, and oil barons. Wasn't it Virginia Woolf herself who said what a woman needs is a room of her own?"

"I don't think she meant it like that."

"They'd be tainted by association, I should think. But no matter. You're never going to finish the job, but maybe you'll make a start, and I do need the place tidied up. And you can talk to Toby."

"Does Toby want to talk to me?" Clemence is embarrassed by the quaver in her voice. Toby has disappeared down the far aisle, surely to hide.

"Toby will do what I tell him to," says Crampton Goldberg. "I write his paycheques, after all. We're closed Monday, for Labour Day, but could you start Tuesday?" But Tuesday morning, Clemence is going to meet with her professor, to begin her new career as an indexer. So they agree on Thursday, and the matter is set.

Eight

"So explain this," says Naomi, whose mouth is currently stuffed with French bread. She takes a moment to swallow. "The desire for an unsuitable attachment. How that's going to fit into your overall scheme. And why you just can't lust after the hot guy."

"Naomi is trying to project-manage me," Clemence says to Jillian. "This is what you do," she says to Naomi, who shakes her head. Naomi has no idea what Clemence is talking about. And Jillian is laughing at both of them, sitting back against the railings on Clemence's balcony, against the purple golden sunset, the dazzling colours even more so when refracted through the bubbly wine in the stemmed plastic glass she is holding aloft.

Clemence is drunk. Clemence is happy.

Clemence says, "I fear sometimes I may have bitten off more than I can chew." It is an evening for disclosures, one more link on a chain stretching back over the decades, since they first became friends when they were still teenagers, Clemence's current circumstances taking them back to those days of material impoverishment. There are only two chairs at her table, and it's too hot to sit inside, and so she's spread a blanket on the balcony, covering up the detritus from the tree, and she's called it a picnic. Springing for the fancy cheeses at the fromagerie and the bread that's almost cake from the boulangerie, and she's feeling Parisian, sophisticated. Her friends have brought wine that probably cost even more than everything else in her elaborate spread, but Clemence is glad. She hasn't been drinking much since beginning her new life. Drinking is not the same without company.

Down below them, Charles Yeung has just finished mowing the lawn, and Clemence is explaining why he can't be the object of her affections, no matter how attractive he appears in the soft evening light.

Clemence tells her friends, "The point is not to have any significant attachment at all, which is a definition of freedom, you know? To be accountable to nobody but myself, and to travel, to discover who I really am by where I ended up."

"Like a tumbleweed," suggests Jillian.

"But not in the middle of a dust bowl. And I'm not saying there is anything wrong with ties and connections. I think connections are the basis of a meaningful life. You know I know that, I mean—here you are! But after so long being tied to something—to Toad, to Toad and me and our marriage, to the *institution*,"—her tongue trips over the consonants—"I wanted to try being untethered in that fundamental way."

"And how's it going?" asks Naomi.

Clemence says, "Well, okay, it's kind of lonely. I've learned I'm not cut out for hermeticism." She stops Jillian before she can say what's next. "And I *know* you told me. I know you knew, but that's not the point. I had to find out myself."

"You need the love!" exclaims Jillian, triumphant. "Because what's eating and praying without it? Like a two-legged table, your spiritual quest. It will topple over."

"And he likes you," says Naomi. "Lawn mower man. The way he looked up and waved. I'd let him hold up my table."

But Clemence disagrees. "What I need is like a placeholder," she says. "An object of fixation, but one that's never going to go anywhere. Something inconsequential." She notes the skepticism on her friends' faces. "And I've thought about this a lot."

"Well, why not try an app, then?" suggested Naomi. "For something casual. Say 'no strings'—they love that."

"But it's not even about sex," says Clemence. "I mean, I already tried that, supposing that meaningless sex might be the solution to what ailed me, but it didn't fill me up at all."

Jillian says, "I mean..."

Clemence tops up her glass. "We're talking spiritually," she insists. "And it didn't do a thing. And I've had time to reflect now." She takes a sip. "I think what I need is a little bit of drama. You know the way it goes when you start something with somebody at work?" She'd met Toad when they worked together in the student union pub a thousand years ago. "And all of a sudden, you're excited about going to work? Even if nothing ever happens there, because it would be inappropriate." (Not true. She had got it on with Toad in the room in the back among boxes of beer nuts.) "And there's this *frisson*." She feels strange saying this word out loud, because it's one of those words she's only seen written down, and Clemence can't quite remember if it means what she thinks it means, but she's thinking of fizz. She's watching the bubbles in Jillian's glass again, and the sun's nearly gone.

"Everyday life just made a little bit more exciting—and it's more about anticipation than anything coming to fruition. I don't want the fruit, I want the blossom." Perhaps she's making no sense at all. "But I have this problem. I mean, I've had it, where I always take the fruit. I can't say no to fruit." This is all getting a bit Book of Genesis. "So maybe it's best if the fruit is a little bit rotten? Or at least pale and dyspeptic. An unsuitable attachment, something inconsequential. Something that wouldn't even get written into a book."

"How is your book going, anyway?" Naomi asks. Ever since Clemence had mused about writing one, no one will let her forget it.

She counters, "When are you going to be getting around to having children?"

Naomi retreats.

"So you want drama," says Jillian. "What you're saying is that you're bored."

"And not horny." Naomi has emptied another bottle of wine. There's row of them now. Mrs. Yeung is going to see them in the recycling and arrive at conclusions—that Clemence has been entertaining visitors, that Clemence is a lush.

"Oh, I'm horny," says Clemence. "But I like that part. I'd honestly thought that my sex drive died, but now it's restarted, and I'd thought it never would. It feels so good to be yearning. I thought I'd never yearn again. But I'm good with being slow but steady. It's like cultivating a flame. No, I just want an object. Is that wrong?"

"Objectification?" asks Jillian. "Isn't that supposed to be wrong?"

"Not when it's a man," affirms Naomi. "That's like reverse racism. It's nonsense. I say you're allowed to make an object out of any man you like. So venture forth. You're only righting the balance."

"It's like she's an authority," says Clemence to Jillian.

"As long as you like what she's saying," says Jillian.

"I'm saying I'm ready for the cake course now," says Naomi, and Clemence has to haul herself back up to her feet, which is even harder to do with the world spinning.

SO THIS IS HOW a woman builds a life, in bits and pieces. You realize there are these little things you're missing—a box of matches, a roll of tape, Q-tips, a needle and thread—and you head out to buy them, many of these available in Crampton Goldberg's little grocery store where you only have to blow the dust off. You pick up a chive plant and put the pot on the deck, snipping odd fronds for seasoning or garnish. You go running once, and only once, but your shoes give you blisters, so you purchase a box of Band-Aids from the pharmacy, along with a small first aid kit since you're already there. Clemence finally buys a can opener, and also a beautiful yellow teapot from the potter at the market in the park because she'd been drinking her tea cup by cup, and the kettle was working overtime. She likes a pot so it can linger, lasting halfway through the morning. She is working on her index, for a biography of Alvin Puddicombe, an obscure mid-twentieth-century regional poet, fuelled by rage and alcohol. He used to beat up his girlfriends. Puddicombe always had girlfriends—what is the matter with women?

Clemence sits at the desk she has made at her kitchen table, and contemplates the logistics of indexing. That she has the power to give this book a kind of shape: Puddicombe, Alvin: Impotence. Improprieties. Infidelities. Intoxication. Where did the impulse come from to fashion such men into legends?

When the first pot of tea is finished, she puts away that work and opens another file. She has been writing. If anybody asks her how that book is going, she still refuses to answer, because she doesn't want to jinx it, but at least it's going now, words on a page. "So this is how a woman builds a life, in bits and pieces," she writes. She never knew how much a box of matches would matter. When she'd been married, she'd had all the material goods a person could desire. Once upon a time, Clemence had been co-owner of six coffee grinders, which is hard to believe now, when going out to buy a simple yellow pencil encompasses an errand. Leading to the need for a sharpener, of course, but she can borrow one from Doug, the agoraphobic artist who lives downstairs. He makes her stand in his doorway sharpening the pencil to a point, the shavings trailing on the floor. He tells her the mess doesn't matter.

It feels good to be creating, sitting at the table, pencil in hand. To be enduring, too—the notion that soon she will have spent an entire season here. Soon the summer will be over, fall will begin, and Clemence will discover all kinds of new things about her new home. How the leaves change and when they'll let go of their branches, and how the light will hit her bed in the morning when those branches are bare, and maybe it will be cool enough that she'll have to acquire another blanket for her bed, but at the moment that seems impossible, far more likely that the heat of the summer will continue forever, just the way that Clemence, only a year ago, couldn't have imagined a world beyond her old life with Toad.

Nine

On Thursdays, Clemence goes to the bookstore and talks to Toby. She doesn't tell the people in her life that this is what she's there for, but she lets everybody know that she's found another job. Her work at the bookstore too is like the box of matches and the needle with thread, another item gathered. The entire block owned by Crampton Goldberg is transformed into someplace different now that Clemence knows its history, and she feels connected to it. This is how a woman builds a life, and she's sorting the books. Mrs. Yeung's church is looking for donations for their upcoming winter jumble sale, and books are always a big seller, she says, a bit of information that makes Clemence feel good about the world for once.

She is performing the same tasks at the bookstore that she has been doing in her own life, establishing order, making space where everything was crowded before.

Cluttering the aisles are boxes of books that have never been opened, and these are mainly used as furniture when a rare customer sits down on them to browse the shelves. Clemence opens one box and finds that the books inside have literally turned to dust, bindings made redundant as the pages disintegrated, but not all the boxes are all as bad as that. In another, she finds vintage editions of V. C. Andrews novels, spines barely cracked. And there's one stuffed with all the copies of *The Pilot's Wife* that she'd been wondering about on her first visit.

She tells Crampton about Mrs. Yeung and the church jumble sale, reminding her that there are more books within the walls of the shop than she could hope to sell. Crampton consents to donate some of the overflow, though partly in the interest of making the shop into less of a fire trap.

"And you're talking to Toby?" she asks. Toby is hiding again, and Clemence will have to head into the maze to find him. To talk to him. She's promised Crampton Goldberg, who insists he needs the company.

But Toby does not agree. Clemence finds him upstairs on a ladder with a roll of duct tape, because there's a hole near the ceiling where mice are getting in, leaving droppings among the microwave cookbooks. No doubt if he slipped up there, that delicate man would wind up in traction, and Clemence resists the flutter in her person at the thought of Toby tied up.

The tape, she suggests to him, might not be the most effective arrangement. Surely mice could chew through such a barrier? And Toby welcomes her feedback as much as he appreciates anything she offers him, which is pretty much not at all.

She stays by him, not to talk, because she has no desire to be a distraction from the matter at hand, to send him toppling, but because if it happened, she'd be able to call an ambulance right away. Breathing a sigh of relief as he climbs down the ladder, returning to safety, but then he trips over a box and she catches him. He lands right in her arms.

Toby is more substantial than she'd imagined—and yes, she'd imagined plenty. This is what a person does with their unsuitable attachments after all, idle fantasies, but in these, it was always more like holding a feather, because he's so slight, but the reality of holding him is that he has all these sharp angles, shoulders and elbows. He has a pimple on his lip, the very worst place for such a thing. Clemence is close enough to note the patchy way his eyebrows are connected, and oh yes, this is intimacy. And the way he has entirely submitted, his whole body gone slack, Clemence wondering how he's managed to lose consciousness without hitting his head.

But Toby is dramatic—after just a few shifts together, she knows this. Although he's not an actor, but a set painter, an artist who had to give up the trade, he'd explained to her, when he developed an allergy to the paint. He'd completed a college diploma, but there's nothing he can do with his training now. And after wasting years on futile dreams, Toby is resentful of anyone whose achievements vaguely resemble success, Clemence discerning that he finds her own presence only vaguely tolerable because he gets to feel superior when he's with her—a strange and novel experience for him—being, after all, the store's full-time employee, while she stops in for a few hours a week on some whim of Crampton Goldberg's.

Toby lives in one of Crampton's apartments, a bachelor above the old shoe store. When his college program was completed and he couldn't find work, Crampton gave him this job, which he doesn't seem to realize is charity. Toby's arrogance, Clemence supposes, is a posture to compensate for his lack of anything to be arrogant about.

"There you go," she tells him, setting him back on his feet. Dust and spiderwebs are caught in his shaggy hair, but this is what happens when you spend long enough in the bookshop. Clemence has taken to having a second bath when she gets home before lunch, washing off the grime, and yes, thinking of Toby's hands on her body as she pours the jug of water over her head and shoulders, and her thoughts of this have been so vivid that it's as though it's actually happened. In fact, when she looked down after he'd fallen and found him in her arms, the scene felt so familiar, and it didn't surprise her that he'd linger.

But of course, it should have. Once Toby regains composure, he jerks away from Clemence, as though she'd startled him, and turns around, refusing to acknowledge that she may have saved his life. He doesn't say a word, and takes off, possibly embarrassed, leaving her among the cookery books, forcing her to follow him back through the store, because this is what Crampton demands of her, and also because it's kind of fun.

He settles back down behind the counter with a book, always a Restoration play, which is when Toby feels that drama peaked, and nothing even half decent has been produced since then, or even before it—don't mention Marlowe or Shakespeare, because he'll pretend he's never heard of them. Clemence takes her seat amid the books and the boxes, resuming the gathering of titles for Mrs. Yeung's jumble. There's an entire box of 1980s Harlequins, with gorgeous covers, all of the women wearing shoulder pads. Would Clemence herself dare to file these away in Women's Fiction? And why not? Who gets to make the distinction?

No, these she's taking away for donation to the church, because she knows somebody's going to snap them up, and they're doing no good to anybody packed away in the bookstore.

She hears the bells at the door, assuming it's Crampton, because Clemence has never known anyone else to walk into the store, and she's afraid to turn around because Toby seems to be ignoring her right now, and Clemence isn't sure if Crampton will hold her accountable for that, and dock her pay, but the footsteps are heavier and she glances over her shoulder to see a tall Black man in a tailored suit. Clemence is slightly gratified—albeit embarrassed—to see that this customer gets the same service she'd received from Toby on her first visit, having to clear his throat three times before Toby lowers his play and notes the customer's presence.

"There's a bell," she calls out to him from her perch. Toby and the customer glance over at her in confusion.

"In case you need to get his attention," she explains. "I mean, for next time," and the man turns back to Toby, explaining that he's looking for books on hats, European millinery history in particular, Toby sending him upstairs to the books about fashion, and then slouching back into his chair, exhausted from the exertion of all that.

Clemence is concerned that Toby is malnourished. He doesn't cook; he barely eats. She's offered to bring him an apple or a banana, but Toby claims that he hates fruit.

"How can you hate fruit?" Clemence demands. "That's like hating 'seasons.' Or 'dessert.'"

"I also hate seasons," says Toby. "I have allergies."

"I just think," says Clemence, unpacking a box of 1970s *National Geographics* that surely belong in the recycling, "that if you took better care of yourself, you might have more energy."

"I've got energy," says Toby, lowering his book again. "My problem is ennui, but that's got nothing to do with diet."

The customer comes back downstairs with an armful of books, and Toby consents to let him make the purchase.

"Has anybody ever come in here and not found what they wanted?" Clemence asks.

"Well, not a lot of people come in," admits Toby, "but yeah, no."

CLEMENCE PACKS THREE BOXES of books to take to the church, a mix of the romances, 1990s Oprah's Book Club titles, and a bunch of paperbacks about true crime and

Satanic panic, which are especially sinister with their pages trimmed in red. She's also found a pile of cowboy novels, essentially romance for boys, and by now she's managed to clear enough space in the bookstore's central aisle that a person might walk down it without having to step over anything. Even Crampton is pleased by the improvement.

She leaves the store with the boxes piled almost higher than her head, although that means she can't see what's in front of her. The balance is precarious.

"You're not moving out, are you?" someone calls on the sidewalk. His face is blocked by her heavy load, but she knows that voice.

Charles removes the top box from her tower.

"Hey," she says, at the sight of his smile.

"You looked like you were struggling," he says, but now he's found himself unsteady, too, a bit of a wobble. He hadn't expected the box to be so heavy. "What have you got in here? Lead weights?" he asks as he regains his balance.

"I wasn't struggling," she says. She wonders what it might be like if they were to meet, both of them unencumbered. If fate is trying to tell her something, setting obstacles in her way.

"Come on, you were about to drop it," says Charles.

Clemence says, "I was fine." She was. But she also says, "Thank you."

"You're not *really* moving out, right?"

"I guess if I were, I'd be going in the wrong direction." This is the way toward home, and they're walking side by side, taking up the entire sidewalk.

He says, "You want me to get that one?" He's got the one box, and she's still carrying two, but she's fine now. He asks her, "Where you going, anyway?"

"The church."

"So she got you." Charles is shaking his head. "I knew she would. She saw you coming. My mother is indefatigable. You know, I told her about your book."

"My book."

"Eat, Pray, Love."

"I didn't write that book," says Clemence, feeling her face getting hot. What was going on here? Who uses words like "indefatigable"?

"Well, shit." Charles puts the box down. "And here I thought you were Elizabeth Gilbert. I told my mom that she had Elizabeth Gilbert living up in her attic, and she's been trying to impress you ever since. You know, she loved *Coyote Ugly.*"

"What?"

"Where are these going?" He picks up the box again, because they've arrived at the church, whose haphazard architecture features at least a dozen entrances.

They head inside the closest one, near where the church office is located, and they're directed to a room where jumble is being collected, already packed with bric-a-brac, sets of dead people's china, and plastic grocery bags exploding with costume jewellery. Clemence and Charles add the boxes of books to the collection, and she takes a minute to look through the rest of the stuff, Clemence explaining, as she riffles through a pile of earnest cross-stitch hangings, that she's not actually attending the church, just facilitating this donation.

"She's got you in the door, though," says Charles. "It's the first step. A slippery slope."

"I don't know," says Clemence. "Somehow you've been able to resist the draw." Charles was as disoriented by the labyrinthine church hallways as she was, so hardly a regular attendee.

"Only because I moved out of the city," he tells her. "And even then, she used to insist I come down, but she also insisted on giving me gas money, and then she decided it was too expensive. She assumes I go to a church out in the suburbs, though. I let her think that."

"You're like the opposite of me," Clemence says, as they weave their way back out of the building. "I grew up in the burbs, and then I moved downtown."

"A little bit of distance," says Charles, "is healthy for any family relationship."

They emerge back into the daylight and begin the rest of the walk toward home.

"You're around a lot, though," says Clemence. "Helping out."

Charles says, "Of course. The church part doesn't matter to me, but I don't want to leave my mom all alone. My brother lives in Florida. We're all she's got. She set everything up so we'd both do well, but one of us has to stick around."

"To do the heavy lifting," says Clemence.

"Not exactly," says Charles. "You ever seen my mom lift? She's small, but mighty. It's why I generally don't like to cross her."

"So what do you do?" asks Clemence, "when you're not carrying other people's burdens, I mean?" They've arrived back at the house and she sits on the step. Charles sits down beside her.

"What do you think I do?" he answers, a smile on his face. Does he know she's staring at his body, at his pecs? Is that why his left biceps is flexing now, just so slightly, almost indiscernible?

She says, "I don't know. Maybe ... you're a mover? Or a builder?" He'd known a thing or two about wiring, but not enough to avoid blowing the fuse, so he likely wasn't an electrician. Clemence was having a hard time understanding him outside of the context of this house, what kind of person he might be beyond it. But maybe he only had the build because of a spectacular home gym. Perhaps he worked a desk job, in computers or accounting, and worked out in the evenings.

But when she dares to voice these further ideas, he accuses her of drawing on racial stereotypes.

"I'm not," she says, indignant. "I have absolutely no idea. What have you given me to go on?"

He rolls his eyes. "I've told you in little ways so many times."

She tries to think back to the conversations they'd had, but all she'd been doing was fixating on his body. "Are you ... a weightlifter?" she asks, feeling like this was something out of "Rumpelstiltskin." Although she already knew his name—this was Charles Yeung, and she really liked him. An unsuitable attachment indeed, but only because such an attachment would lead her to trouble.

And Charles tells her, as though he wants to make that trouble inevitable, "I'm an English teacher. High school." The last thing she would have expected. He tells her that he loves it, that his whole world is books and reading, and he gets to do it for a living. The students, sometimes, he could take or leave, depending on the day, but he lives for literature. Spelling out every single syllable, softening the consonants like a song. His favourite book is Toni Morrison's *Song of Solomon*, the best novel he'd read lately was *On Earth We're Briefly Gorgeous*, by Ocean Vuong, and he had a copy of *Minor Feelings*, by Cathy Park Hong, in his car that he wanted to lend to her. As long as she promised to give it back. "I'm kind of possessive about my books," he says.

She swears that she'll take good care of it, and they walk down to where his car is parked on the street. Charles's car is a mess and he has to dig through several layers of papers and fast food wrappers to find the book, and though she doubts he will, she's proven wrong when he pulls it out of the pile, exactly where he'd said it would be.

"My filing system is unorthodox," he explains, "but it works." He places the book in her hands like it's something precious, and she knows it will be. And then he reaches for her face, to stroke her hair, she thinks—but it's only to pull out a dust bunny stuck behind her ear.

"It's from the bookstore," she tries to explain. She doesn't want Charles to think that she's coated in filth on the regular, although with a car like that, he'd have to be a real jerk to judge her.

He lets the dust bunny fall to the sidewalk, where it

rolls into the gutter, and Clemence thinks again about the tumbleweed. She thinks, *Out of the fire and into another fire*. She thinks, *No*.

Charles Yeung is not going to move in to kiss her. Because you don't do that to someone from whose head you've just picked a ball of ancient dust, even *literary* dust.

But he does say, "You know, I *was* trying to impress you. Dropping hints. It's not every day a writer moves into my mother's attic. I wanted to let you know that I had some literary cred. I've taught *Romeo and Juliet* a thousand times."

"Like, you've read a book or two."

He says, "I have."

"Thank you for lending me this one," she says, clutching the paperback to her bosom. "I'll care for it well. You'll find not a single page dog-eared upon its return."

He says, "And you won't use it as a coaster?"

She says, "I swear. And listen, thanks for helping me carry the books."

Charles smiles. "Anything for the jumble sale."

Clemence says, "Well, obviously." And oh, the tension between them, like a trap door that could spring open beneath her feet, and she knows she'd be falling, falling, falling. She sidesteps, away from him, and then a twirl, like a whirlwind, away.

Ten

There is news: her sister Prudence is pregnant again, though Clemence is not sure this constitutes news because Prudence has been pregnant throughout most of the last decade. What is different this time is that nobody knows, except Clemence. While previous announcements had arrived momentously at holiday dinners, or via cute videos sent by mass email (the recycled "I'm Going to Be a Big ~~Sister~~ Brother" T-shirt was a theme), this time Prudence breaks the news half-heartedly while stripping wallpaper, the occasion for which she'd invited Clemence to dinner. Prudence never invites anybody over without giving them a chore, something Clemence can't stand, and she would have declined the invitation, as had been her habit since moving back home, except something in the way her sister had punctuated her texts had led Clemence to believe more was going on.

And so that weekend she'd taken a bus out of the

city toward the suburbs, not the northern ones where Charles lives, but this time west, leaning her head on the window and thinking about Charles while trying not to, the world beside the highway speeding by. She is patient when Sandro fails to be waiting upon her arrival, because Prudence's family is always late. Prudence has them on a regimented system, but it runs about twenty minutes behind everybody else's, and now here is Sandro, driving the small bus that constitutes their family vehicle. He doesn't even put the car into park, taking off again before she's got the door closed, let alone fastened her seat belt, slamming on the brakes as he arrives at an unexpected stop sign, flinging out his right arm to stop her from flying through the windshield and/or (is she imagining this now?) copping a feel of her left breast.

"Sandro is European," is the Lathbury family's explanation for everything unusual or inappropriate about their sole remaining son-in-law, plus he's a professor, and so it's impossible to tell if these are the factors in play or if he's just weird. Sandro has always been flirtatious, the kisses he bestows as greetings a little too intimate, and he delivers compliments such as, "The way that blouse hugs your bosom is most appealing."

It would have been sleazier if he'd taken pains to hide it, or if Prudence herself didn't just roll her eyes when he behaved this way, as though it were a minor annoyance, a little quirk, and so Clemence tries the same approach. Recalling what her sister had said at the barbecue, that Sandro supposes that Clemence wants to sleep with him. She folds her arms over her chest just to be extra clear about boundaries, and starts telling Sandro about her own professor and the book on Alvin Puddicombe, whom Sandro has never heard of. Sandro believes that nothing that isn't Italian could possibly constitute literature anyway (his pronunciation of "literature" is "lit-*tore*-a-ture" and she doesn't hate it) and he wants to make sure that Clemence is getting a fair wage for her work.

The work women do, Sandro reminds her, as if she doesn't know, is rarely permitted its fair value—and this is what Clemence is thinking about now as she and her sister strip the wallpaper from the dining room, a hideous pink floral that had been hanging since they moved in. Sandro considers himself a feminist, and an attentive father, and he is—with this family, at least; things had been very different when he'd been married before. On feminist grounds, Sandro had objected to Prudence's resistance to hormonal birth control, but he'd also been supportive when she insisted they employ a more natural method because it was her body, her choice. "The fertility awareness method," Prudence explains. "But maybe we should have been more aware."

And now she is six weeks pregnant. Again. "All the baby stuff," she says. "I thought it was over. It's only been in the last year or so that I've rediscovered sleep." She hasn't told Sandro yet. "He'll be fine either way, but he'll also say 'I told you so.' He never really believed in fertility awareness in the first place."

Prudence is standing up on a ladder. The ceilings in here are so tall, the floor-to-ceiling windows revealing the backyard where Sandro is leading the kids in soccer drills. The only reason Prudence can be so open with her disclosures is that she's not making eye contact. She's got her back to her sister, and it's more like a monologue.

Clemence, up on another ladder, manages to loosen a corner, and peels back a strip in a satisfying release. Too bad it can't all be like this. She knows to stay quiet, to let Prudence say what she needs to say. When Prudence desires feedback, she'll will ask for it. Clemence continues to peel the paper and she waits, and tries to think about Toby instead of Charles, fixating on the one best suited to being her unsuitable attachment.

Of course, an abortion is an option, says Prudence. She's still got some time to decide. Prudence had had an abortion when she was seventeen, in high school, which she's still quite clear is the best decision she ever made, until she married Sandro. She's not opposed in principle. "But it's not quite in keeping with the spirit of all this, you know? So many kids—what difference is one more?"

"But you're talking about a family, not a flash mob," says Clemence. "And what you want matters, too. A lot." She is thinking of what she was wanting when Charles leaned in to—she thought—kiss her. She is thinking that she apparently has absolutely no will, and can't control herself, and Prudence is the living embodiment of what happens when a person lets those impulses take over.

"Before, I was never ambivalent." Prudence steps down from her ladder and stands back to examine her work so far. "I didn't understand how anyone could be, if they're not seventeen. Ambivalent about a baby? A baby is a blessing!" She turns around to face her sister. "But this time it all just seems so overwhelming."

This time? "I guess you know what you're getting into."

"I do, and it's a lot. Pregnancy does a number on you. My hemorrhoids have hemorrhoids."

"That's good to know." It wasn't.

"It is," insists Prudence. "Because nobody tells you these things. And I like being a mother. You know that. I *love* it. It's my whole life, and I'm fine with that, and so it seems weird that I can't accept this with open arms. Like what kind of a mother am I, then, really?"

"One who acknowledges her limits?" Clemence and Prudence are now sitting on the bottom steps of their ladders. "There's nothing wrong with that." Limits are important. Clemence hasn't felt this connected to her sister in years.

"I needed to tell you, to talk to somebody who wouldn't judge," says Prudence. "I mean, you're not exactly pro-family values."

"Hey, I have family values," Clemence says. "I'm here, aren't I? My sister needed me. With household tasks and other things. That's family values."

"I just mean you're not Catholic," says Prudence. "And you can see there's more than one side of things, other possibilities. You know there's never just one answer."

"Wouldn't it be easier if there were?" says Clemence.

"But getting to decide is the point," says Prudence. "No matter what the outcome is. It's about the process, and what I needed today was to process this."

"And to take down the wallpaper."

"That, too. Listen, don't mention anything." They hear the sounds of the family coming in. And Clemence, naturally, promised that she wouldn't say a word. Now engulfed in the noise and hubbub of her sister's household, she can see what Prudence means—what difference would one more make? But also, when she visits her sister, Clemence usually needs two days to recover. Roberto walks into the dining room, and immediately kicks over the bucket of water by Clemence's ladder, the deluge soaking her socks, and little Enzo has already scrambled around her, making his way to the top. Lila hiking up her shorts to show her mother the scrape on her thigh from falling down on the sprinkler, and Alessia is yelling at her smallest brother. One more child might be the point to tip the whole thing into chaos, although Clemence recalls thinking the same with each of her sister's pregnancies. She is glad that this cacophonous family life exists, but she's never desired it for herself. The things she wants are different, and she insists on that, the right of women to want different things, and this was why her sister had called her here, for this perspective. In addition to the manual labour.

CLEMENCE LEAVES HER PHONE at home when she goes to the bookstore, because the huge *Cellphones OFF* sign by the door conveys the message that she should, and the only time Toby has gone out of his way to note her presence in the store was the time he told her off for checking her texts.

"I thought the sign meant I had to turn my *ringer* off," Clemence protested, but Toby said no, it meant she had to power down the whole thing altogether, which turned out to be fine because she couldn't get a signal anyway, the three-plus layers of hardcovers lining the walls not permitting one to permeate the building. Otherwise she might have snuck around to the shadowy corner where foreign language erotica was, and checked her phone while hidden there.

But she's been checking her phone a whole lot less anyway, which means, two weeks after the wallpaper afternoon, that she's already waited well into the evening before finally reading and responding to a text message from her sister Grace: "CALL ME!" Grace answering the phone and railing against Clemence for being so hard to reach these days. "How am I even supposed to know you're alive?" she asks. Clemence has stopped using social media. "I keep checking for updates," says Grace, "but there's been nothing since that bird at your backyard feeder last May. What's going on there?"

Clemence explains that she's abandoned the virtual realm for the actual, for things that can be touched and held, and whose satisfactions are much less ephemeral.

Grace tells her she sounds like a space cadet. "Anyway, Clem, Prudence is pregnant." Confidential. This is supposed to be the kind of call where two sisters discuss the third sister in concerned tones, and pretend it isn't gossip.

"She told you?" Clemence has only just come home after spending the afternoon in the library hard at work on Puddicombe's index. It's stuffy in her apartment, and she walks across the room to open up the door.

"She told *you*?" Grace is asking.

And Clemence says, "Yes," without thinking. Without thinking about how this is Grace's trigger, being left out of the trinity. She's going to flip, and she does, because Prudence hasn't said a word to her yet. "Why did I have to hear it from Mom?"

"I think it's been complicated," says Clemence. "I don't know. You could ask her."

"I don't want to have to ask her," says Grace. "How come you got to hear it first? You haven't lived in town for seven years, and all of a sudden you're the centre of the loop."

Don't tell Grace she's being childish. Don't tell Grace she's being childish. "Grace, you're being childish," says Clemence's worst self, and Grace explodes. Clemence sets her phone down on the table and goes to put the kettle on.

Picking up the phone again a few minutes later to hear Grace saying, "Do you know what I mean?"

Clemence says, "I do. You're right."

Grace says, "It means a lot to hear you say that."

"Of course." Clemence settling down on her bed, whose lumpiness she's grown accustomed to. The only thing adorning it is a crisp white sheet, and it feels cool against her skin. And Grace is talking about their sister now, how their mother isn't sure how Prudence is taking it.

"Well, Prudence isn't even sure how she's taking it. It was an accident."

"It was?"

"The fertility awareness method."

"Oh, for fuck's sake," says Grace, who often returns to her tirade on the heteronormative privilege of the nuclear family. "Do you know what I'd have to do to get pregnant by accident? How far out of my way I'd have to go? It's not fair."

"Maybe you should have married Sandro."

Grace says, "Gross." There are phones ringing in the background.

"You're at work." Grace is a social worker.

"I'm on my dinner break," says Grace.

The kettle is boiling, and Clemence gets up again to fill her teapot. "Why don't you call Prudence and talk to her?" she suggests.

"You know I can't do that." Prudence is occupied all hours of the day by her children's activities, and once the children are in bed, she's too tired to talk. "Besides, I didn't want to talk to her. I wanted to talk *about* her."

Clemence says, "Fair enough." She places the lid on her teapot. "The twins are okay?"

"The twins are fine. They're at Mandarin tonight."

"You're not Chinese."

"If I was, they'd probably know Mandarin already. Anyway, it's the only program we could get them into. It's a skill, at least. Looks good on a CV."

"They're four years old!"

"Clemence, they're three."

"No, I knew that." She hadn't. "But isn't that even more absurd?"

Grace doesn't want to pursue this. She says, "Mom said you got a job in a bookstore?"

"Kind of. I'm mostly sorting stuff, moving boxes around."

"Sounds like you're definitely thriving."

And Clemence can't tell if Grace is making fun of her.

CLEMENCE HARD-BOILS TWO EGGS for dinner, and mixes them in a bowl with some mayo, salt, and pepper, and a few clippings from the chives growing outside. She's got the tail end of a loaf of bread, with only a bit of mould growing on one slice. She cuts off the mould, keeping the rest, and eats the sandwich lying in bed, crumbs falling down around her on the sheet, which concerns nobody except herself. When it comes time for bed, she'll brush them to the floor and, because she chooses not to think deeply about the mouldy part, her meal is delicious. *And could this be considered thriving*, she wonders, recalling her sister's words. To be cobbling together a life out of scraps and other people's discarded furniture? She actually thinks it might be. Something about it is substantial in a way her previous existence had never been.

The following afternoon she has a call with Jillian's friend Sarah, who writes the newsletter about women and their remarkable stories.

"I don't know that I'm so remarkable, though," Clemence notes.

Sarah tells her, "Everybody says that."

Clemence talks to her about the plan she'd had, like

Eat, Pray, Love. "My own personal odyssey," she explains, but the voyages are all in her head. "I wanted to start from nothing and see what I'd become." All these women, the spinsters and maiden aunts who'd made their lives in single rooms. "Less Elizabeth Gilbert, and more your Auntie Mildred." Not everything needs to be so dramatic, she means. Not everybody is meant to be Odysseus.

And what is she discovering, Sarah asks?

"That no woman is an island," Clemence answers. "No matter how hard she tries." The cat walks in through the patio door, as if to underline the point, and Clemence gets up to fetch him a saucer of milk. "And when you move more slowly, or even not at all, you notice things. Instead of a pilgrimage, you get to be where you are."

"It's like the opposite of optimization."

"Completely." This woman gets her. Sarah has been divorced herself, years before. She talks about these opportunities when it all falls apart and you get to figure out what kind of life you want to lead, what kind of person you want to be. All the possibilities inherent in disaster.

"*From Bridal Blogger to Serene Spinster*?"

"Sadly, being divorced means I don't get to be a spinster," says Clemence. "Which, I think, is one of the great tragedies of my life. Still, the angle's a little reductive, don't you think?"

"Reduction," Sarah reminds her, "is the point of an angle, after all."

"I don't want to be reduced," says Clemence. "And maybe that's *my* point. I don't know where I'm going, but what if that's okay? I've spent my whole life jumping from one institution to another, and I don't want to do that anymore."

"Jillian said you're writing a book."

"No, I'm making a life." Any book Clemence wrote now would have to be like a recipe book, but for more than just meals. So self-referential that she isn't sure it would resonate with somebody else, but she wouldn't care if it didn't. Clemence has been writing to please herself, for the very first time, and it's integral to her becoming. How could she know anything if she didn't write it down?

Sarah asks her to send a photo to accompany the piece, and Clemence realizes she hasn't seen an image of herself in months, besides the reflection of her face in the cloudy mirror in her bathroom. Easing off her social media habits has changed her practice, and she thinks about how this was one area in their marriage in which Toad had come in handy. He'd known her best side, and where she should stand for the good light, and he was always happy to photograph her outfits of the day, and take pictures of her in bed in the morning (after having showered and changed into fresh pyjamas) inhaling the scent of a cup of coffee with her eyes closed. She doesn't do any of that anymore, such obsessive documentation, as though an experience hadn't actually existed until it was made virtual. No woman is an island, but these days Clemence's self-regard seems to be, which is almost like a superpower. She's not interested in external feedback, in the likes and the follows, and the doses of dopamine they result in. Fearing judgment, perhaps—this might be the slightest part of it after everything that happened with Toad. But it's also part of her wider project of liberation. Clemence doesn't need to know what she looks like, or what anybody else thinks about what she looks like, because she knows what she *feels* like, and she is in tune with those feelings for the first time in her life.

But of course, it's still a familiar face that greets her when she turns her phone camera on and flips the screen to selfie mode. Smiling without even trying, like she would at the sight of an old friend. Her chin-length bob has grown out and she hasn't even thought about getting it cut, because then she'd have to get it cut again, and she has no desire for that kind of commitment. She doesn't want any commitments, and so her hair is long and wild. She's not wearing any makeup, the lines around her eyes on display, but her skin looks good—she's well rested, and eating wholesome food these days, full of good fats and heritage grains. She's wearing a loose-fitting cotton dress because it's still too warm to wear anything else, never mind that it's autumn, and the colour is flattering. Clemence likes how she looks; can it be so easy? Too easy—she almost feels compelled to find fault with the woman before her now, like a habit. It feels rude not to, to be so pleased with oneself. But nope. Clemence just doesn't care, and she has missed her face, she's fond of her face, and she clicks the photo to capture it as is. She sends it off to Jillian's friend Sarah who will put it on the internet for everybody to see, and the prospect should be terrifying, but she doesn't mind. The only things that concern Clemence these days are the things that are right in front of her.

Eleven

On Sunday morning, Clemence wakes to someone pounding on her door, and flies out of bed convinced the house is on fire before she remembers that she's naked.

But the house is not on fire. Instead, Mrs. Yeung has come to take her to church. Marching into the apartment as if she owns the place, which she does, grabbing the sheet off the bed and handing it to Clemence so she can cover her person. Explaining that Clemence has ten minutes to get dressed and come downstairs, and then she stops, pointing to where the air conditioner sits abandoned in the corner, a pashmina shawl draped on top for decoration. "I paid six hundred dollars for that," says Mrs. Yeung.

"You did?" That's a lot: a sizable proportion of Clemence's rent.

"Well, I managed to talk him down. You aren't using it?"

"Not right now," says Clemence. "It's October." She'd

got by most of the summer without it, so she hardly needs it now, and the appliance takes up so much room, but it seems mean to ask Charles to carry it all the way downstairs again. Or could this be the opportunity she'd been waiting for? How available is Charles, anyway? Or could she feign a bathroom leak? Something else that might need fixing?

"Ten minutes now," says Mrs. Yeung, returning to the task at hand. "Come on, get going."

And because Clemence feels guilty about the six hundred dollars, even talked down from, not to mention having answered her door buck-naked, she has no choice but to comply. Throwing some water on her face, and clothes on her body, she just has time to quickly brush her teeth before she runs down to the porch to meet Mrs. Yeung, who hands her a blueberry muffin.

"In case you haven't had breakfast," she says, and Clemence follows her down to the street, and then up the sidewalk as she talks about the church. "It's always quiet in the summer, but the congregation is returning now that everybody's back to their usual routines." Although, when they arrive, there are perhaps twenty people sitting in the sanctuary, a mix of white and Asian faces, most of them elderly. Mrs. Yeung settles Clemence in a pew, explaining that the Korean church used to hold a separate service, though they shared the building, but eventually the two congregations came together. Churchgoers are a dying breed, seeking solidarity where they find it.

The huge church building takes up an entire block, its curious architectural mix demonstrating that when times were good, the church had been added on to over and over again. Once upon a time there had been money for that, to grow and think big, but now the roof was crumbling. Literally. The jumble sale, Mrs. Yeung explains, is raising money for a new one, their goal still far off on the horizon. Plus there are all the social programs, people lined up for the food bank every Monday evening, and Clemence has seen them there, lines of needy people stretching all the way down the street. Such desperation, a few decades ago, would have constituted an emergency, but now the emergency was routine. The social safety net was stretched so thin, but it was the church's role to step up, no matter the challenge.

When the service begins, this appears to be its message, English contributions delivered by an earnest white woman with a round face and a freshly shaved head, who at first appears to be playing dress-up in her sombre robes. She seems so young, and Clemence wonders at the path that delivered her here. No one Clemence had ever known had become a member of the clergy. She'd never even realized it was an option.

The church sanctuary is refreshingly cool and bright, tall windows opening to the air with a complicated system of strings and pulleys, and old-fashioned fans whirring above, stirring the breeze. A man plays the organ, his hunched back to the giant room, and Clemence realizes she'd been hearing his music from her bed on Sunday mornings, but so faint in the distance as to be almost indiscernible. In the sanctuary, however, the sound is loud and forceful, in defiance of all the empty pews. At the end of the service, they are all called on to stand up and shake hands with a neighbour, but the only person within reach of Clemence is Mrs. Yeung.

Coffee and cake are served in the courtyard, which manages to bring everyone closer. The cake is banana bread with a cream cheese frosting, which Clemence feels wholly justifies her attendance this morning. She might even come back. Her mouth is full of the cake when the minister approaches, introducing herself as Reverend Michelle, waiting patiently, expectantly, for Clemence to respond once she's finished chewing. Mrs. Yeung stepping in to explain who Clemence is and that she'd brought her that morning, proudly, like Clemence was a prize.

"So you like it, right?" Mrs. Yeung proposes as they walked home together. "It's so convenient, so close. They're nice people. Good cake. Grape juice for communion. We need young people. And Charles told me you're looking for a spiritual path."

"He told you that?"

"Like Reese Witherspoon in that movie. The wild one."

"Well, not exactly."

"I didn't think *exactly*," says Mrs. Yeung. "I've never seen you carrying a backpack. But the church is just up the street. You don't even need a backpack."

"I can help with the jumble sale," offers Clemence. "Collect more books. You're going to need a lot of jumble if you're going to build a new roof and feed the hungry."

"That's what the prayer is for," says Mrs. Yeung, throwing her hands in the air. "So no church for you, then."

"Probably not the Sunday-morning kind." That banana bread, though.

"You know, it's not healthy to sleep in the nude." Mrs. Yeung leans over to pick at the lawn, to pull out a dandelion by its roots. Straightening up again. "And what if the house *had* been on fire?"

"Then I think being naked would be the least of my problems."

But Mrs. Yeung isn't listening. "The lawn needs mowing."

"Is Charles coming to do it?"

"Summer's over." Clemence waited for her to elaborate. "He's back at school now. He doesn't have time."

Clemence says, "Oh."

Mrs. Yeung turns to look at her sharply. "You're going to miss him!"

"I mean, he's a nice guy."

"You know he's married."

"I ... didn't." As though this had nothing to do with anything, except it really did, more than Clemence would have supposed. This news feels like the ground giving out beneath her shaky legs.

"Yup, he's taken," Mrs. Yeung is prattling on. "Off the market. You've had the wrong idea and you're going to have to do your husband-hunting somewhere else."

"That's not—" Clemence is indignant. She's just been force-marched to church by this woman who's now she's treating her like some man-hungry predator, which is hardly a fair exchange. "He was just friendly." He was also flirtatious. And now she's furious at having been sucked into his game.

"He *is* friendly," agrees Mrs. Yeung. "He's a very nice boy, and everybody thinks so. Especially the girls." She winks. She actually winks.

"It's not like that at all," Clemence asserts, or at least she tries to, but she's completely discombobulated and her voice has gone strange so that she sounds like a wailing and sputtering mess.

"His wife is a very nice girl. A nice Korean girl. She's a doctor. Very busy. That's why you haven't seen her. They have been together for a long, long time."

"Good for them," says Clemence, thinking fast to regain some ground here. Thinking stupid, perhaps, because then she blurts out, "But I have a boyfriend."

Mrs. Yeung stops short. "You do?" Clemence nods. "You've never brought him home."

"So I think it's you who's had the wrong idea," Clemence says. Which is true, regardless of her attraction to Charles, because Mrs. Yeung doesn't understand her intentions at all. "I'm not a husband hunter. I've had all the husband a person needs for one lifetime. So, I mean, I'm glad his wife is a nice girl—or a woman. But that's got nothing to do with me."

"She's a doctor."

"You said that." Clemence is done here, for once Clemence is winning, and on that note she heads up the steps to the porch. "I'll keep collecting for the jumble," she calls over her shoulder, but no way is she going back to church.

Twelve

Alvin Puddicombe wrote poems about the black eyes he'd administered to his wives, how they pained him, comparing the shades of bruising to ever-changing twilight, and he blamed the drink, he blamed himself, he blamed the women, too, the raging fires that burned inside them, and Clemence thinks that the Mrs. Puddicombes didn't rage enough, and surely all of them ganging up to kill him would have been a fitting end to his most storied life. His fifth and final wife, Dolores, was seventeen when they met and twenty-five when Puddicombe met his demise at the age of eighty-seven. She'd nursed him on his deathbed. Dolores published three volumes of poetry herself, plus an autobiography called *Memoirs of a Muse,* which Professor Edmund Fairfax does not reference in his own book, whose index Clemence is contractually obliged to finish within the next two weeks. She'd looked up Dolores Puddicombe's memoir online, and it had not received favourable reviews.

The cat comes in again and jumps onto Clemence's lap, his bushy tail in her face, so she is unable to work, but it's time to make another pot of tea, anyway. Just an excuse—Puddicombe's book is getting her down; he's so loathsome. She'd read some of his poems in anthologies back in high school, albeit not the one about the black eyes, and she recalls finding all of it romantic at the time, the tortured artist, the women touched by his genius, and she used to think that this was what love was.

Clemence opens up a can of tuna, spooning out half for the cat, and they sit side by side on the floor splitting the snack, except Clemence's is mixed with mayonnaise and she eats it with a fork. She is troubled by how much she wants the cat to stay around, how much she likes his presence. She also listens out for other people in the house, the sounds making her feel less lonely, and she is forever anticipating the sound of somebody, anybody, coming up the stairs. What does it mean to be this dissatisfied by her own company? Has she utterly failed in being an excellent woman already?

Clemence is still dying inside about her conversation with Mrs. Yeung, and even more about how despondent she'd been ever since. She's been separated from Toad for no time at all, and she's already hung up on another man. Charles, the least suitable unsuitable attachment Clemence could imagine, and yes, why does she require an attachment, anyway? Naomi doesn't. It's not impossible to be without one, but then Clemence is weak-willed. This is her defining characteristic. For example, she should be continuing her work on that misogynist bastard's biography right now, but she's sharing a pack of protein with a cat with three unopened letters from her husband's lawyer piled on the table before her. She doesn't want to think about her husband, and this cat doesn't even belong to her.

"Somebody's taking care of you," she says, rubbing under his chin, and now she feels self-conscious again, even if only the cat is listening. "And I mean, that's cool," she continues. "But there is something to be said for caring for yourself."

Bailey examines Clemence with his single eye. No doubt he knows all about that, a strong-willed, solitary feline who goes where he wants to go, and Clemence is worried she's insulted him, implying he's codependent, or unable to stand on his own four feet. But the cat isn't bothered, since he stays by her side, permitting her to continue petting his length. His long hair sheds all over the floor, but she doesn't mind, because sweeping it up again is so satisfying and the hair is beautiful, iridescent, blue. It's a chore so different from the indexing or from her tasks at the bookstore, which never seem to be finished, where every step forward leads to another mess of things still to be accomplished. This she especially likes about living alone, that the only messes made are her own. Or the cat's. No one else's drinking glasses are left by the sink, or clothes on the floor, and she doesn't mind the ring around the bathtub, because one's own filth is so familiar.

Other people are a lot of work. Prudence is no longer speaking to her, Clemence has heard from her mother.

Grace told Prudence that Clemence had reported that her pregnancy was not necessarily good news—which wasn't what Clemence had said *exactly*—and Prudence hadn't received that well, unimpressed at hearing her ambivalence expressed third-hand.

"I spent a whole afternoon stripping her wallpaper," Clemence protested to her mother on the phone.

"Oh, Pru will come around," says Bonnie. "You know how she is. Plus the hormones."

But I have hormones, too, thinks Clemence. Especially if "hormones" means "feelings." This wasn't fair. She'd done nothing wrong. Grace had misconstrued things, as usual, and then blabbed it all to everyone.

Clemence gets up off the floor and brushes the cat hair from her hands. Sitting on her bed is the copy of the book that Charles has lent to her, *Minor Feelings*, essays about being Asian in America. His name is inscribed on the inside cover, and she studies his handwriting, the neat and tidy letters: *C. Yeung*. And even though his pen does not appear again inside the book, she'd starts imagining coded messages between the lines, something personal, as though this is a book intended for her eyes only. Like an invitation into Charles's soul—would she think the same if Toby made her read one of his seventeenth-century plays? But he wouldn't. Toby doesn't care what Clemence reads one way or another. This book that Charles pressed into her hands resonates on a deeper level. Essays about art and poetry, and friendship, growing up as the child of immigrants, and about race, recontextualizing the familiar in her mind. Clemence loved the book, and that

Charles had loaned it to her without an agenda, when he had a wife—it only made her admire him more. Affection was a trap.

She would have to return *Minor Feelings*. Or did she have to, really? Feasibly, couldn't she keep the book and never speak of this again? Moving on from the humiliation of her conversation with Charles's mother—there might come a day when Clemence would see the book on her shelf and not remember where it came from. Though this was unlikely. His name was on the inside cover and Charles had made her promise not to use it as a coaster, so clearly the book matters to him. Clemence isn't making something out of nothing. She absolutely has to return it.

And for better or worse, Clemence knows a route to make this happen. She puts the cat out, shuts up her apartment, and heads downstairs, book in hand, to knock on Mrs. Yeung's door. Maybe with something to prove, to show this woman that there had been a connection between Clemence and her son after all, something tangible enough that you could hold it in your hand, which was what Clemence was doing now, like an offering. "It's Charles's," she says, "and I wanted to make sure it got back to him."

Mrs. Yeung takes it, suspiciously. "He gave this to you?"

"Just to borrow," says Clemence. "I read it. It was very good."

Mrs. Yeung is unconvinced. "He has too many books already."

"I think this one is important," says Clemence.

Mrs. Yeung shrugs, and tosses it onto the table behind her in the hall. She says, "We're sorting tomorrow. You coming?" For the jumble sale. Clemence thinks it's curious that her whole life lately has become about sorting through junk in search of treasure. But she remembers Reverend Michelle, and the church roof, and the lineups for the food bank, and this seems like one way to make a difference. To make up for the self-indulgence of the rest of her day, lumpy bed aside.

Mrs. Yeung says, "How's your boyfriend?"

"My boyfriend?"

"You said it. 'I have a boyfriend.' But you have no boyfriend?"

"Not everyone needs a boyfriend," says Clemence.

"They do if they say they have a boyfriend," says Mrs. Yeung. "Unless they're lying."

She was lying. "I wasn't lying," says Clemence.

"I want to meet him," says Mrs. Yeung. "Your boyfriend. I haven't seen you bringing him by here. Because you're sneaking him in?"

"There's no sneaking," says Clemence. She should have kept Charles's book. "We work together. At the bookstore." It was convenient. Why not? She gets paid to talk to Toby anyway. Two birds, one stone.

"You're not sleeping together?" The question is preposterous. And not only because they're supposed to be talking about *Toby*. "It's okay," Mrs. Yeung waves her hand in the air like magic. "None of my business. You're not my daughter. Young people can to do what they like, even if they live under my roof. I am a very open-minded landlord. Just don't be disturbing the neighbours."

"I'm not disturbing anyone," says Clemence.

"See, this is why I don't like renting to women. Everything is more complicated."

Thirteen

Crampton receives new stock at the grocery store every Thursday, which Clemence finds surprising, because it didn't seem like the store received new stock ever, but she knows now that if she goes in on Thursday after her shift at the bookstore, she has a good chance of finding bread and milk whose best-before dates are still on the horizon. She also thinks it might please Crampton to have a customer, but Crampton doesn't seem bothered either way. Apparently she makes enough selling cigarettes to subsidize the loss from the rest. She sees no problem with this approach, and that she keeps her store at all, she explains, is community service. Not everybody has the energy to make the trek up to the superstore, or can afford the luxury of having groceries delivered.

"Once," she tells Clemence, "the store was the centre of the neighbourhood. When my mother ran this place, she knew everyone. We used to do sandwiches up here at the counter." But the neighbourhood is changing. Crampton says, "It's always been changing." Someone has started sleeping in a tent popped up in front of the organic dog food store, and it won't be long before there'll be no sign that either the tent or the business had ever been there. "Not all change is bad, though," Crampton adds. And change, at least, is how you know that a neighbourhood is alive.

Clemence wants to talk to her about updating the window displays, but Crampton dismisses her suggestions. "I've been running this business since before you were born."

But the problem is that's exactly what it looks like. There are cans of SPAM that have been on the shelf ever since then.

Crampton says, "Don't start. It didn't work the last time."

"The last time?"

"Don't you people have anything better to do than walk up and down the street criticizing the way I run my businesses?"

"'You people'?" *Who* people? "I've come to buy cheese," says Clemence. Not the fancy cheese, those ones that are soft and come in a wheel, but just a brick of cheddar, perfect for a tuna melt. "I really don't know what you're talking about."

And so Crampton tells her about the time the tyrannical woman who runs the artisan market got involved with the Business Improvement Association and tried to get bylaw enforcement officers to issue tickets because her windows were so filthy. "There aren't even bylaws about that. So you can leave my windows alone."

"Oh," says Clemence. She wouldn't have mentioned anything if she'd realized this was a sore spot. She was mostly here in pursuit of the tuna melt. "Hey listen, I need a grater, too." The one that came with her apartment is rusty. Crampton's shop has a tangle of dusty housewares down the far aisle, from which Clemence had already bought a Pyrex measuring cup. It was the first vintage item she'd purchased that wasn't second-hand.

She unearths the grater and Crampton rings it all up. "So, I hear you've been going to church," she notes, feigning nonchalance but doing it poorly.

"I only went once," says Clemence. "How did you know?"

"I've got spies." Crampton doesn't even smile as she says this. "I didn't take you for the churchgoing type, what with the rabid feminism."

"I went to church once. It's not rabid." Clemence can't keep up with the onslaught of accusations. "I'm helping with the sale, the jumble."

"You mean *junk*," Crampton says as she packs Clemence's shopping in the plastic bag with the smiley face that she insists on every time.

AFTER HER SATISFYING LUNCH, Clemence walks up the street to the bookshop, goes inside and right up to the desk where she rings the bell obnoxiously.

"You're back," Toby says. He doesn't even put his book

down. He's not reading a play today, instead the collected poetry of John Dryden.

"Are you tired of drama?" Clemence asks him, and now he lowers the book, looking confused. "The book, I mean," she continues. "You're reading poetry. I didn't know you did that."

"Why are you here?" Toby asks. "This is the part of the day where I don't have to talk to you or anyone."

"Some job you've got."

"You should talk," says Toby.

And Clemence sings, "I do!" Toby's apparent lack of a personality seems to give Clemence permission to behave in ways that magnify her own to a most absurd degree. She says, "Toby, I'm kind of bored. We didn't even talk that much this morning. Do you get a break? Do you want to go get a coffee? I could buy you a muffin?"

Toby shakes his head. "I'm gluten-free."

"You eat every meal at Burger King!"

"Burger King gluten isn't the kind that gives me trouble."

"But that doesn't make any sense," says Clemence. "And you know, there are entire cafés now that don't bother with gluten at all."

Toby says, "Why?"

"Why what?"

"Why are you doing this to me?"

"To you?"

"Don't you have any friends or something?"

Which was bit rich coming from him, Clemence thinks. "They're all at work."

"But *I'm* at work."

"I think your work," Clemence says, "is a bit more flexible?"

And it is. Apparently Toby is free to take breaks when he chooses, flipping the sign in the window (or not—he says it doesn't matter) and off they go to the coffee shop up by the fromagerie where they have gluten-free cupcakes. But then it turns out he's also allergic to cocoa, so he's out of luck. He doesn't drink coffee, either. The place has a gluten-free madeleine, though, so he contents himself with that.

"Like Proust," says Clemence.

"You've read Proust?" asks Toby, mildly animated at this.

And Clemence is forced to confess that no, she hasn't. "But I don't imagine you have either," she says, "seeing as he never wrote a single Restoration play." And Toby laughs! Well, kind of.

The lighting in the coffee shop is dim, but interesting, strands of naked bulbs undulating from the ceiling, and Toby looks healthier here, the shadows underneath his eyes not as pronounced. He is also less solipsistic than Clemence had given him credit for, asking her, "Why don't you get a job? A better one? More than three hours a week, if you're bored, I mean."

Clemence thinks about his question. She tells him, "Right now, I'm taking a break from all that, from routine and striving. I'm having a reset. Even just being bored is a novel experience—I don't think I've been bored for more than five minutes since I was eleven." Clemence has spent years with her days and her life booked up so that she'd never been able to take a moment to think about where she was going or what any of it meant. "Which is how I got here, I guess. And what I need is a recalibration." She wants him to know, though: "But I actually do have friends."

"Sure," says Toby. But he doesn't sound sure. Though Toby doesn't have much truck with friends anyway. He doesn't see the point, he says, and Clemence wonders if she and Toby have more in common than she thinks, if her current recalibration is putting her on the road to becoming a weird recluse. Toby is lonely, Clemence suspects, and evidently Crampton thinks so too, because she's paying Clemence a wage to engage him in conversation, but Toby doesn't appear to think that his loneliness is a problem, or at least one that needs addressing with the presence of actual people.

Clemence says, "I envy you, actually. You seem okay on your own. The point of all this, for me, is to become accustomed to my own company, but I'm terrified the end result might end up being that I don't even like it. My company, I mean." She tenses. She can't believe she said that. She hardly even knew she *felt* that way, but she does, and the thing about Toby responding to everything Clemence says and does as though she's strange and unfathomable is that it permits her to be as strange and unfathomable as she'd like, and maybe more, because he'd never notice the difference.

Toby says, "No."

"No?"

"You're good company," Toby clarifies.

"Really?"

"You bought me a snack." He shrugs. She's also bought him a small carton of milk, and she's surprised to find that his digestive system can tolerate lactose, the rest of him seeming so fragile. *Toby contains multitudes*, she thinks, but maybe she's giving him too much credit. He's just tipped the carton back to get to the dregs, milk running all over his shirt.

Clemence says, "Want to walk me home?"

"Why?"

"I bought you a snack, remember? It's only polite."

And so he goes through the motions, awkwardly holding the door for her as they exit, but stumbling over his feet in the process and hitting his head on the frame.

"Well, now you *really* have to walk me home," says Clemence, after ducking back inside to grab a pile of napkins.

"Why?"

"Because I've got a first aid kit, and you're bleeding."

Toby panics. "Is it serious?" Clemence is pressing some of the napkins against his head. "Do you think I'm going to have to get stitches?" He touches the wound, getting blood on his hands. Clemence foists the rest of the napkins upon him.

"You don't need stitches," she says, hoping she sounds more certain than she is. Because there does seem to be a lot of blood for a cut that's mainly superficial. The napkins Toby has pressed against his head right now are soaked through already. Thankfully, her house is close, even though Toby winces as she leads him up to the porch, and she isn't sure he'll be able to make it all the way to her room at the top, but somehow he manages, stopping only three times to catch his breath. When they arrive at her door, the napkins are disintegrated, and there's blood all over his hand and face, and Toby looks like he's been in an explosion.

Clemence leads him into the bathroom, helping him sit down on the edge of the tub. She wets a washcloth, holding it gently to the wound, and he's submitted to her entirely. Whereas before, it's been only resistance, Toby darting around corners and bounding up ladders to escape her, she's touching him now, and his eyes are closed, almost as if in pleasure. His eyelashes are impossibly long, and she's tempted to kiss those full lips, to push her luck ever so far, but no doubt that would jerk him right out of whatever state he is in. Toby would leap away and run out the door, or have an anaphylactic reaction to her lip balm, and Clemence would never see him again, which would be inconvenient for all kinds of reasons. So she doesn't, because she doesn't want to kiss Toby anyway, she just likes his lips, which part gently into an almost smile as she holds the warm washcloth against his brow.

"You don't need stitches," she tells his again, softly so not to disturb the spell. "You're just bleeding a lot." It was starting to let up, she thought, though maybe this was wishful thinking.

"I have a clotting disorder," Toby whispers. "Thankfully mild."

"I have Band-Aids," she tells him. But Toby is allergic

to Band-Aids, it turns out, something in the adhesive that gives him a rash, so she has to get out the first aid kit properly, feeling so capable, unrolling the gauze and cutting off a square with the pair of tiny scissors. Ordinary medical tape will be fine, he says. He tells her that she's a good nurse, which nobody has said to Clemence in her life.

Once the bandage is sorted, Toby follows her out of the bathroom and perches on the edge of her bed, moving pillows out of the way to make this possible.

"How are you feeling?" she asks.

He says, "Dizzy." He sounds woozy. It was only a surface wound, and if he'd showed up at the hospital for stitches, they would have laughed at him. But now he's seen his reflection in the mirror, that clean bandage against his pale white forehead, and he imagines himself to have survived great peril. "I'll have to monitor this. It might be a concussion."

"It's not, it's just a scrape." Clemence wants to offer him something—a drink? She has milk. Does he want more milk? But he doesn't. He's happy to accept a glass of water, though.

"Got to replenish my fluids." Toby is the most ridiculous human being Clemence has ever known in her life, and she knows her family, so that's saying a lot. He drinks the water and confesses: "I know Crampton is paying you to talk to me. She told me. She isn't nice, but she's never sneaky. She thinks I need to get out more, that I'm too isolated."

"Well, maybe she's right."

"I don't know," he says. "People aren't really my thing."

And something in Clemence's expression must betray the hurt she feels when she hears him say that, after all this trouble, because he rushes to reassure her, a rare display of empathy: "You, well. I mean, *you're* actually okay." Sounding as though this revelation surprises him, too. And then he looks around the room suspiciously. "What I don't understand, though—is she paying you *now*?"

"Now?"

"Your shift is over. You'd left for the day."

"Well, maybe I need someone to talk to, too," says Clemence. "It's not all about the profit."

"Good, since you can't profit much. Is it even worth it?"

"I like the books," says Clemence. She pulls a chair out from her little table and sits down across from Toby. The bleeding has stopped. The bandage on his head is still pristine, and makes him look more like a tortured nineteenth-century poet than ever. "And getting rid of Women's Fiction. I want to do that. I'm making progress." She'd already moved over Jane Austen, and was making room for the Brontës after dumping Dan Browns and Michael Crichtons. They were going to be donated to the jumble. Clemence was confused about how they'd ever made it into Literature in the first place.

"I just stick them wherever there's room," Toby admits. "We don't get around to organizing much."

"I can tell," Clemence says.

"I should probably get back to work, though," he says. "I'm allowed to take breaks, duck out for a few minutes, but it's been a while now. Somebody might notice."

"Nobody will notice."

"Still." Toby stands up. "I'm less dizzy." Shaking his head sideways as though to dislodge something from his right ear. "Thank you," he tells her.

"I'll walk you down," says Clemence, trailing him down the two sets of stairs to the foyer. And just before he opens the outside door, she calls, "Stop!" He turns around, alarmed. "Just, I mean. Hold on a sec." And then she knocks at Mrs. Yeung's door across the hall, and her landlady opens it as though she'd been standing there waiting on the other side, which is mostly likely. Clemence says to her, "I wanted to introduce you. Toby, this is Mrs. Yeung," and both of them are polite enough, neither seemingly struck by the strangeness of the interaction, because possibly for Mrs. Yeung and Toby, things are weird all the time, particularly where Clemence Lathbury is concerned.

Mrs. Yeung comes out on the porch to wait while Clemence walks Toby down to the sidewalk, and Clemence is conscious of her eyes on them. Silently, she is imploring Toby not to lose his footing, to remain upright and fulfill his part in this role she's cast him in, which he's nearly finished performing and he's done so well.

He stops and turns to her. "This was nice," he says, as though surprised, and Clemence knows what he means. "Other than the blood."

"The blood's never the best part of anything."

"Thank you for the bandage," he says, his voice a murmur. Lingering. What is he waiting for? What is Mrs. Yeung waiting for? And what is *she* waiting for, Clemence asks herself, for crying out loud, so she follows through.

Standing up on her tiptoes to deliver a kiss to those big cushion lips, a quick one, nothing fancy, but still, he stumbles backwards and says, "Whoa." He doesn't fall down though. She'll give him that.

"See you at work," she says, her voice just low enough that Mrs. Yeung might imagine she's bestowing an intimacy. And then he turns and flees, and Clemence hopes that from a distance it doesn't actually look like that's what he's doing.

She waits, watching him go, his wild hair flying, his narrow back but large shoulders, getting smaller and smaller. How his pants are too short. If Clemence stands here long enough, will Mrs. Yeung have turned around and gone back inside?

But no, she is waiting, arms folded. She looks delighted. "So that's him?" she calls. "That's your boyfriend? Because he looks like a child. And what's with the bandage?"

"He hit his head."

"I don't like him," says Mrs. Yeung.

Clemence says, "Okay." It's none of her business, anyway.

"There's no life in him. He looks like a vampire. You, you're fat and healthy. It's a bad match. Does he expect you to feed him?"

"Well, I can't, really. He's got a lot of intolerances. He's kind of delicate."

"My son is more attractive."

Clemence doesn't speak. This is a trap.

"Charles eats everything. The meat, the gluten..."

"Good for him. And he's married to a doctor."

"Did he tell you that?"

"No, you did," says Clemence. She is suddenly very tired.

"Hang on." Mrs. Yeung disappears back into her apartment. Charles's book is still sitting on the table in her foyer. Clemence thinks about whether she'll ever see Charles again. She hears his mother banging around in the kitchen, and keeps waiting. She wonders when the Yeungs moved up to the first floor. Students live in the basement now, even though the space is dark and dingy.

Mrs. Yeung comes out again with a mason jar. "It's soup," she says, thrusting it into Clemence's hands. "For your boyfriend. None of the gluten. Tell him it's vegan."

"It is?"

Mrs. Yeung shrugs. "More or less. It's good for him. Good for strengthening."

Clemence thanks her, and turns to head upstairs.

Mrs. Yeung calls, "I'll tell Charles you say hello? Next time I speak to him?"

"Sure," says Clemence, appreciating this woman's formidable use of emotional torture. When combined with her kindness and generosity, the effect was absolutely discombobulating, and most people would just surrender.

"I'll tell him you brought your boyfriend by. That I met Tony."

"It's Toby."

"That part," says Mrs. Young, not wrongly, "doesn't matter at all."

Fourteen

Bonnie Lathbury drives downtown and takes Clemence out for sushi, telling her that if she apologizes to her sister, Sandro will hook her up with one of his colleagues for an editing job.

"I can't read Italian," says Clemence.

"It's a *translation*." Bonnie efficiently moves the wasabi away from her California roll. She and Roger don't do spice. "Just say you're sorry. I don't understand the point of you moving all the way back here if you're only going to be on the outs."

"That wasn't up to me!" says Clemence. "Prudence is being dramatic."

"Prudence is being Prudence," says Bonnie, eyeing her carefully. "Besides, I think you'll need the money."

Clemence nods, picking up the last sweet potato tempura; this is true.

Bonnie's still watching her.

"What?" Clemence asks, with her mouth full.

"Toad called."

Clemence chokes, which is distressing, but also opportune because, as she struggles to breathe, she doesn't have to hear what comes next, or say anything herself, and maybe this could be a convenient way to go … except that she doesn't really want to die, and the tempura is easily dislodged from her throat. Bonnie refills her water glass, and Clemence takes a sip, wondering how long she can drag this out for, if she might get away without saying a word.

But no. Bonnie says, "We thought you'd been in touch with the lawyer. You told us you'd been." Clemence is not going to get away with this at all.

"I didn't say that, *exactly*."

"You said you were dealing with it."

"And I *was*," Clemence protests. "I mean, I was going to. I still am. Just …" She picks up a dab of wasabi and uses her chopsticks to mix it into her soy sauce. "When I'm ready." She can't look at her mother now. She knows how feeble she sounds, though in theory the plan had made a great deal of sense.

"He needs to know about the house," says Bonnie. The townhouse that she and Toad owned together, where he lives alone now. Clemence still owns half of it. He'll have to buy her out eventually, and yes, that would help her finances more than some editing job, although still not enough for her to be able to afford a place in this city. "You need to move forward."

But isn't that been exactly what she's been doing? Leaving her whole life behind, and Toad is welcome to it, to all of it. Clemence hoping that if she waited long enough, Toad would forget he ever knew her, forget what she'd done. Does she even need her half of their house? If she gave it to him outright, could that be atonement?

"But you don't need 'atonement,'" says Bonnie. "You just need to take responsibility for your own life. Especially the parts that are bound up with his. He deserves that. He doesn't deserve much, but he deserves *that*." And Clemence is surprised to hear this from her mother, which Bonnie reads in her expression. "Oh, come on now, you know I never really liked the guy."

But Clemence hadn't known. Her father, maybe, but never her mother. She'd always supposed her husband to be the chosen son-in-law, the one without a previous family, the one who wasn't a pervert. All that, and Toad still couldn't come out on top.

"He took you away. He made your world so small," Bonnie laments. "But what was I supposed to do? If I said anything, you wouldn't have listened to me. I don't even know if you're listening to me now."

"No, I am," Clemence says. Especially the parts about how she didn't need atonement. "How's he doing, anyway?" she dares to ask. The real reason all those letters remain unopened was because she didn't want to know. It was a terrible kind of power to be able to wreck a man's entire life. "Was he crying?" She's got her eyes squeezed shut. She doesn't want to know.

"Well, no."

Clemence's eyes fly open to stare at her mother in amazement. This was all she'd been waiting to hear—and yet...

"I mean, not *at first*," Bonnie clarifies. "He was holding it together, then he broke down partway through. He's not doing well, and I don't think it's helping him any, your avoidance." And then she says, in a more sympathetic tone, "And I don't think it's helping you much, either." She says, and not for the first time, "Clemence, the whole world doesn't only exist in your head."

Clemence says, "I'll talk to him." Sooner or later, it was going to have to happen.

"You will," says her mother, popping the last piece of dragon roll into her mouth. "Because I gave him your number."

"You what?"

Bonnie shrugs.

"Okay," Clemence says. It was always going to come to this. "And I'll talk to Prudence." Which seems to do the trick, for now, because the fraught conversation is over. She and her mother order green tea ice cream, and finish their meal feeling easy with each other. Clemence is telling her about the bookshop. "Just a few hours a week, but the stuff I'm turning up is fascinating. And you know that I'm volunteering at the church."

Her mother says, "I didn't." And now she's worried that Clemence has gone and joined a cult. She's imagining hippies in a storefront, the women dressed like *Little House on the Prairie*, and whatever had happened to her neighbour Muriel Adelman's niece who convinced her parents to invest their life savings in a pyramid scheme, then ran away to Montana and nobody's seen her since.

"It's not like the Adelmans' niece. This one's an actual

church," Clemence assures her mother. "St. Saviour's, established in 1872. They only meet on Sunday mornings and they've got an organ and everything, so you know it's legit. I went to just one service, but I'm still helping out. It's a community thing. They're raising money for a new roof and to feed the homeless."

"That *sounds* pretty reasonable," Bonnie admits.

"And it's not your life savings they're after. They want your jumble."

"Jumble?"

"Housewares, crockery, costume jewellery, old books, and bric-a-brac. Whatever it is that's cluttering up your drawers and closets that might be of good use to somebody else."

"And they don't make you wear a bonnet?"

"Mom, the women don't even wear fancy hats. It's a very progressive church."

CLEMENCE HAS TO MAKE an appointment to call her older sister, who is more difficult to reach than anyone else Clemence knows. The kids are back to school now, which means that Prudence is up to her ears in lesson plans and glitter glue, and when she's not running the home-school, she's sleeping, which makes it sound like Prudence is avoiding her, but Prudence is so occupied that she doesn't even have time to avoid her sister, because she'd have to go out of her way to do that.

Bonnie coordinates the whole thing, letting Clemence know that Pru is available on Tuesday morning at six thirty, and so Clemence has to set an alarm for the for the first time in months. Usually the church bells are what manage to rouse her in the mornings (*oranges and lemons*), and they don't start until eight o'clock.

Prudence answers, and the first thing Clemence says is, "I'm sorry." They haven't spoken since the wallpaper stripping. Alvin Puddicombe's index will be finished by the end of the week, and Clemence is proud of her work, that it might be the most subversive index in the history of indexing. Anyone who reaches the book's conclusion and imagines the poet's violence and misogyny excused will find otherwise within the pages that follow: *B* is for buffoonery; *M* is for moral standards (lax); *P* is for the poems that Puddicombe plagiarized from his second-last girlfriend (who was called Patricia).

P is also for pragmatism. Clemence hadn't done anything wrong, but she needs the editing job from Sandro's colleague.

Prudence is still explaining the extent of this betrayal. "When I confide in you, it's *confidential*. I told you not to tell anyone, and especially not Grace. This is tough for her. I know it is."

"But I *didn't* tell Grace," says Clemence. She never tells Grace anything. She shouldn't even speak to Grace, because look where it gets her. "She already knew—Mom told her. It's Mom you shouldn't have confided in."

"But Mom wasn't the one who told Grace that I didn't want this baby. You made me sound *callous*, Clemence. That was never what I said."

"And I never told her that," says Clemence. "I know

you're not callous. I would never have said anything at all, but she just got me on the phone, and I thought everything was all out in the open. I misjudged. And I'm sorry." She'd said it twice. And she was sorry. But she also needed this to be over. "And you know how she twists things."

"I do," says Prudence, after a pause. So they're on the same side again. "Maybe I overreacted." Clemence lets this stand. "I'm actually looking forward to it, you know. This baby. One more go-around. Sandro says he's getting a vasectomy. He said our fertility awareness is lacking."

"He's not wrong."

"And he mentioned it to his doctor, who asked him if he was really sure. She told Sandro to think of any future partners and what they might want."

"How many families is Sandro going to have?" asks Clemence.

"He's determined that ours will be his final one. He says any future partners will have to lump it. That they'll probably be busy wrangling the scads of children I've born to him, anyway."

"And where will you be?" asks Clemence.

"Hopefully sipping a stiff drink on a tropical island. Anyway, I suppose you'll want to know about this editing job ..."

And for the sake of family harmony, Clemence pretends not to know what her sister is talking about as she scrambles for a pen and paper to write down the details.

Fifteen

Clemence dreams about Toby, about his lips, and in the dream those lips do more than just receive her fleeting kiss, and when she wakes up in the morning, she's unable to distinguish between Toby in reality and everything that happened in her head, which is confusing and embarrassing. She knows that when she sees him, she will blush, and any discerning person will be able to tell that something's going on, and luckily Toby isn't discerning in the slightest, but this doesn't make Clemence feel any more confident about the matter.

She meets Jillian in High Park and they go for a walk. Jillian's is the kind of lifestyle in which the suffix "power" gets applied to various items and activities, including juices, lifting, brokering, and yes, walking, and so Clemence finds herself chasing her friend up and down the hiking trails. She has worn inappropriate shoes, flimsy slip-ons, which make her heels hurt, but she doesn't complain, because Jillian has made time for this in her busy day, time for friendship and physical fitness. Jillian is also clearly in much better shape than Clemence, because she doesn't get winded at all.

"I think you've gotten off track," she calls out over her shoulder, moving a tree branch that snaps back and hits Clemence in the face. "I thought the point of all this was to forget about men, to be your own centre. To fill your life with other things—that's what you said. A spiritual pilgrimage. But you're acting as silly as a schoolgirl. No offence."

There is none taken. Jillian is right. And now they've arrived at a rock face, and Clemence's heart falls at the premise of having to scale it, because even in the right shoes, it would have been impossible, but luckily there is another path that winds around it, and Clemence follows her friend along that trail.

"I think I was confused," says Clemence, "about the difference between going off one man and going off all men in general. I'd forgotten there were men who aren't Toad. And I'd forgotten what it felt like to lust after those men. To feel that tension. The anticipation of a kiss. Jillian, it's fun. It's like my soul has come back to life. Do you know what a relief that is? Do you know that I've been masturbating so much that I've triggered my carpal tunnel?"

"Is that good news?" asks Jillian.

"I think so."

"I know a good physiotherapist."

"It's not desperate yet. I bought a brace at the drug store. It might also be my office set-up. The kitchen table in my place is not exactly ergonomic, and I've got this new editing project."

"Love poems."

"They're pretty erotic," says Clemence. "Sometimes I wonder if everyone affiliated with Sandro is a sexual deviant. Let's just say I have to take lots of breaks."

"Clemence!" Jillian hurls a pinecone at her head, and it hurts. "You're making me uncomfortable." But Jillian brings it out in Clemence, with her straitlacedness and unflappability. Sometimes Clemence wants to make Jillian flap. It's not healthy to keep so much pent up inside.

And maybe Jillian agrees, because she almost explodes with the following sentence: "I'm having an affair with my therapist." These woods are empty and expansive, and Jillian's exclamation echoes on the breeze.

"What?" Clemence feels displaced. She's supposed to be the outlandish one. She had been on the cusp of disclosing that Toad is trying to get in touch—his familiar number lit up on her phone yesterday, and she'd felt a dread so potent and familiar that it felt like being married to him—but she's refusing to answer his calls. "*You have a therapist?*" Clemence is not being funny—this is the greatest surprise of her friend's revelation. "And isn't that wildly inappropriate?"

"You're not the only one who gets to have a shadow side." And then Jillian charges away into a thicket.

Clemence follows, getting burrs stuck all over her cardigan, and probably in her hair. During this whole outing, she'd felt like Jillian was trying to get away from her, and now she realizes she wasn't wrong. But when she finally reaches her friend, Jillian has stopped moving, perched on a big rock under a maple tree. Looking up, Clemence sees that the leaves are beginning to turn.

Jillian is crying. Clemence sits down beside her and tentatively moves close enough to put her arms around her. Jillian has never been touchy-feely, but she consents to this, collapsing in Clemence's embrace. She says, "It's so fucked up. I know it's so fucked up. And nobody knows, except Jeremy."

"Jeremy knows?"

"He wants me to report him, but I can't. I don't feel like he was taking advantage. It just happened. I was as responsible as he was. I wanted it."

"But Jeremy knows?" Clemence doesn't get it.

"It's over now. Mostly."

"Mostly?"

"Jeremy doesn't know that part. Clemence, I'm a terrible person."

"You're not." She isn't. But this isn't Jillian, either. What's going on here? Jillian is sensible, and this is lunacy. "But this is a lot."

"So, like, I know," says Jillian, "is what I'm saying. About what you're going through. I understand. Do you know that when Jeremy and I have sex, we have to schedule it on the Google Calendar? Do you know what that does to a couple, to have this regimented, impossible, exhausting, never-ending onslaught of a life?"

Clemence says, "Kind of." But she'd never had it that bad. Things had been rough with her and Toad, but this sounded like a different kind of awful. They didn't have kids and she didn't really love him, which made the stakes so much lower when she walked away. "So what are you going to do?" She finds Jillian's efficiency remarkable—as with friendship and physical fitness, Jillian didn't have time to have an affair and go to therapy, so she decided to do both at once.

Jillian says, "I think I'm going to do nothing. Kind of anticlimactic, right? To go on this journey and end up right where I started, but it's not like that. I feel different now. All those things I took for granted, and then once they were on the line, I realized I didn't want to lose them after all—my marriage, our family. And I've been lucky. Jeremy wants to work through it. Of course he does. Six months ago, that would have been the whole problem, how accommodating he can be. Sometimes it's like living with a balloon instead of a person, you know? He just floats and here I am losing my mind, but he's always exactly the same, and I just want him to have a reaction. I want him to be furious, too, instead of so docile. But if both of us were furious, everything would explode. I see that now. One of has to be the accepting one, the forgiving one, and I'm so damn lucky that's how he is. I didn't understand before. I didn't understand what I'd be losing if I lost him, but now I know."

They sit in silence, listening to the whistle of a cardinal somewhere overhead. Jillian moves closer, and lays her head on Clemence's shoulder.

"What does it mean, 'mostly' over?" Clemence finally asks.

"Well, I mean, I'm not seeing him as a therapist anymore."

Clemence laughs, as she is supposed to. "But who does that?" She turns to face her friend. "If you went public about this, he'd be in all kinds of trouble. And who else has he done this to?"

"He's been going through a crisis. He got divorced, then his mother died, and his half-brother is an incel, and he needs to sell the house, but the brother refuses to come out of the basement."

"Where did you find this guy?"

"On Yelp."

"Jillian!" Clemence cannot fit all these details into her scheme of reality. "You're supposed to be the smart one."

"His rating was great, and I needed an appointment in a hurry. He got me in the very next day." Jillian pulls out her phone and checks the time. "We should keep walking." She takes off again.

"You just don't want to face me," Clemence calls after her.

"I don't want to be late for my three o'clock," says Jillian once Clemence has caught up. But she says, "Thank you for listening. And for not hating me."

"How could I hate you?" Clemence asks her. "Honestly, hearing your story, I kind of hate myself less. So, like, I *love* you." They walked a little farther, and the parking lot appeared in the distance. "If it's over, though, shouldn't it be *actually* over?" Fuzzy boundaries were dangerous. "What does Jeremy think of that?"

"You'll be not shocked to learned that Jeremy has been remarkably easygoing. He wants to give me the space to figure out what I need to know. He says that when I'm ready, he'll be waiting."

"And that's an offer that doesn't expire?"

"I don't think so."

"You don't want to chance it, though."

Jillian says, "I know that now."

"Does Naomi know?"

"I'm not going to tell you."

"Why not?"

"Because if she does know, you're going to call her and talk about it for hours and try to analyze how messed up it all is, and I don't want you to do that."

"We care about you."

"I know, but I don't want the two of you talking about me behind my back if I'm not there."

"If you're there, it kind of defeats the purpose talking about you behind your back."

Jillian says, "Exactly." They arrive at her car, and she changes out of her athleisure wear like a magic trick, back into a suit with high heels, dropping off Clemence on her way back downtown to the office.

CLEMENCE MAKES A SOFT-BOILED egg for dinner, and eats it feeling like a baby. Even her spoon is small, the tiniest of all her utensils with a slightly bent handle. As with everything she has found in her kitchen, she wonders about its provenance, and the journey any item would have had to take to end up as part of the hodgepodge that is her furnished bachelor apartment. She thinks about how that's gendered, too—where do all the bachelorettes get to live? Never mind the divorcees, she considers the arbitrariness of these distinctions. And how can there possibly be order at all in a universe in which Jillian has been cheating on Jeremy? With her *therapist*?

Clemence is forced to use all the strength she possesses not to text Naomi. Even though it really wouldn't be so disloyal as Jillian is making out. No, instead she'd be trying to understand how Jillian could do something so out of character. If she could talk about it with Naomi, she'd be able (maybe?) to hash out some sense of it, to put the broken pieces of her perceptions back together into something recognizable, but instead she's on her own. Poor Jeremy. As accommodating as Jillian is rigid, but if things work out, this will be the reason why—in addition to Jillian's fundamental goodness. Clemence and Toad were never very compatible anyway, beyond how well they photographed together, complementary at first glance, but that was only superficial. Clemence doesn't miss her husband at all, and she hopes—that initial heartbreak aside—he will come to feel the same. Being lonely together was lonelier than being on her own.

Which she knows for a fact now, four months into this new adventure. Clemence has not yet worn out her own company entirely. She can eat an egg with a tiny spoon, and nobody asks her any questions, and she can go to bed early, or stay up very late. She can sleep in the nude, and walk around all morning draped in a bedsheet. She can measure the hours by the church bells, and never attend another service, instead sitting out on her balcony, feeling autumn's chill setting in, rereading *The Republic of Love*, a novel she's read a thousand times, and nobody's going to make a snide remark. Clemence realizes her main aversion to the cataloguing system at the bookstore is that those had been Toad's distinctions, too, between frothy women's books and literature that was worth one's while. Although he tended to read mostly non-fiction, anyway, and then would fail to finish those books. A copy of *Guns, Germs, and Steel* had been sitting on his bedside as long as she'd known him. Worthwhile in itself—Clemence read it. She has never gotten over the chapter about the impossibility of domesticating the zebra. Because certainly people have tried. But zebras are stubborn creatures, and prone to biting, digging in their teeth, and refusing to let go.

Sixteen

Clemence sees Toby for the first time since she started dreaming of Toby, for the first time since she kissed him—although Toby usually has Charles's body when she finds him in those dreams, and sometimes he's actually Charles altogether. Even though these days, with school back in session and the allure of his sexy doctor wife, Clemence doesn't see Charles at all, and it's Toby who arrives in her life every Thursday on those morning shifts for which Crampton pays her with ancient bills stuffed in recycled envelopes.

Clemence had wondered if things with Toby might be different after what transpired the day of the head wound, but at first it's hard to tell because he's got his face in a book, more conspicuously than usual. She can't even see if the wound has healed, and he refuses to look up. So she waits; but surely they've developed a rapport. Why does this feel like they've gone back to the beginning?

Because Toby stays frozen, his whole body clenched. She goes to ring the bell, and only then does he speak: "Please don't. I can't stand that sound." He's still hiding.

She says, "Nobody at any level of literacy could spend that long on a single page. I know you're not reading." Reaching over the desk to push the book down, and there he is—that face, those lips, those sad eyes, and the cut on his head is healing well. Proud of her first aid, she reaches out to touch the wound, but Toby recoils.

"What?"

"I don't understand what you're doing," Toby says. "Are you making fun of me? Is this a joke? Because I don't get it."

"I was just—" says Clemence, but she actually doesn't know what she's doing, either. This was never supposed to be part of the script.

"Like maybe it's an elaborate set-up?" he continues. "With Crampton, and that old lady at your house. I don't understand, but I don't appreciate being someone's joke." He's speaking very deliberately, and Clemence can tell that he'd practised these lines, and honestly it only makes him more endearing more because she can see the inner workings of his heart. Oh, Toby.

She doesn't want to further upset him. "She made you soup," Clemence tells him. "My landlady, Mrs. Yeung." She has carried the jar over in her bag, and now she takes it out and puts in on the counter. "You should put it in the fridge. It's very good soup. And nobody is making fun of you." Her voice is quiet and calm. No sudden moves. "I'm here for the books."

"You have to talk to me." He accepts the soup. He's picked up the jar, is examining its contents.

"But I like that part." She shrugs. "I like you." She really does, inexplicably. "Is that okay?"

"Maybe?"

"I'll try not to bother you," she says. "Leave you to your reading for now," and she tiptoes over to Women's Fiction, looking back once to see that he's watching her. She waves, and he waves back. He's not quite smiling, but she can see that he could be if he tried.

A person has to be the change they wish to see in the world, Clemence thinks, as she once again sets about the task of rearranging shelves in a bookstore crowded beyond capacity. Her ex-husband never believed this, scoffing at her self-importance. "You're just one cog in one wheel of a system," he'd say. "A system set up for your failure." Whenever she'd complain that the system didn't work, he'd counter that it was working precisely the way it was intended to, for the rich to profit and the oppressed to be oppressed, and what was the point of anything short of a revolution, which was never going to happen? This was how Toad justified his work as an analyst for an international mining conglomerate, destroying pristine acres of Bolivian rainforest in the process. When she'd first met him, he had dreams of being a botanist.

Maybe Clemence hasn't changed the world, but she's changed *her* world, and who is to say that doesn't matter? She spent so many years being complacent, going with the flow, and she'd been miserable. And now she's not miserable anymore, she's even happy, or approaching something like it. She has purpose in a way she never did when she was writing about wedding gowns and bridesmaid shoes. The cogs all count for something, is what she's thinking, as she's envisioning "Classics" and "Modern Fiction" shelves. Much less offensive to her own sensibilities, women's stories up there with all the others. She wonders if this ever might be a place where people browse. If they got rid of the dust, they'd be able to welcome shoppers with respiratory ailments. What if they took away some of the books stacked in front of the window and dared to let in a bit of light?

"Toby?" she calls, and she knows he's heard her because she hears him sigh. "Would you ever think of bringing chairs in here?"

"We've already got a chair," he points out, and he's right. There's a big cozy chair across from the cash, except it's easy to miss, stacked high with boxes of books and piles of books.

"But like, what if we had chairs that people could sit on? Somewhere comfortable to sit where they could browse through their books?"

"They could go to the library," he says. "They don't even mind if you sleep there."

Clemence stands up and heads over to face him again, everything less strange between them now that they're talking. "I'm thinking of ways to freshen things up."

"Fresh is a stretch," says Toby. "If you were looking for something fresh, wouldn't you go someplace else?"

"But that's the point. Wouldn't it be good if the store

was even a little bit busier?" Toby's grimace suggests that he doesn't think so. "Isn't the point of a store to attract customers? This place is off-putting. The first time I walked in, I almost turned around and walked back out again."

"Most people do," says Toby. "Not a bug; it's a feature."

"But it's not sustainable," says Clemence. "And all these books with nobody to read them—it's a tragedy." She turns back to the shop and looks around.

Toby says, "The books are fine. What can we do about it, anyway?"

Clemence says, "Now you sound like my husband."

"You have a husband?" His voice rising an octave or higher.

Clemence faces him again, eyeing his expression carefully, which is mainly confusion. "Well, my ex," she says. "It's not official yet. But it might as well be. I've got to get used to saying 'my ex.'"

"You've never mentioned him." Is it possible he's bothered by this?

"He's not very remarkable," says Clemence. "My ex. Which was kind of the problem. I mean, you might like him." This is an outright lie. "A lot of people do." That part is true. "I wasn't the right person to appreciate his qualities." This is one hundred percent an absolute fact. Clemence says, "I think you're not interested in attracting customers because you don't like the idea of anybody showing up here to bother you."

"Well, yeah," says Toby. "Why do you think I work here? And now you've disturbed the whole equilibrium, and you want to find a way to bring in more people? Can you imagine this entire building filled up with people like you?"

Clemence says, "If only." It's actually her dream. A building filled up with people who are conscientious in their lifestyle choices, value books, and who would purchase ocean-friendly sustainable tinned fish if given the option. "Can you imagine? Each and every one of those people buying and reading books? Bringing you soup?"

"And rearranging the bookshelves."

"I am being the change I wish to see in the world, Toby. You should be proud of me. And if it weren't for me, Crampton might be making *you* do all this reorganizing work. I feel like you should be grateful."

"But if it weren't for you," says Toby, "there wouldn't be reorganizing work at all. And I'd be reading my book. And I wouldn't have hit my head."

Clemence is tired of him now. "Well, then read away," she says, her hand gestures a little too embarrassingly theatrical. "Don't let me stop you." Toby really can be a jerk. And why does she even care? It would actually suit his interests to conform to her fantasies, and it's not her fault if he doesn't see that. If he insists on remaining the primary character in his own pitiful life, instead of embracing all she has to offer. Which is, well, mainly, a little excitement, something bright to punctuate the days with, to let the sunshine in. Isn't that what Crampton is paying her for?

She has removed the *Women's Fiction* and *Literature* signs already, yellowed papers dotted with white spots where thumbtacks had stuck them up for decades. She is using damp paper towel to wipe down the shelves she's clearing, dust that's been accumulating for almost a century. Made up of shed skin cells of so many people who must be dead by now, and she considers whether she ought to be showing more respect, if there ought to be some kind of ceremony. Most of the ceremonies and rituals Clemence knows are superficial, devoid of meaning. *Something borrowed, something blue.* As though a rhyme makes up for vacuity. When Clemence married Toad, they'd made arrangements for a blue ribbon to be woven into her bouquet, but at the end of the day she'd realized this detail had been forgotten. And, Clemence wonders, is this why the marriage had gone so wrong? How does a person get to know things, the real things, things that connect one to knowledge and wisdom stretching back for centuries?

Clemence feels a hallowedness in the presence of these books, which is what she'd been missing at the church service. And then, almost as though they know what she'd been thinking, had picked up on her vague blasphemy, the church bells start chiming the hour, all twelve of them, signalling that her shift at the bookstore is over.

Rising, Clemence straightens her clothes, and gathers used paper towels for the garbage. Not intending to say another word to Toby, because he'd been rude. Because, evidently, he didn't even want to talk to her, anyway. But she has to walk past him at the desk, because it's unavoidable, and when she does, she's both surprised and not surprised to see that he's lowered his book already.

"You're going home now?" he asks, and she nods. "You want me to walk you there?" he offers.

"Why?" she asks. Now she's the one being rude.

"That time you bought me a snack," he says. "It's only polite."

"Those aren't terms existing in perpetuity," she says. "You don't have to."

He says, "I know," laying his book down. He follows her out of the store, flipping to the *Closed* sign, and Clemence doesn't feel compelled to fill the comfortable silence as they make their way along the sidewalk, around the corner and down her street. He stops at the bottom of her steps, and shrugs. "Here you are," he says.

But the next part surprises her. She really hadn't thought he had it in him ... and then he goes and blows her mind by kissing her, on the lips, even. Not even a peck. Eyes clenched shut and he's kind of lurching toward her so there is absolutely no contact between their bodies, so yes, it's as strange and awkward as all that, but also it really isn't. And then it's finished, and before Clemence has even a moment to process what's happened, Toby is gone. Leaping up the street like some untamed gazelle, arms flailing, running like somebody who's being chased.

Seventeen

The next week, the piece about Clemence goes up on Jillian's friend Sarah's newsletter, and it sets off a furor, which is the way of the internet. Though the piece, at first glance, appears unprovocative. Sarah has written about Clemence ending her marriage, simplifying her life, seeking out that proverbial room of one's own. But Clemence ends up getting hate mail, and the post goes viral among certain groups on social media taking umbrage with Clemence's appropriation of spinsterdom. "Trying it on like it's a costume," one person accuses her, and they find it rich that Clemence is being posited as an authority on the matter after having been single for just a handful of months. In the post, Sarah has written about spinsterdom's new vogue, and the readers are angry about that part, too, because, of course, single women have always been here.

The feedback is not all negative. Other readers email Clemence to say her story is empowering, inspiring. Sarah sends a note reminding her that people hate any kind of woman who takes up space, and this is true, though Clemence can see both sides. It's different, of course—she has acquired her life, her tiny room, her tinned fish, and borrowed cat all by choice. But that women get to make that choice at all, and that a life unencumbered by a husband and family would be the thing they choose—isn't that significant? Just one more remarkable way of refusing the question of how to be a woman?

Clemence's room becomes smaller as the seasons turn, her French doors closed against autumn's chill. Mrs. Yeung turns on the furnace, an intimidating rumble from the bowels of the house, and for two days, everything smells like burning dust. The heat barely reaches Clemence's perch, which is fine now, but might be a problem in January. The tree outside her window stays green longer than many of the others in the neighbourhood, but soon it will be changing, too. Nothing in Clemence's new world ever stays still, which is another difference from her life before. The subdivision where she'd lived with Toad was newly built, the trees spindly and barely there, West Coast weather invariable throughout the year. From where she sits now, Clemence realizes that she's become cut off from all things cyclical during the years of her marriage. She'd had her IUD removed a few weeks ago, her period properly returning after years of being so light, and she welcomed it, because it was one more reminder that she was alive inside a body that had its own processes, and she was even conscious of this with every exhalation, the magnificent fact of her breath, her blood, her heartbeat.

Clemence feels like she is bursting with vigour, and it could be her diet—eggs, oily fish, and excellent cheese—or maybe it's Toby. Could it possibly be Toby? Could ever a person such as Toby have the ability to provoke a reaction like this? To turn an ordinary streetscape into a musical theatre production, Clemence feeling as though she's dancing on her way to the bookstore, *floating*, even, and it seems as though everybody she encounters—the butcher, the baker, the artisanal beeswax candlestick-maker—is in on it, too?

"Good morning," calls out Cindy, the librarian, on her way to work for the day, and Clemence salutes her from across the street, barely resisting the urge to pirouette, to click her heels, but they're clicking in her mind. The sky is blue and the trees are gold and orange, a psychedelic feast for the eyes. A delivery van drives by and the driver wolf-whistles out the window at her, which Clemence takes as a message from the universe, that she is here, and she is seen, and she's connected to the world around her, a world moving, unceasingly. All day long those church bells chime hour upon the hour.

And more chimes as she enters the bookstore, which Toby takes no notice of, as usual. If he's been waiting for her, he doesn't show it, everything between them as strange and awkward as it's ever been, except it's even stranger, because Toby is in on it, too, and he's just as bewildering to her as she is to him, or as she is to herself, for that matter. It's like trying to find your way in the dark, and this is the case, quite literally, as Toby arrives in the aisle where Clemence is sorting Anita Brookner, taking her hand, leading her around past Literature all the way to the closet under the staircase with the cryptic sign on the door, the remnant of some long ago attempt at order: *Ursa Major—Asia Minor.* The closet serves as a storage space for (guess what) more books, except the light bulb burned out years ago, and no one has replaced it, so what any of those books might be is a mystery.

Their redolence, however, is overwhelming, the rich and pulpy smell of cheap mass-market paperbacks, pages with an edge of mildew, but in a good way, in that way that smells like coming home to people like Clemence and Toby who discovered themselves through books and reading. Clemence is leaning back against these books and while she can't see the stacks of them, she knows them, the same way she knows Toby standing in the dark before her, with breath that smells like toothpaste. It's obvious to Clemence where all this is leading, but Toby still has to check. Because he's the opposite of smooth, instead a strong proponent of friction, which is to say consent. Turns out spending a lifetime as a misfit with an utter lack of guile has left Toby especially aware of how a person might be taken advantage of. He doesn't want to be that guy.

"Can I kiss you, please?" he asks, the tension between them mounting, because they've been standing there in the dark, just breathing, staring in the direction of each other, but also into the abyss. Truthfully, at this point,

Clemence would have consented if Toby had asked to devour her whole. She feels as though every nerve in her body is alert and reaching for him, and it's been so long since she's been this close to anyone. And even longer since she was and it was absolutely where she wanted to be.

When Clemence breathes a yes, Toby draws nearer, and it's in the darkness where everything between them makes sense. That she'd be tasting him, his tongue in her mouth, his soft lips meeting hers, and this is the first time she's experienced Toby approximating anything close to physical fluency, because he knows what to do. She reaches out to pull him closer, to stroke the untrimmed hair growing thickly from his temples. Toby's hair is lush—who would have thought it? And all she wants, based on the strength of his kiss, is to feel his hands all over her body, but his hands are nowhere. Hanging still by his sides, she presumes, because she cannot see them, but she's also distracted by his mouth, the way his tongue is tracing her lips. Opening her mouth wider, she can't help emitting the smallest of moans, despite herself. Placing her hands on his chest, to feel his body, too, to show him what she wants him to do to her. And he's all bones, skin and bones, presumably, under his shirt and his sweater, and she wants to be tearing the clothing off him now. Feeling like a dam has burst, and there's no stopping the flow, because water will go where it wants to.

She tells him, "Touch me." A whisper. His shoulders are wide, but his frame is so delicate. *Hollow bones*, she thinks. She doesn't want to break him, but also she really wants to break him, and she wants to have him break her, too. She needs him to touch her, finally.

He asks her, "Can I?"

She says, "Yes," the word trailing long, like something aching, and it is. He lays his hand against her hip and she gasps at the electricity, the darkness concentrating every sensation, and she wonders if he feels it, too.

He moves his hand up her body, as she reaches under his sweater, his shirt. To feel his skin, and his body is so warm. That part surprises her—Toby is dyspeptic, allergic, and so vulnerable that she hadn't supposed it would be welcoming to touch him, the soft hair on his stomach, and she can tell by his stiffening muscles that he's conscious of her there. She can feel it in the way he holds his breath. Following his example, she asks, "Is this okay?" Both of them proceeding, step by step, ever so slowly, and she's overwhelmed by the eroticism of this. That they are both consumed, because he can barely nod against her neck and breathe, "Uh-huh." This is tantalizing, agonizing, and wonderful, to feel so slowly his hand tracing the edge of her left breast, through her clothes and everything.

He stops. "Does that feel good?" And of course it does, because why else would she be melting into a puddle, but he needs to hear her say it, so she does.

"So good." And you might think that this is the most ridiculous intimate scenario in which Clemence has ever found herself, necking with Toby the pale book man in the darkness of the musty closet, likely exposing herself to tuberculosis, but then you'd be forgetting about Clemence and Larry and Lisa next door. Larry with the receding hairline and the long, grey ponytail, and maybe Clemence has a thing for men with untidy hair, this is true, but she really (promise) never had a thing for Larry at all. Although if that's true, why is she thinking about Larry right now, as she's gently biting Toby's lip, careful not to draw blood, because she remembers what happened when he hit his head? Because of the distance from there to here is the answer to that question, how absolutely at home Clemence feels at this moment, in her body. It's so different in every way, and not because it's dark, because her vision has never been so clear.

Don't think of Larry, Clemence reminds herself. She's never been very good at keeping her mind in one place, because it prefers to take off on meandering journeys. Clemence has to rein it in, think of Toby. The toothpaste taste of Toby, and she wonders if he'd brushed his teeth with intention. If he'd been planning this, or it was spur of the moment, the way he'd waltzed up the aisle and led her to this private place, Ursa Major—Asia Minor. And his face is stuck in her neck now, and she's inhaling his hair, Head & Shoulders shampoo, and she's running her hand up and down his spine, fingers a whisper on his vertebrae, and his bones are so protruding that it's a wonder he doesn't snap. What a thing to wonder so much about someone and then finally to be touching their body.

He stops. "This is okay?"

"Okay," she confirms, urging him back to the matters at hand, as he kisses her collarbone. His hand on her breast is still tentative, so she pulls it closer to affirm things, and starts sucking on his earlobe, her yearning building at the touch of his fingers, and it's been a long time for her since an encounter had built up so slowly. The intensity so concentrated. It might be possible to be satisfied if this was all there was ... but no. Clemence wants it all.

"We should stop." He steps back.

She says, "No," the word trailing like something out of a tragedy, or perhaps just in the way of a whining child, and reaches to pull him closer, knocking a precarious stack of paperbacks to the ground with her elbow. They both ignore this, returning to kissing, until Toby pulls away again.

"We can't lose our heads," he says.

"Why not?" But he's right. One thing leading to another. What would Jillian say? Although Jillian these days might say anything. "What would Jillian have said before she'd become unhinged?" might be the most appropriate question of all to consider at this moment, and here she and Toby would be in agreement. Time to step back, but metaphorically, because there's not enough room in the closest, and to take a deep breath, also a metaphor, because the air in the closet is too stuffy for that. Jillian would probably recommend they get out of the closet altogether, and they do, emerging into the light with blinking eyes, and the bookshop really does not seem so dim after you've been snogging in a cave.

Instead, the space is almost luminous, the two of them standing around, adjusting their clothes, smoothing their hair, untucked and rumpled by the books about gardening and hedgerows, and Gertrude Jekyll, whom Clemence likes to imagine as Mr. Hyde's far more salubrious sister.

Bookstores are so distracting. She has always found it difficult to have conversations in these spaces, to not be looking over someone's shoulder at the beautiful book on peonies high up on the shelf, but Clemence is a far cry from Toby, who struggles with conversations everywhere. Get him in a closet, though, and he really comes to life.

Clemence puts her hand on his shoulder, imploring him to wait for a moment. Otherwise, he would have walked away from her without a word. "That was nice," she says. "I like you, Toby." It will be complicated to process their encounter now that they're standing in the daylight.

"Thank you," he says. He doesn't look at her. Out here, he's lost all his verve, his instincts. It's like they're back to their very first meeting again, and all he wants to do is hide behind a book.

Which only makes her want him more.

And what kind of game is this? What has Toby done to her, to Clemence, who had been determined to never again want anybody ever, when she'd specifically chosen him for his lack of desirability? Because someone like him should not be able to reduce Clemence to jelly, but this is what he's done.

Eighteen

Mrs. Yeung puts Clemence in put in charge of promoting the jumble sale, and Clemence has ideas about social media and email marketing. About targeting local influencers, and everybody on the committee humours her in this respect, but they insist that she has to do posters, too. The church has a laser printer, they keep reminding her, which must have been remarkable once upon a time. Reverend Michelle prints the posters using last year's template with the dates adjusted, and Clemence walks around the neighbourhood with a big roll of packing tape on her arm like a bangle, sticking those posters to poles and fence posts and community boards. She convinces Crampton to stick one in the window at the grocery store, though she has to clean away the grime with a wet cloth before the poster can be visible through the glass. In addition to being sensitive about her windows, Crampton isn't crazy about the cause—she's been furious at St. Saviour's since she was a child and made to feel unwelcome at the Sunday school picnic on account of her father being Jewish.

Which Clemence understands entirely. "But I don't think they do that anymore," she says.

"They had Neapolitan ice cream," says Crampton, not listening, still far away in her memory. "I've always had an affinity for stripes. I wanted to try it, but the other mothers made me leave. They said it wasn't appropriate."

"Neapolitan isn't very good."

Crampton eyes snap back open. "It would be years before I knew that for myself." Clemence struggles to imagine Crampton as a child, or eating ice cream for that matter. Surely she was born wearing a tweed suit with her grey hair closely cropped. She explains, "It was our neighbour who brought me to the picnic. I used to hang around her place, because my father was always working, and my mother had just died. I'm sure I was a nuisance, but she was kind, and after what happened that day, she was mortified, though I'm not sure if it was for my sake or her own."

"And what did your father think?" They are standing outside, looking in through the window, and out in the fresh air, Crampton is most forthcoming. As though leaving her shop has broken the spell that Clemence has long suspected Crampton lives under, the kind that freezes time entirely.

Crampton dismisses Clemence with a wave. "My father didn't care. He hated the church. He told me I was a fool to bother with them, anyway. And I vowed to never have anything to do with them again. So I haven't. Until you came along and started pilfering my books for your jumble."

"I didn't pilfer! You gave me permission."

"I gave you codswallop," says Crampton, and then she faces Clemence head-on. "What I want to know is, what did you do to Toby? Because either something's going on, or he's been attacked by a vacuum cleaner."

Clemence tries to keep a poker face. "I have no idea what you're talking about." She really doesn't. Mostly.

Crampton actually cracks a smile. "I have to say that you've impressed me. Your nerve at demanding to reorganize my bookstore was really something, but that you've somehow compelled Toby to be intimate with another human being." She shakes her head in amazement. "They should give out prizes for that."

Clemence is not sure how to take this, if Crampton is mocking Toby, but also is it so far-fetched that Toby might find Clemence desirable? He'd practically dragged her into the closet. She feels like telling Crampton this, but restrains herself. "I *like* Toby," is all she says.

And Crampton says, "Then you're smarter than I first took you for, because Toby is brilliant, and gentle, and good. The world needs to be a kinder place for strange people. So many of us would benefit. I don't know anyone who wouldn't."

"Toby's not so strange," Clemence says, if only to be polite.

Crampton says, "Then you don't know him yet. He only gets stranger the more that you do, but beyond that sickly exterior, he's got the most surprising vitality. And you must be a fairly substantial person yourself if he's put his book down." Looking at Clemence narrowly now. "He *did* put his book down, right?"

"He did."

Crampton's tiny eyes actually sparkle with glee, and she rubs her hands like an evil sprite. "And so this is the reason I let you put your poster in my window," she says, "even in violation of a decades-old grudge. I don't violate my grudges for just anybody, you know."

THAT WEEKEND CLEMENCE IS forced to take an afternoon off from her usual practice of lounging in her daybed eating apple slices and blue cheese off a chipped china plate while fantasizing about her body being ravaged by someone who is kind of Toby, but a little more John Keats, complete with Charles Yeung's biceps. She's currently steeped in the erotic poetry translation, and she's actually glad to have a reason to shift her mind to other things, although her sister's twins' fourth birthday party probably wouldn't have been the diversion she would have chosen.

But the birthday party is the diversion she has, and it's such common knowledge her days are wide open that she could hardly make excuses. "I would prefer to stay home alone with my filthy thoughts" wouldn't go over well, and while filthy thoughts are a movable feast, it's impossible to think most of them in the midst of a children's birthday party. When Clemence arrives home again at the end of the day, she will write three paragraphs about how remarkable it is that the presence of one's siblings' offspring can quell any urges toward activities that lead to reproduction.

But right now in the middle of the party, she's been fixed up with sangria, so she's doing all right, and with so many grandchildren to occupy her, Clemence's mother leaves her alone. The children are risking their lives on a bouncy castle that's been squeezed into Grace and Allison's tiny backyard, their screams at ear-splitting levels, and Clemence's dad is sitting beside her, but she'd have to yell to talk to him, so she doesn't, and they both prefer it this way, the only peace for miles around. Bonnie and Prudence are hiding bags of candy for a treasure hunt, and they're arguing because Prudence's kids aren't supposed to have sugar and so she wants to hide the treasures too well. And Grace and Allison are arguing because this is what happens whenever they have people over, Grace getting all stressed out and anxious, ending up yelling at everyone, which nobody minds too much because Allison is a professional caterer, so the hors d'oeuvres alone are worth it. Even if Allison smokes, that remarkable thing, and Clemence is always a little afraid she's going to uncover a bit of cigarette ash dropped in her sausage roll.

Jarvis has shimmied up the top of the bouncy castle now, and is perched on the roof, which Clemence suspects isn't meant to be part of the play area, but no one's going to call him out, not just because it's his birthday, but because his parents don't believe in constraining their children's spirits. "The most dangerous thing a child can be exposed to is too much 'Be careful,'" is one of Grace's favourite axioms, also convenient because it serves as a dig at Bonnie, who was a very nervous mother. And this is why Clemence decides to get up and distract Bonnie before she realizes what Jarvis is up to, partly to keep the peace but also because she is tempted to screech, "Be careful!" herself. Putting down her glass, she takes Bonnie by the elbow, leading her inside, out of one chaos into another kind, because there is music blasting from the living room, that incessant song about a horse on the old town road.

She locates the speaker and turns the volume down, just as her mother says, "So you're seeing someone."

Clemence is caught off guard. "How did you know?" she asks, instead of denying outright, which would have been more accurate, anyway, because it's not like she and Toby have some kind of formal arrangement. "Seeing somebody" implies a person she isn't kissing the dark, someone who isn't Toby and so prone to rashes and outbreaks, which she can't explain in a way her mother would understand.

And then Prudence walks in as this exchange is happening, just to make everything more complicated. "I knew it!" she screeches, clutching her virgin cocktail to her burgeoning belly whose burgeoningness is so unremarkable after all these years. And Clemence is sometimes grateful that her sister is always pregnant, because of how it takes attention away from the fact that Clemence never will be. Fingers crossed. Her favourite thing about no longer being married is that nobody asks about it anymore. Prudence easing her body down onto the couch—she's already huge, and she has months to go. "Spill the beans," she instructs.

But there are no beans. Not really. "I mean, it's complicated." It always is for Clemence, her family expecting her stories to map onto their preconceived notions of how a woman's life should go, but Clemence keeps disrupting the narrative. "I'm not seeing somebody exactly."

"Polyamory!" Prudence claps her hands in delight. "Sandro called it. He saw the whole thing a mile off. He and Mom had a bet."

"A bet?"

"Not about polyamory," says Bonnie, who's made visibly uncomfortable by the word. "He said you looked like you were in love."

"He said you looked like you were getting boned," Prudence corrects her. "Sandro is usually right about these things. He said it's in the complexion. So who are they?"

"They?"

"Your, um, partners," says Bonnie, who finds the vocabulary awkward, but will embrace her daughters' happiness wherever and with whomever they find it. She just doesn't want to be left out of the loop.

"Tell us why you're glowing, Clem," urges Prudence.

And should she tell them it's oily fish? Coupled with plenty of sleep? Or should she tell them it's Toby, though she's sure it's not that. The only thing Toby has done to her skin is to irritate where the parts of his beard he missed shaving had rubbed against her neck.

"It's not really anything," she tells them, but they don't believe her. She imagines if she'd brought Toby with her, what they'd make of him. What he'd make of them, how long he might last in the midst of this chaos. Toby is impossibly incongruous. She cuts her mother off before she goes to speak again, "And I promise it's not polyamory." One Toby is enough. But her mother and Prudence are waiting, demanding to know more. "It's this guy who works with me at the bookshop. But I mean, it's nothing. We kissed once. And that was all." But yes, the whole experience has been running through her mind on a film reel ever since then. "No one's getting boned," she promises.

"Maybe no one's getting boned *yet*," says Prudence. "It's like Sandro has a sixth sense sometimes."

"Well, he is European," offers Bonnie, thoughtfully. "And now I owe him twenty dollars."

"I think it's healthy," says Prudence, as they all get up and move into the kitchen to help with the cake. "It's good that you're starting to move on from—"

Don't mention Toad, Clemence telepaths to her sister, who must get the message because her words trail off. Good. Clemence doesn't want their mother to ask if she's been in touch with Toad yet, and she's actually glad she hasn't been, because doesn't that prove that Clemence left him behind months and miles ago? That she *has* moved on? Why must she be getting boned in order for everyone to see that? Especially when she has so much else to show for how far she's come since then?

In the kitchen, Allison is assembling a seven-layer cake

made of rainbow stripes, scraping off the icing on the side in a deconstructed style.

"Now that's different," says Bonnie under her breath, which is what she always says when anybody varies from the motherhood practices she set in stone in the late 1980s. Bonnie's fancy birthday cakes were those with coins wrapped in wax paper baked inside. She'd had to stop when it was one of Prudence's kids' birthdays and somebody swallowed a dime.

And because Juniper and Jarvis are twins, there are actually two seven-layer rainbow cakes, lit with sparklers, and Clemence is called up to carry the other one outside. Holding the cake out beyond her so the sparkler doesn't spark in her face, or set her hair on fire, but the cake is heavy and awkward, and she doesn't want to drop it, and how does anybody manage to hold it all and not get burned?

Nineteen

The bookstore window gets smashed sometime during the night on Sunday, which Crampton discovers in the morning. Nothing appears stolen, though it would be hard to tell. Piles of paperbacks stacked up against the pane are now spilled out onto the sidewalk, surrounded by shattered glass that glistens in the sun like diamonds. Whoever did it did it for the impact, for the sound and the fury, but things are quiet now as Clemence comes around the corner to pitch in with the cleanup. Pedestrians do delicate sidesteps around the mess. Crampton hands Clemence a broom, and she starts to sweep, Crampton picking up the books, returning them the same piles they'd been stacked in for decades.

She needs to open the grocery store and while the bookstore doesn't open until noon, she asks Clemence to wait around anyway for Tom to arrive and put up plywood in the window until the new pane can be installed. Tom is Crampton's handyman—she uses him for everything. Not because his work is good, but because he's never put his rates up in the half century he's been working for her. Crampton is not rattled by the destruction of the window—these things happen. A lifetime on the block, she says, has taught her that much.

And so Clemence continues the cleanup, discreetly disposing of books so overtaken by mould they're no longer saleable, and scooping out a few more volumes for the jumble sale, which is coming up fast. She's created a Facebook event, but the only people who've RSVP'd are her family, determined to support her, even though she's told them they don't have to. What Clemence needs is to drum up local hype—she's been contacting vendors from the artisan market to see if they might want to buy tables. A few sellers of succulents and a potter or two would offer a whole different vibe to the jumble sale, plus that woman selling tiny pots of local honey from the hives she keeps on the roof of the Montessori school. Jillian's friend Sarah has promised to promote it both in her newsletter and in the community newspaper she writes for, happy to pay Clemence back for all the clicks her profile's outrage generated. Naomi has offered her own marketing expertise, pro bono, and if the Facebook event doesn't pick up steam, Clemence will probably take her up on that. There's a poster up in the bookstore by the door, but since nobody goes into the bookstore, it's mostly symbolic.

Tom the handyman arrives, sauntering in with a hammer hanging from the loop on the back of his denim overalls. Clemence wonders how he drives his truck like that, if he has to sit on the hammer, and if that's awkward, but everything is awkward with Tom, and the hammer is the least of it. Tom is impossibly slow. Slow to move, to process, to get to the end of a sentence. He'll look at a thing and say, "Well, now . . ." Until you think you've lost him, but then he'll say another couple of words before he trails off again. It's fortunate his rates are low, because if he billed by the hour, Crampton would be paying him forever. Clemence watches Tom cut what's left of the glass from the frame, and then amble over to his truck to see if he has a piece of plywood that will fit.

It takes all morning. Clemence goes inside, clearing off the chair near the door and getting comfortable there. She picks up a sun-damaged novel called *Family Happiness*, which turns out to be a collection of short stories about a woman having an affair. Not what she'd expected with a title like that, and Clemence checks to make sure that the main character doesn't lie down on train tracks at the end, which seems the common fate for wives who commit adultery.

But no: (*spoiler alert*) the adulteress doesn't die. She doesn't even get found out or in trouble, and she loves her husband, and she loves her children, and there's just this other facet of her life that is a retreat from all the rest of it and which she requires in order to be her truest self. An indulgent fantasy, this book is, and Clemence adores it, reading it cover to cover before Tom has finally bumbled around enough to be finished with his work, the plywood panel making the bookstore even darker than usual. Clemence has to use her phone light to read by.

As the church bells are ringing twelve, Toby arrives. expecting neither Clemence nor the damage.

"Crampton called me," she explains. Crampton hadn't called Toby because Toby doesn't have a phone. And this is what Clemence has been waiting for as she's been reading, anticipating this moment, her first encounter with Toby since what happened in the closet. From where she's sitting in the chair, Toby looks imposing, his face all in shadows. She can't read his expression, but she wants to. She rises to meet him, to tell him, "There is something I need to ask you about." And this time she's the one who so easily leads them to the small room under the stairs, where everything gets lost in darkness and you have to feel your way.

AT THE CHURCH, the jumble is overflowing, and there's scarcely enough space for the latest box Clemence brings from the bookstore. All she can do is pile it on top of another box and hope the tower doesn't topple. Reverend Michelle is there scoping out the scene, looking concerned. The jumble sale absolutely has to be a success, and not just to feed the hungry and to raise the roof, but because if it isn't, the church will be left with the further problem of what to do with all this stuff.

"Although to be fair," Reverend Michelle admits, "we have room to store it. We have rooms upon rooms. So much space, but that's not much good without a roof above it." The parishioners who'd spent the twentieth century growing the building had never envisioned a time when resources at St. Saviour's would be this scarce.

Clemence tells her about her social media plans and connections with vendors from the artisan market. Jumble sales, she explains, have retro charm, but they're also very much of the moment in terms of the economy, the environment, and the public appetite for all things vintage. There are vendors at the artisan market who make their living selling jumble. "The key is curation," she says, and tries not to think about the shoebox full of headless Barbies somebody donated, and the plastic bag stuffed with worn-out slippers with no mates.

All this stuff—it's overwhelming to behold. If a person was determined, they might unearth a few treasures, but most of it is anything but. Ugly mugs from tourist attractions, and amateur folk art projects. Clemence and Toad used to make regular donations of household junk to second-hand stores, their household seemingly lighter every time they did, but it would never be long before they'd start finding even more things to get rid of. Stuff multiplies. Though they'd never ventured inside any of the stores they'd made the donations to. Toad didn't like the smell of second-hand, and their townhouse had a distinctly modern aesthetic that made vintage items seem unsuitable. And how the tables have turned, Clemence thinks now, in that—the books from Crampton's aside—she couldn't rustle up a second-hand donation if she tried. Instead, she is eyeing the stock for things she's in need of—an egg beater among the kitchen stuff whose shine keeps catching her eye.

Mrs. Yeung arrives with her clipboard, ready to officiate. She is fluent in *Robert's Rules of Order*, and insists that minutes be taken no matter how informal the meeting. When the rest of the group is present, everyone sips bad coffee from Styrofoam cups, and just before proceedings are about to begin, Clemence's phone starts to buzz, the buzzing curiously amplified by whatever synthetic material the tabletop is made of. It's a rude interruption. Nobody else on the committee even has a phone on the table, let alone one impertinent enough to start buzzing before the call to order.

"You want to take that?" Reverend Michelle asks Clemence kindly, ignoring the rest of the committee's nasty looks.

But Clemence—without even flipping her phone over to see who's calling—knows she doesn't, because there is only one person who would be calling, the most dogged human being she's ever met, and she still doesn't want to talk to him. She'd come halfway across the continent to escape him. Feeling virtuous, for once, because she has a reasonable excuse to not take the call, which is that *she happens to be in a meeting.* Once she picks up her phone and directs Toad to voicemail—which is already full and she wouldn't know how to check it even if she wanted to—the meeting can begin.

Last spring's jumble sale, the treasurer reports, brought in a grand profit of seventy-five dollars, and Clemence wonders if they ought to do something about their pricing. But that's not possible, someone else explains, because they'd had signs specially done up and laminated with the prices displayed, and it would mean the signs were out of date.

"Committees are exhausting," Clemence says to Mrs. Yeung on their walk home together.

Mrs. Yeung murmurs her agreement. "People are an interesting project, though," she says, "and that's why I keep going." She turns to Clemence with a mischievous grin. "You know today Charles is coming downtown?"

And then she rushes ahead, Clemence trying to keep up, which means she can't possibly play it cool as she asks, "But how would I know that? I haven't talked to Charles." She couldn't have. They never exchanged numbers, which only seemed strange until she'd learned about his wife.

Mrs. Yeung says, "Oh sure." Dismissively. "You don't even think of Charles, right?" Is she winking? She's a remarkably awful woman to be the mother of such a nice guy. "He's donating jumble. He said he didn't have anything and then I told him you'd joined the committee, and I guess he changed his mind." What even was this?

"I guess he'll be bringing his wife." Clemence would like to meet her, for real. To see Superwoman in person.

"Who knows?" shrugs Mrs. Yeung. They'd finally reached their front door. "She's very busy."

"She's a doctor," Clemence adds.

"You know her?"

"You told me."

"Did I," says Mrs. Yeung, but it's not a question.

Twenty

Clemence takes her work outside because it's warm out, and it might be one of the last autumn days on which she can sit on the balcony. She needs to finish up her edits on those love poems. She's thinking about the seasons, and wondering if the editing work has infected her brain, if she'll still feel as amorous when she's moved on to her next project, which is indexing a book called *Love Means Having to Say You're Sorry*, written by a feminist psychologist colleague of Grace's who's hoping to make it big with a marriage counselling podcast. Clemence expects such a project will extinguish her sex drive like a snuffer, but then the snuffer is an image that makes her think of sudden dark, the room under the stairs, and what she'd done there with Toby that morning. Slowly, so slowly, Toby always tentative, setting the tone, and she respects these boundaries, whereas usually she'd rush into the whole thing sidelong. Clemence is too impulsive, she knows, and so this is an interesting experiment, one thing leading to another, waiting to see what happens next, her eyes closed so she can almost anticipate where he's going to touch her. His hand under her top, cool against her skin, and the way he whispers, "Your skin is so soft."

Reaching under her shirt now, just to feel what he felt, which is a curious kind of intimacy. And she's keeping her eye on the street down below, waiting for Charles, or not *for* Charles, exactly, but it's the same thing, another experiment. She wants to see what happens, clearly, because Charles could come and go and she'd never even know he'd been here, and no doubt this has happened several times since September. Which she's fine with, Charles living his own life, teaching his classes, living up there in the suburbs with his fine doctor wife, and Clemence only knows him because of this brief moment when their worlds collided. A misunderstanding on her part. Perhaps they could have been friends, but maybe even that is a stretch. She's a tenant in his mother's rooming house. It wouldn't be the sexiest set-up, even without a wife.

And perhaps this is just where she is these days, erotic love poems or not. If you put any man in front of Clemence right now, she'll probably fall in love. She's vulnerable, which is why she's continuing to steer clear of Toad and his lawyer. It's been such a tender time. And if ever there was a gamut, Charles to Toby is it, so her feelings are likely not about either of these men at all, and Clemence is reading far too much into everything. As she is prone to doing. Part of the appeal of Toad, to be honest.

Toad was an easy read—short works, large print, with plenty of white space. There had been a time when she'd thought this was good for her, but then she'd forgotten how to feel things or even that she could.

Was life better when it was complicated? Impossibly knotted up with the feelings and experiences of others? And this thought brings to Clemence's mind an image of a macramé wall hanging someone donated to the jumble, a treasure in a bag that was otherwise mouldy bath mats. The question has her thinking of jumble in general, its chaos and messiness, all those awful things that nobody wants, but here and there is something perfect, like it had been waiting for her. The macramé owl was like that. And what were the odds of it finding its way into her hands? Such remarkable serendipity. How could you not love a world that could set you up in this way?

The question is still hanging in Clemence's mind as Charles's car, still familiar, appears on the street. He stops out front and pops the trunk, emerging from the vehicle like a vision. She'd wondered in the last few months if she'd just imagined that he looked this good, but no. He's at a distance now, but she'd seen him up close, and it was real. Or so she'd thought. Clemence had also thought he was available, and interested in her, so it's possible she knows nothing at all. Except that she can't take her eyes off him. Willing him to look up at her, and then willing him not to, because what's she even doing? Would he understand that she's simply out here enjoying the weather?

Maybe. Because he does look up, as though he's heard her longing, and he breaks into a smile that might be the easiest, most beautiful expression she's ever seen. As though maybe everything doesn't have to be so complicated after all, and easy-to-read is preferable. Charles raises his hand to wave, and she waves back, and she stands up so he doesn't think she is hiding.

But he has a wife. Charles Yeung has a wonderful wife, who at this moment is likely saving somebody's life in an intensive care unit. And Clemence has Toby, anyway, her unsuitable attachment, even though he's more suitable than she'd initially supposed. Certainly suitable for her purposes right now, which is the important thing. Clemence doesn't want to marry Toby, but Clemence doesn't want to marry anyone, and shouldn't that mean there's no reason why she can't go downstairs and see Charles?

This is not big deal, and yet—she'd dressed up for this, put on lipstick. She would have changed her clothes, anyway, after spending the morning in the bookshop and the meeting sorting jumble at the church, with all the grime inherent. The last thing she needs is Charles Yeung picking another dust bunny off her body, and she's recalling the tension of that moment as she goes outside. She can't decide if it had been wonderful or awful. She knows she looks good, though, and she can tell he thinks so too by the way he takes her in, head to toe, as she walks down the steps to the street where he's been unloading his car.

He says, "Hello, stranger," and here she'd been wondering if she'd merely imagined his allure, the dazzling effect his presence had on her. Turns out no. Which means that it's a terrible idea after all, her coming all the way down here to greet him. That wave from the balcony should have sufficed, and it wouldn't have got her into this kind of trouble, tangled up in feelings for a guy who's married, when she'd spent a good forty minutes earlier that afternoon kissing somebody else.

To Charles, however, she simply says, "You've got jumble." And has a stupider sentence ever been said by a human being in all of history? Absolutely not, and for some reason she even has to surpass it: "Of all the jumble sales in all the towns in all the world, you had to donate to mine."

"So it's your jumble sale now, eh?" Charles has closed his trunk, and reaches to pick up the boxes he's unloaded. Clemence comes over to take on some of the load—the boxes aren't as heavy as others they've carried together. She helps bring them up to the porch. He says, "I think my mother might have something to say about that."

"Well, I *am* in charge of publicity." Her tone is joking, but as she's speaking, she realizes it actually means something to her, this responsibility. Except that Charles has spent his entire life around the churchwomen and knows too much to be impressed. Besides, Charles is a teacher. He's somebody's husband. His whole life is rife with purpose, and so whatever Clemence has going on seems paltry in comparison.

"So is that where you've been hiding, then?" They leave the boxes by the door and sit down at the top of the steps. "At the jumble sale? Busy with publicity?"

"I've been around," says Clemence. "I'd say you're the one who's disappeared."

"We're like ships in the night, I guess," says Charles. "I've been missing you." The kind of remark that Clemence might have read a lot into before she knew about his wife, Dr. Wonderful. Charles Yeung, it turns out, is just remarkably warm and effusive—he must get it from his dad's side. He says, "My mom's been keeping me up to date, though. You've got a hot Italian boyfriend." Clemence doesn't know how to respond to that—neither the adjectives nor the noun having any bearing on her reality. What has Mrs. Yeung been saying? "She made him soup, she said. A guy named Tony. You know, my mom's not going to make her soup for just anyone. He must be a special kind of fellow."

Or just one who looks as though he's severely in need of vitamins and nutrients. And Clemence says, "Oh, *Toby.*" As though it had been the name that threw her. She can't tell Charles that Toby isn't actually her boyfriend, since he only thinks he is because Clemence told his mother so. Clemence is surprised that Mrs. Yeung has found her remarkable enough to mention to Charles at all. "He did like her soup," she says.

"Everyone likes her soup."

"Well, Toby's pretty particular."

Charles says, "Oh, really."

And Clemence wonders if she and Charles are capable of having a conversation that isn't borderline flirtatious; if he is like this with everyone. Why are they talking about Toby? She changes the subject. "How's your wife?" But now this is even worse than what she'd said about the jumble sale.

Charles regards her strangely, confused. "She's fine," he says, more a question than an answer.

"I bet she also likes your mother's soup."

"Actually, she doesn't," says Charles.

"Ah, the exception that proves the rule."

Charles says, "She and my mother don't get along too well, to be honest. Not a lot of love lost. Or soup exchanged."

"Oh," says Clemence. "That must be—difficult." It's surprising.

Charles shrugs. "It is what it is." Fiddling with his hands. "Anyway, I've got the stuff for donation." He gestures toward the boxes. "So at least there's that. Nice to pare things down. It feels good, you know?" And Clemence nods because he seems to expect her to. "It's important to just get on with things."

"Things like jumble sales," says Clemence. She wonders if he's making fun of the slightness of her life.

But he seems serious. "Exactly." Both of them turning around as his mother comes out to the porch, and she speaks to him severely in Korean. Turns out she's angry that he's late, that she's been waiting for him. She switches to English, and tells him she hopes his donation is up to par. That he's not one of those people who bring her their boxes and boxes of garbage. She mentions the mouldy bath mats, and Charles promises her that there's no such thing. "Clothes, mainly," he says. "And some stuff from the kitchen that I never use. I had three juicers. Who needs three juicers? I don't even drink juice."

He's not staying—just dropping by. "Of course you

are," says his mother in exasperation, but she's prepared three plastic bags stuffed with food containers for Charles to take home with him. Including—as Clemence can see through the straining bag—the soup. For once, Mrs. Yeung doesn't mention Charles's wife, and she's almost kindly as she and Clemence walk him back to his car. Though maybe it's because she wants her son to come back downtown before too long since the tiles in the upstairs shower need replacing. Charles tells her that he'll definitely try.

"Definitely try," says Mrs. Yeung, as the car disappears at the end of the street. Charles had hugged her, and administered to Clemence an affectionate touch on the shoulder. "That's how he says no way and hopes I won't notice," she adds.

"You know, I can recommend a handyman," Clemence says. She would have to get Tom's contact details from Crampton. And she knows that Mrs. Yeung is about to protest that she can't afford it, but Clemence interrupts her. "He might surprise you. He's not particularly efficient, but apparently he's even worse at putting up his rates."

Inside the foyer, they begin going through Charles's boxes, one of which is entirely women's clothing. Good designer stuff, too, and Clemence is perusing for her own interest until it becomes clear that Charles's wife is very small. A blessing in disguise, perhaps, because how embarrassing would it be to have him—or, heaven forbid, *his wife*—show up at the house one day to find Clemence wearing clothes intended for the jumble?

She takes the set of knives in the other box, though. Mrs. Yeung urges her to, in compensation for her volunteer service, and also because they'd had to instate rules about selling knives as jumble since the year someone was nearly stabbed in an altercation about whose turn it was to refill the coffee urn. Church basements were tense places—it was best to avoid weapons altogether.

And so Clemence has something new and shiny in her kitchen now, sharp knives where all the others are dull to the point of useless. Which hasn't mattered much, because the only thing she slices is cheese, but these new knives make her consider expanding her culinary horizons. She removes an apple from the bowl on the counter just to experience the difference, how easy a thing can be if you only have the right tools. The apple falling into perfect sections, which she places on a plate, and then she sits down at the table to eat them, thinking of Charles, and of Toby, and inexplicability. About how she is utterly failing in her quest to live the *Eat, Pray, Love* without the love. She doesn't even really have the "eat" part, because she can't afford restaurants, and she has only a hot plate. She thinks about all the great women whose culinary genius might have been quashed by the absence of a proper kitchen—imagine the bolognese sauces we might have been permitted had some of these maiden aunts been in possession of a decent saucepan? The advances in bread-baking, but for want of an oven. An oven—all those years she'd had an oven, a huge state-of-the-art model that was as complicated to program as a spaceship, and she'd taken it for granted. Even just the smell of something baking or roasting signalled home.

For the first time since she'd come here, Clemence's room of her own seems kind of meagre, and she turns around to glare at the knife set on her counter, because it's the knife set that's at fault. Rendering everything else dull and shabby in comparison, when there is nothing she can do about it. The church bells chiming a question, seven times: What if she's actually wasting her wild and precious life?

Twenty-One

Jillian and Jeremy have been seeing a therapist, a different therapist, one they didn't find on Yelp and who has prescribed that they partake in scheduled date nights. Jeremy texted Clemence to ask if she might help—the prospect of Jillian having to scrounge for child care for these date nights could be the straw that breaks their marriage's back, and Jeremy doesn't want that. So he's wondering if Clemence might be able to babysit. Careful to emphasize that Clemence is not a babysitter; he knows she's not a babysitter. He doesn't want to cause offence by suggesting she's a babysitter, and Clemence goes off—what's wrong with being a babysitter? Care work is work and it's work that she values, and she's certainly not too good for that. To suggest as much as sexism, and Jeremy texts back, "Whoa whoa whoa." He just meant that Clemence wasn't really into kids.

Which she isn't, but Jillian's daughters are non-feral as kids go, plus while Clemence really isn't into kids, she wants to play a role in preserving the institution that is Jillian and Jeremy. She is a tiny bit concerned that philandering and divorce are contagious, and feels responsible. Also, they are going to pay her, and every little bit helps. Even better? Naomi has agreed to come over to keep her company, and Jillian had finally told her about Dr. Yelp, so she and Clemence can sit down together and make sense of the whole thing once the kids are in bed.

Hannah and Chloe are the kind of children who could make Clemence almost consider having kids, or at least see the point of the exercise, because they are smart and funny and entirely responsible for their own toileting habits. They make microwave popcorn and get dressed into matching pyjamas, and Clemence notes that caring for them is actually more fulfilling and less weird than talking to Toby, plus it pays better. But of course, Toby himself comes with benefits, which Clemence finds herself discussing with Naomi when she arrives after work, long after the kids' bedtime. Naomi has brought wine, and the two of them are curled up on the couch to hang out for the first time in ages.

"But I thought the whole reason for an unsuitable attachment was so you wouldn't get attached," says Naomi.

"I don't know if you'd call it attached," says Clemence.

"Not even at the lips?" asks Naomi, who's been filled in on all the details. The way the whole thing with Toby is a bit like that junior high school party game where you're kissing in the closet, except it goes on well beyond seven minutes, but stops mainly at groping and those deep passionate kisses that are so intimate and rapt that it feels like getting off, and every time they come back out into the light, Clemence's legs are weak, she's dizzy, and it's hard to walk. They've upset all kinds of stacks in the closet, and now paperbacks litter the floor. She's imagined lying down on them, the softness of their worn paper and cracked spines, how it might feel like a bed—what a mattress. Clemence has imagined a lot of things. "The closet thing is weird," says Naomi. "What's up with that?"

"I guess because it's private," says Clemence. She's picking dust bunnies out of her hair all the time now. But she also loves it, the closet under the stairs, Ursa Major—Asia Minor. The way that she can't see what she's doing in there, which means somehow that she doesn't have to think about it, either. That what happens with Toby exists on another plane, and when she tries to explain to anybody else it doesn't make sense. It sounds stupid and sordid, and Toby's weird. Of course, Toby is weird. But in the darkness, his weirdness seems to matter less, and she loves the way he makes her feel, the slow and steady desire. She'd never known desire to be steady, instead of overwhelming *want* and satiation—too much and then nothing. But oh, the way he can eke her out, pulling feelings from places she didn't she could feel.

"But it's only kissing, you said," clarifies Naomi.

"There's nothing *only* about it." And Naomi nods. She gets it. Naomi has no interest in the strings and drama that accompany relationships. Naomi is Clemence's guru in opting out of the narratives society offers a woman for how her life is supposed to be. She is married to her job, and it's an inspiring, fruitful relationship, and every few weeks she hooks up with partners via various apps for the creative and wild sex that's outlined beforehand in startling specificity. There is a trapeze folded into a dresser drawer in Naomi's spare room that Clemence only knows about from the two weeks she was staying there, and she can't envision how a person could begin to use it. If she asked, Naomi would explain it to her, but some things are best left to the imagination. All of which is to say that Naomi, of all people, understands what a kiss can be.

"But do you think you'd still want to kiss him if that closet had a functioning light bulb? And if the answer is no, what does that mean?" Clemence thinks about this, and Naomi continues, "And if the answer is no, I think that's okay. Not everything needs to be dragged out into the light of day. But I think it's important you really want what you want, is what I'm saying. Isn't that kind of the point of wanting after all?"

And here, they begin to talk about Jillian, about how what she wants is Jeremy, but not with the way that things are, and how her affair with the therapist was a cry for help.

"Jillian never cries for help like normal people," says Naomi. In crying for help, as in all things, Jillian would be extraordinary.

"Weren't you stunned when she told you?" Clemence

asks. She needs Naomi to be stunned. Naomi's signature pose is refusing to be rattled, but surely this one thing must have shaken her. "Especially the part about Yelp."

"Especially the part about Yelp," says Naomi. "Because Jillian is usually so responsible. You'd think she'd get a decent referral, you know? She doesn't trust Yelp to find a dry cleaner, so it seems strange she'd use it for a therapist."

"But maybe a Yelp therapist was precisely what she was looking for. It all makes sense. You know Jillian and her way with precision. A good therapist wouldn't have been useful to her, but a bad one permitted her to act out in a most fulfilling fashion. And now look—she and Jeremy are out on a date together. She says it's like their relationship has been renewed and he's finally invested after a few years of coasting on autopilot."

"But maybe that's just luck," says Naomi. "It all could have unfolded very differently."

"I want to report him," says Clemence. "The therapist. But she knows that I will, so she won't tell me his name."

"I know his name," says Naomi. "He's the first result when you look up therapists on Yelp."

"We could leave a review."

"An honest review."

"Oh yes, let's write that review," and Naomi pulls out her phone and they start composing a paragraph about the therapist who'd preyed upon their friend. One star.

Twenty-Two

Clemence can't stop thinking about it, though: Why *does* everything with Toby have to happen in the dark? Despite Mrs. Yeung's assessment, she pretty's sure Toby isn't a vampire, although he probably has some medical condition that is analogous. But all the same, she wants to bring him out into the light. She wants to invite him over to her place for dinner, taking into account his varied dietary needs, of course. Her brand-new second-hand knife set has inspired her.

Clemence stops by the bookshop and makes the proposal, giving him absolutely no opportunity to decline. She tells him when to arrive. She says she'll meet him on the porch; there's no need to ring the bell and alert the entire household. Confirming that she knows he can't eat gluten, and yes, he's sensitive to soy. And while he indeed drinks milk, he can't handle cheese. Clemence is aware of what she's getting into, refusing to be waylaid by any of his excuses.

The menu will be a challenge, though, with Toby's requirements and the fact that she'll have to cook on a hot plate. Clemence goes up to the main street to shop, skipping Crampton's grocery store with its decrepit produce, no doubt doused in pesticides. Crampton thinks that organics are a scam, and she might be right, Clemence considers, as she checks out the stock at the health food store that's opened up next to the cheese place. The store has a smoothie bar, and she wonders if they're paying the beautiful people to sit in the window sipping through paper straws, because such people seem to come and go in rotation. Clemence has been hoping to buy a cauliflower, except the ones in this place cost as much as an actual steak.

But Clemence feels obligated to support the health food store, which had been kind enough to display a poster for the jumble sale in their window alongside the beautiful people. So she purchases the cauliflower which, the woman on the cash assures her, has never been treated with pesticides and was actually picked from an urban farm just this morning. And Clemence also buys some local vegan cheese, the kind made from something that isn't cashews because Toby is also allergic to nuts. A fancy sorbet for dessert, and she's got a bottle of wine at home already. This meal, she thinks, is a feat of engineering, but she's inspired by the challenge and enjoys putting it all together.

Once everything is prepared, and she's got herself ready, Clemence goes downstairs to wait for Toby and she's also still wondering if he'll actually show up. Toby had said he was coming, and his schedule is wide open, as far as Clemence knows, apart from his shifts at the bookstore. The rest of his life he spends in his apartment on his computer, where he's part of an online gaming community, but they won't mind if he skips an evening here and there, he tells her. "They think that you're my girlfriend," he's told her in a droll, ironic tone, and Clemence is mortified to feel her heart skip a beat, and then even more concerned that Toby seems to consider this a stretch. As if the idea is that ridiculous.

But there he is, right on time, and she greets him, knowing she looks good in her black tunic with a lavender scarf and matching earrings, an effect that's cute but not trying hard. And Toby definitely isn't trying hard, either, wearing the only outfit she's ever seen him in, jeans and a wrinkled button-down that's tucked in too tight. His expression is confused and he seems out of place, which is also part of his usual look.

"I thought we could try something different," Clemence tries to explain on the way up the stairs. "Might be nice to know you in another kind of context." And useful as well. To see Toby in the daylight, or at least by bulb light, and it's a relief to note that he does not appear to have any kind of open sore right now. He's also brought her a bottle of wine, albeit one coated in a thick layer of dust, like it's been sitting around his apartment for a hundred years, but Clemence sort of thinks of dust as *their* solid matter, the same way other couples might have a song, so it's actually a sweet gesture.

When they arrive at the top of the house at her door, she's more nervous than when she'd brought him over while he was bleeding. Because the path forward then was determined: stanch that wound. But now where she's taking him might lead anywhere. Her stomach all fizzy, and she hates this, because isn't the point of a relationship with Toby that she doesn't have to dissolve into bubbles? Maybe the whole affair is a mistake, but they've come too far—and climbed too many stairs—to turn back now.

Dinner is ready and waiting. She's fashioned a macaroni cheese dish except with cauliflower instead of pasta, boiled and then diced with the new sharp knives, and she'd been thinking about Charles's kitchen as she prepared the meal, what kind of spaceship it must be for knives like these to be discarded as jumble. She and Charles, Clemence had reminded herself, live in very different worlds, and maybe it's not even especially significant after all that they both like books. Because who doesn't like books, really? Toby also likes books and here he is sitting at her table. Clemence needs to focus on the here and now, and not just what happens to be bright and shiny (and/or muscly).

They sip wine from her plastic glasses over stilted conversation about the weather and then the housing crisis, a stiltedness that Clemence can't decide is the result of general awkwardness or sexual tension, but at least the glasses have stems, and Toby isn't snobbish at all about that sort of thing. Clemence has a corkscrew, because Naomi and Jillian had presented her with one as a housewarming gift on the night they came over to drink on the balcony. Toby breaks the cork as he's opening the wine, pieces falling down into the bottle, which doesn't seem to bother him in the slightest.

"I'll just pick the bits out," he says, dipping his fingers in their glasses, and she really can't object, because she's been happy enough to let him stick his fingers into all kinds of other places.

The wine is good, and Toby seems relatively enthusiastic as she serves the main course, which doesn't appear at all appetizing, a palette of beige. He promises her it's fine, and Clemence finally sits down before him at her own place. She has lit a tea light for ambience, the effect rendering Toby even more ghostly than usual. The cauliflower tastes better than it looks, or at least as good as a vegetable substitute for pasta could hope to taste, especially one cooked on a hot plate, but maybe that's a low bar. Clemence and Toby are in the midst of a conversation about the virtues of vegan cheese, because he's tried many brands and has strong feelings, and so does she, because it's *cheese* after all (or is it?), and then he stops in the middle of his sentence.

She says, "What."

He says, "Nothing." Looking everywhere but in her direction, his eyes darting. Toby is nervous. Something is wrong. He rattles his fork on the edge of the plate an unconscious gesture.

"Are you allergic?" Does Toby carry an EpiPen? "What's happening?" Clemence doesn't want to panic, but now it's too late.

Toby says, "It's fine." He's a terrible liar. This table is too small for two. This room is claustrophobic. "It's fine," he repeats, as though assuring himself. Taking a deep breath, he stops rattling the fork, whose prongs he now administers to the slop on his plate with the precision of a surgeon.

"What is it?" Clemence leans over to see.

"Get back!" He covers the plate with his hand. His voice is sharp. Then he softens his tone: "It's nothing." Still not letting her see the plate, he picks up his fork again. "Mmmm," he says as he chews, such an unconvincing portrayal of a person enjoying what he's eating.

"You don't like it."

His mouth is full, but he stuffs in more. "I'm eating," he tells her anyway, in a tone of consternation. "It's delicious." Almost mockingly. He says, "Yum." This is awful.

The meal is not good. Clemence knows it's not good, though that's not entirely her fault—the fact of her non-kitchen, plus Toby's dietary requirements are ridiculous, not to mention obnoxiously inconsistent. But he doesn't need to pretend. He's humiliating her now, and she's had enough of this. What is the point of trying to please a person so prone to pickiness and fuss? "Just stop," she says, giving up entirely. Reaching across the table to take his plate, but he won't let it go, his grip surprisingly strong. He won't let her take it. He won't let her see. "What is it?" she demands.

"I think," Toby says. "It's a caterpillar?" Releasing his grip. And he's right. A fat green caterpillar on the edge of his plate, one with yellow stripes, the archetype of caterpillars, struck down in the prime of its life in a pot of boiling water. Finished off by vegan cheese sauce if the boiling wasn't enough.

If there could be anything more absurd than Toby himself sitting at her table, the caterpillar is it. Clemence can't believe this, collapsing back into her chair, the plate in her hands. This is a nightmare. "I washed it, I swear." Though perhaps not so carefully. With organic produce, she figured, you didn't have to. But surely a decent rinse ought to have done the job. With an insect that big, wouldn't she have been able to see it? Hacking the cauliflower to pieces with her fancy knife, she'd spied nothing at all. The creature must have been clinging to life on an underside of the floret, manoeuvring out of the way to escape her shiny blade. It was certainly dead now, as she prodded it with her finger. Would the situation be more or less gross if the caterpillar were living?

Toby says, "It's fine. I mean, it's not like I ate it. Not even close. And I didn't want to make a big deal out of it. You'd gone to all this trouble. You—"

She tells him, "Stop." Toby has never before seemed so achingly human, which is to say, aware and concerned with the feelings of another. Toby is trying and this is intoxicating. "Stop talking." The food itself was never the point of this meal, instead the opportunity for them to be together in a different kind of light, or any light at all. So that Clemence could know for sure that their arrangement, while atypical, was nothing she had to be ashamed of, or one that compromised her dignity. This man, who was squeamish as all get-out, had nearly eaten a caterpillar to preserve her honour, had stuffed his mouth with cauliflower that was caterpillar-compromised. And now all Clemence wants to do is kiss that mouth. She's crossed her fingers that he's carrying that one brand of condom that won't give him a rash. She wants to bring Toby to her daybed and throw all the throw cushions to the floor, and she does all this while telling him, "I want to do everything. Okay? Everything. You can ask, if you want to, but you don't have to."

THE SEX IS MIDDLING. Here the whole dream fizzles. It's exactly what you'd expect with someone like Toby, who's fragile, delicate, and whiny in a way it's easy to forget about when he's sticking his tongue down your throat and has his hand up your shirt in a closet. In her bed, though, he's lost whatever physical fluidity he might possess in the dark. He bumps his head on the bedframe, and later possibly dislocates his shoulder, and when one thing simply leads to the next thing, it's much less dazzling than the overwhelming anticipation of waiting. The getting is not as rewarding as wanting is, which is probably a good thing to learn.

But Clemence nearly fed him a caterpillar, so she holds none of this against him, and while she's disappointed that their lovemaking was not transportive, she knows he's a good person, and he makes her feel good, too. He's got an ice pack on his head, but his skinny arms are wrapped around her, and she is listening to his heart beat in his pale, scraggy chest. *Beat. Beat.* And then nothing. And then it beats again.

She looks up at him with a confused expression, and

he knows what she's asking. "I have a heart murmur," he explains.

"Of course, you do." It is a miracle that Toby is alive, and that he didn't expire when he came inside her, and now she's imagining how that would have panned out. What Mrs. Yeung would have thought of the drama, and what a burden to carry a body, however slight, down all those stairs. It's such curious, angular body, too. She admires it the way she'd admire an abstract sculpture—it's *interesting*. Toby has beautiful pink nipples, the colour of his lips, and she can't help kissing them. And he's kissing her hair, and this is the good part, the two of them more comfortable naked than they've ever been with clothes on, which should probably be the rule.

"I like the way," he tells her, with his face buried in her hair, "that you aren't preoccupied with defining what *this* is."

"This?" She lets his nipple go. She hasn't been preoccupied, but only because it hadn't occurred to her. Yet. She might even never have been preoccupied at all, but it bothered her now that preoccupation seemed clearly out of bounds.

"Us," Toby clarifies.

And Clemence looks up, resting her chin on her hand. "So there's an us?" she asks. After all, he started it.

"Well, no," he tells her. "That's what I'm saying."

"And you like that?"

"Kind of?" Toby's not perceptive, but he knows he's misstepped. He's tentative now, has lost his ease. He tries to explain. "Sometimes I feel like maybe I'm dreaming. See, here's how it is. This beautiful woman walks into my life, and she kisses me, and she keeps kissing me." He stops, and suddenly looks concerned. "Crampton's not paying you for this, is she?"

Clemence tells him no, she's off the clock. This is strictly voluntary.

"It's not usually so easy for me, believe it or not," he says. Oh, Clemence can believe it. "Frankly, it's been a while, and people were saying that since I spend all my time in an antiquarian bookshop and my closest companion is in her eighties, it was probably going to be a while more. But there you were, and we just had sex, and you don't seem to want to tie me down."

"You don't want to be tied down?" asks Clemence.

"If you're talking sexually, I'm definitely open to it," he says. "But in terms of relationships, I've tried it, and I just don't think that I'm that way inclined."

"You're not a one-woman man?" she asks him, wondering where he's going with this. Surely Toby is not so spoiled for choice.

"I think I'm more a no-woman man," he says. "I'm not good at these things. People get upset with me. It's very disruptive. I hate conflict because it gives me anxious diarrhea."

"Toby." She wants him to stop. "Nobody *likes* conflict."

"Some people do," he insists. "The women who go out with me. And every time they tell me that with them it will be different. Now granted, I'm talking about a limited dataset. There haven't been so many. But it never goes well. And I don't want that to happen with you. Because I like you too much."

"That might be," says Clemence, "the sweetest, strangest declaration of affection I've ever received from anyone."

"You're kind of sweet and strange yourself," says Toby, and Clemence wants to melt into the moment entirely. Its perfection. There is no template for this, and no reason why it should work or make sense, but here in her lumpy daybed with Toby is precisely where she wants to be. She likes him, too. He's totally weird, but it doesn't even matter. Tracing her fingers along the curious red bumps along his upper arm, which she hasn't noticed before, and they're particularly enflamed, so it's strange she hadn't. Are they hives?

"What's this?" she asks him.

And he sighs. "Do you, by any chance, happen to have a cat?"

Twenty-Three

"So it went well," she says to Jillian the following Friday as Jillian's getting ready for another date with her husband. "Once the swelling went down." His entire arm had blown up like a balloon, and Clemence was anxious about it, but Toby wasn't bothered.

"These days, as long as it's not anaphylactic," he'd told her, "I barely even notice." He'd gone home, though—he didn't want to make it worse. Yes, he was allergic to cats, even part-time cats. He's also allergic to gerbils and hamsters and rabbits, and probably dogs, but he's never been close enough to one to find out. Toby hates dogs.

"He hates dogs?" Jillian is aghast. Jillian doesn't have any pets because she doesn't have time to clean up after them, but she's on the board of a group that flies in rescues from South America.

And Clemence has to assure her that Toby likes dogs well enough as long as he doesn't have to be around them, which seems fair, even though it's a total lie. Because she doesn't want Jillian to think Toby is a monster. She wants Jillian to tell her that all this is okay. She needs permission.

"I don't know," says Jillian, who's applying mascara before her vanity mirror. Jillian's bedroom is four times the size of Clemence's entire apartment. It's only been renovated twice since they moved in, which means Jillian must be mildly satisfied with it. And no wonder. Everything is white—the wooden floors, the beams, the slanted ceiling. Jillian sleeps in an attic, too, like Clemence, but she has the rest of the house to go with it. Her bed seems bigger than king size. Her bed is an island, and Clemence is perched upon it cross-legged, watching her friend get ready. Their couples therapist had told them that the ritual is important. She says Jillian and Jeremy have to make an effort.

An effort for Jillian requires an hour of preparation, however, while Jeremy can appear as is. He's downstairs now, feeding the children their dinner, but this gives Jillian and Clemence time to talk. Everybody wants to talk to Clemence now that they know she's slept with the guy from the bookshop. Her first time with anyone since leaving Toad.

"Although the last time wasn't with Toad," Clemence clarifies. Everybody forgets the chronology.

"Oh yeah, the neighbours," recalls Jillian. The most ill-advised escapade of Clemence's lifetime, but she is free now. She is free to make all the bad decisions in the world, and nobody gets hurt.

"Nobody gets hurt, except maybe *you.*" Jillian is holding two different earrings up to her face, trying to decide between them.

"Pick the long ones," says Clemence. They almost sweep her shoulders. If Jillian's meant to make an effort, she might as well go all in. "And I'm not getting hurt."

"Not yet." Jillian picks the other pair.

"Not everything turns out badly, you know," Clemence tells her friend.

And Jillian says, "I know that. Your situation, however, seems specifically engineered to do so. Isn't that the point?"

"Well, not right now," says Clemence. "In the meantime, we're both happy with the arrangement."

"And what about when he wants more than that?"

"He won't, see? That's the thing. He doesn't do relationships, all those unnecessary ties."

"But you said the sex wasn't even good. And if that's all there is?"

"It was good!" Clemence protests. "I mean, it wasn't that good. But I've had worse."

"Not a ringing endorsement."

"It isn't about the sex, though."

"Well, what's it about, then? If he doesn't want to have a relationship."

"But I don't want a relationship, either," says Clemence.

"I fear," says Jillian, applying one more coat of lipstick and standing up in front of her mirror, appearing like perfection incarnate, "that you are selling yourself short, my friend."

"But I'm not selling anything," Clemence protests. "Everything is about capitalism with you."

"It's a metaphor."

"All this," says Clemence, using her hand to sweep the room, to indicate, "it's so much work. Like you said, you've got to make an effort. And that's so hard. I don't want everything to be so hard. And with Toby it's *easy*. Do you know how refreshing that is?"

"But the thing with effort, you know," says Jillian, "is that you reap what you sow."

"I don't want to sow," says Clemence, flopping back onto the bed. "I don't even want to reap. The grasshopper and the ant—forget that. Life is not a parable."

Jillian walks across the room and closes the door. Comes back and sits down on the bed beside Clemence. "I saw him again. This week. Bob." Bob. Dr. Bob. What a name to put your whole life on the line for.

She says, "Jillian, no!" What is the point of this? All the effort, the lipstick. Clemence giving up her Friday nights in order for this marriage to be saved. "Please tell me you didn't sleep with him?"

"Well," says Jillian, dragging the one word out long. "I didn't really enjoy it. And surely that's some kind of progress?"

"Can't you just delete his number from your phone? Like, cut him out of your life altogether?"

Jillian is shaking her head. "He says I need closure. We're working through it."

"So suddenly he's a therapist again? Jillian, this guy doesn't have your best interests in mind."

Jillian shushes her. "I'm just saying I understand what you're going through. That not everything has to make sense from the outside."

"What about Jeremy?" What about what she'd said before about feeling free to make bad decisions without the chance of hurting somebody in the process.

"He's very patient."

"He knows?"

"Well, not everything. But he knows there's progress. That's all he needs to know."

"And what about your new therapist? What does she think of this plan?"

"Don't be scolding, Clemence. It doesn't suit you." When Jillian is wounded, she turns to steel. "How come you are the only one who gets to make up your own story?"

"Because I am a goddamn mess, that's why," says Clemence. "Whereas you are Jillian, and your husband is a saint, and you have two wonderful children who need you not to blow their world apart."

"And do you know what a heavy load that is to carry?" asks Jillian. "Don't you think I might want to put it down once in a while?" She says, "Bob understands that." The dramatic flair on his name incongruous with what his name is. Clemence can't help wishing his name was something more romantic—Rafe, or Antony.

"Jillian," she says.

But Jillian stops her. "I'm just saying that progress doesn't always look like progress. I get that. But I also think you deserve someone who knows how excellent you are. In a way that Todd never did."

"I guess I ended up justifying his low expectations."

"I think he never appreciated you for who you are, so what else were you supposed to do?" Jillian puts her arms around her friend.

"Remember," says Clemence, "when we thought our weddings were the end of the story? That this was what happily ever after would be?"

"When there is no such thing," says Jillian.

"As happy?" Clemence doesn't want to believe that.

"As ever after," says Jillian. "Because the story goes on and on."

"If you're lucky."

"We're both lucky," says Jillian.

And Clemence says, "Don't I know it."

Twenty-Four

Clemence tries to keep the cat out, but he scratches at the door, imploring her through the window with his single steady eye. Bailey, now accustomed to tinned fish, refuses to quit her, and Clemence is not sure what she'd do if it came down to an ultimatum: him or Toby. The cat is less trouble, and way better groomed. Somebody is taking care of him just fine, and Clemence likes that, too, her complete lack of responsibility for his well-being. Bailey comes and goes, an arrangement Clemence is quite sure she'd be incapable with a lover. With anyone who isn't a feline, she is too subject to obsession.

Because it's true that she thinks of Toby constantly, and she thinks of Charles, and she even wonders about Toad now, though she wishes she didn't. At a distance, Toad has become an object of vague fascination. His number on her phone, a string of digits she barely recognizes, because she never saw them back when he was one of her contacts.

Her primary contact, her literal next of kin, but it's different now, and Toad is persistent, that number showing up at least twice a week, and Clemence knows she should accept the call and talk to him, but she doesn't have it in her. "Not yet," she says, when friends and family urge her to get it over with, by which she possibly means "not ever," and she's curious to see how long she can get away with this, being utterly unaccountable for all her sins and failings. Her arrangement with Toby just another of these things, and she wonders what Toad would make of it if he knew. She wonders if Toad has made arrangements of his own, but this she is having the hardest time imagining. Toad was so set in the life they'd made together that she can easily believe he's carried on without her, still sleeping in their bed, leaving her side untouched, barely having to make the bed in the morning, but he would. And that Clemence could have ducked out of that life with so little effect is the reason she couldn't bear to stay.

This cat though, Bailey, who seems to know his name even though Clemence made it up—he abjectly refuses to be apart from her. When she doesn't open the door, he starts howling. *Is it me or the fish?* Clemence wonders, and she always gives in. Letting him slip inside, but closing the door behind him—it's cold out, and the attic is already so drafty. Clemence is layered in sweaters, but the chill is hard to shake. The place seems much smaller all shut up like this. When it was summer and the doors were open, she'd felt connected to the world up there in the treetops with her patchy view of the sky, the sounds of the world drifting into her apartment—car horns, people shouting, birdsong, the jangly music of the ice cream van. And the church bells' chime, marking off the hours, proving that even when she felt like she was languishing, she wasn't.

But the church bells sound farther away now, the world shut out with a deadbolt.

Clemence knows that burglars—or theoretical ones at least—might try to access a home through a third-floor balcony, though it mostly seems unlikely. They'd have to be the kind of people who scale walls and leap from rooftops, and the only creature Clemence knows who can do this is the cat. Who jumps up onto her bed to make a nest among the pillows, and she should shoo him away, because the bed is the worst place—she's thinking of Toby and his allergies. But the cat looks so cozy, and her bed looks so cozy with Bailey in it, examining her. Their three eyes are locked. Clemence knows she'll be the one to look away first. He's a judgy cat, too, which you can tell by his expression. But this is what Clemence likes about him, appreciates. He's judging her, but he keeps coming back. In her mind, she wears this like a badge of honour.

TOBY DOESN'T COME BACK, but on the off chance that he might, Clemence gathers up her sheets and blankets in the morning, once the cat has departed, and takes the dandered bundle to the laundromat up the road from the bookshop. En route, she begins to notice the trail of destruction—her posters for the jumble sale have been violently removed from utility poles, torn to pieces, taped up corners the only evidence they'd ever hung there. A few remain intact, but these have been marred by a scrawl in red Sharpie: *RACIST SCUM*, it says, which is perplexing. Clemence stands there staring, her laundry getting heavy. She's trying to figure it out. Scum perhaps she could entertain, but why *racist*? She thinks of Crampton and that long-ago church picnic, but Crampton wouldn't have done that to her posters. If Crampton had a problem with Clemence, she would have told her to her face.

She continues on her way considering that someone else might hate St. Saviour's as much as Crampton does, but could the church really be called *racist*? The congregation is more than half Korean. Not that this necessarily brings immunity to racism, but it made the accusation particularly curious. The posters were destroyed or defaced all the way up the street. Across the road, she can see the same thing on the other side. Ripped paper litters the sidewalk, blowing up against her feet. Clemence removes one of the defaced posters from a utility pole and folds it into her pocket—evidence.

The laundromat is quiet, a benefit of the early hour. Clemence stuffs her sheets into the smallest machine to save a dollar, and uses that dollar to supplement the chai latte she buys at the counter. Because yes, this laundromat has a barista. Crampton says that soon normal people won't be able to live here. Ridiculous rents are now justified by this being an organic smoothie district, meanwhile homeless people line up for food packages distributed by a church whose roof is crumbling. Soon the people with houses will also be standing in line, if the price of organic cauliflower is anything to go by.

Every day there are flyers stuffed into the mailbox at Clemence's house, developers begging Mrs. Yeung to sell. She could do it, too, and live comfortably ever after, as she deserves to, but then where would Doug the agoraphobic artist live, and the guy who lives next door to him whose addictions are why Mrs. Yeung keeps her Naloxone kit handy? And the Korean students who come and go, looking for a place to stay and somebody who's not out to scam them? Where would Clemence live? She certainly couldn't afford laundromat chai lattes if she were paying market rates. Her life, she knows, would be miserable, drudgery. Working such long hours that she'd only be able to do her laundry when the place was packed and all the machines were full. Her life would have none of its spaciousness. She was lucky, she knew—but also this surely wasn't so much to ask for.

RACIST SCUM. Clemence sits at the counter in the window with her drink and waits for her cycle to complete, watching passersby to see if any of them are clutching a red marker. Are jumble sales racist? Somebody had donated a miniature lawn jockey, but Reverend Michelle had seen it first, plucking it out of the donations pile for immediate disposal. She was aware of these things. The church congregation had an anti-racism committee whose meetings were held before the jumble sale organizers', and made up of many of the same individuals.

The washer dings, and Clemence moves her sheets to the dryer, returning to her seat to pull her phone from her bag. She has a bad feeling about all this, and the several unread texts she's received underline it. She goes to the events page she'd set up for the sale, her suspicions confirmed by angry screeds, nearly unintelligible, beneath every single one of her postings. So this isn't just the work of some unhinged person on the sidewalk with a red marker—this person has internet access, too. The postings made from a series of fake accounts whose names were rows of numbers and their avatars empty. All written by the same person, it seemed, who used all caps, spurned punctuation marks, and supposed the St. Saviour's jumble sale to be a scourge on the community.

But there are so many scourges, Clemence thinks. How would a person settle on this one? When there were baristas in laundromats, and renovictions, and therapists preying on their clients via Yelp? Not to mention warmongers, weapons dealers, and cyberterrorists. How could the jumble sale be it? She tries to read the posts to understand, but they don't make any sense. There's no mention of racism, either. People are confusing and difficult, which is why Clemence avoided involvement with committees in the past. Influenced by Toad on this point, and he wasn't wrong. When they'd moved into their neighbourhood, she'd signed up for the homeowners' association, but Toad made her quit after she kept coming home from meetings upset that all their plans were about cracking down on guerrilla gardeners and kids on skateboards. "It's not worth it," he told her, and it wasn't, so Clemence resigned, but not before planting a bed of sunflowers on the boulevard to spite them, and some of the flowers even bloomed.

Clemence inhales the freshly laundered bundle that she carries down the street, past the carnage of her publicity campaign. Thinking about Toad, because laundry is a trigger—he'd read that book about tidying up and insisted on his drawers being organized like that, but Clemence could never get the folds right. She'd been so unhappy in their marriage, and she wonders why she's so reluctant to face him now that it's finally over. She's still traumatized by the shock of his tears, and by how much she doesn't want to have to be responsible for that. She doesn't want his heartbreak to be her burden, but is there also a chance there's more to her aversion? Could she still be afraid to let their life together go? Because otherwise, why not just be done with it?

It doesn't make sense, but then neither does Clemence upending her stable existence and moving across the country into a rooming house, choosing to sleep on a mattress that countless others have slept on, cooking all her meals on a hot plate, and living just below the poverty line. She knows this. But she has spent her entire adult life, until these last few months, making smart and practical choices, doing all the right things, such a miserable, magic-drained existence, and why was that okay, and this new life of hers requires an explanation? And yes, maybe she is angry, too, tired of feeling like a human wrecking ball, when it hadn't been only her fault that so little of what was left was salvageable, and maybe never had been worth keeping in the first place.

If Toad knew about the RACIST SCUM, he'd say he'd told her so. All efforts come to trouble. He'd remind her that this is why she shouldn't even try, and maybe this is another reason why she doesn't want to speak to him again.

When she arrives home, Mrs. Yeung is standing in the front hall with Tom the handyman, both of them squinting up at a stain on the ceiling.

"There's a leak," says Mrs. Yeung.

"It's a really old leak," says Clemence. The stain was not recent, was likely older than Clemence herself.

"Yes, but Mr. Jankowski thinks we might be able to fix it."

"Mr. Who?" Tom the handyman. He waves at her, somewhat sheepishly. "Actually fix it?" Who even does that anymore? Wouldn't it make more sense to wait, and sell the house to someone who would only come and gut it all?

"Have you been camping?" Mrs. Yeung asks.

Clemence says, "What?"

Mrs. Yeung points at her bundle. "Sleeping out. Maybe you built a fort. I don't know—why are you walking around carrying your bed like that?"

"Laundry," says Clemence.

"Where's your laundry basket?"

"I don't *have* a laundry basket." She and Toad had laundry baskets. Growing up, her mother had laundry baskets. Laundry baskets weren't the kind of item that one had to go out of her way to find—they just *were*. Clemence clutching her bundle closer—all the heat had gone out of it—says, "Listen, there's something happening." Telling Mrs. Yeung about the posters, and the red marker, and the spam all over Facebook. She pulls the sullied poster she'd saved out of her pocket.

"'Racist scum'?" Mrs. Yeung is perplexed.

Clemence says, "I have no idea what's going on."

"It seems like," begins Tom the handyman, in his slow and steady way, "that somebody out there hates jumble sales. Is what it looks like. If you're asking me."

Clemence says, "But what are we going to do?"

"No question. We'll cancel the jumble sale." Mrs. Yeung decides.

"Really?"

"*No.* Who cares? There's always somebody who's angry about something with these things. All publicity is good publicity."

Tom the handyman says (slowly), "You know, I've heard people say that."

Mrs. Yeung says, "Good work, Clemence. You're doing your job. Getting the word out."

"But they ripped the posters down."

Mrs. Yeung shrugs. "So put more up. It's paper. Grows on trees." She waves Clemence on. "It's fine."

"You're sure?" asks Clemence. "'Racist scum'?" She shakes the poster in her hand for emphasis.

"Does that say 'racist'?" asks Mrs. Yeung. "Isn't that an *F*, not an *R*?"

And Clemence examines the poster again. It is true. On the first poster she'd seen and some of the others, the letter had been considerably *R*-like, but the penmanship is hardly impeccable. And the word on the poster she was holding now does seem to start with an *F*.

"Facist," she sounds out now, rhyming the word with "racist." And then something clicks. "Oh. *Fascist.*" Whoever had defaced the posters is furious, and also can't spell. "Fascist scum. It says we're 'fascist.' I mean, that's okay then, right?"

Tom the handyman looks confused. "You really think so?"

"Well, I mean, if that's what they're upset about, I could let them have it. I'm probably more racist than I'm fascist. It seems less personal somehow."

"I don't think you are very fascist at all," says Mrs. Yeung, consolingly.

Clemence says, "Thank you." Happy to accept whatever approval her landlady is willing to offer.

Twenty-Five

Clemence tells her story to Dr. Penelope Harkness, who's written the book on marriage and is now developing the podcast. She tells her about Toad, and Larry and Lisa, and returning to her hometown for a new life on her own terms. She imagines that Dr. Harkness will have to add a new chapter to her marriage book, and invite her to be a guest on the pod. She likes the idea of being an object of fascination, anticipates raising Dr. Harkness's sculpted eyebrows—but the eyebrows remain unmoved. Which is not surprising. Dr. Harkness's entire face is plastic, which Clemence imagines is partly the result of too much surgery, but also necessary in her line of work. Or does Penelope Harkness simply think Clemence is boring?

And Penelope Harkness just makes a humming noise, a *hmmm* of acknowledgement perhaps. She certainly doesn't probe for details. She is meeting with Clemence for the purpose of her index, and Clemence thinks about how much time she spends sorting through other people's stuff these days.

"I guess you get a lot of people pouring their heart out to you," she says, to fill the awkward silence.

"It does happen," says Dr. Penelope, who has not been forthcoming about her personal life. Her home is silent, austere. There are no photographs, and it might as well be a museum. She seems more like a statue than a person. Her hair is perfect and as unmoving as her eyebrows. She has published four books previously, all of them bestsellers, but this is the first one that she's publishing herself. Dr. Penelope is all business. Clemence doubts she's even listed on Yelp. She isn't what Clemence had been expecting based on the connection through her sister Grace. Grace's friends tend to be more authentic, wearing hearts on their sleeves, often literally in the form of elaborate tattoos. Whereas Dr. Penelope's skin is pristine. Her arms are white and smooth—not even a freckle.

Love Means Having to Say You're Sorry is a guide to repairing broken marriages, about communication and apologizing and taking responsibility for one's actions. And Clemence imagines how it would have felt to have this book come into her life a year ago, if Toad had brought it home and placed it in her hands. She thinks about how much of their love was about saying sorry over and over again. Clemence had disappointed her husband a thousand times, and it was mutual. Toad was excruciatingly annoying—every time he breathed it sounded like a sigh.

Clemence had spent a lot of time apologizing to Toad,

but never in the way Dr. Penelope intended. The only thing she had been genuinely sorry for was all of it, that she hadn't listened to that voice in her head that first night they were out together, that she'd allowed everything to happen knowing it was ultimately unsustainable. Which wasn't fair to Toad, who wasn't a bad person, and deserved a partner who believed in him, and for a while she'd tried to be that partner, faking it until she was making it, but that didn't work, and Clemence was sorry about this, too. That she'd been faking everything, and any apology she'd delivered would also have been fakery, and the slow torture of it all could have gone on forever.

She asks Dr. Penelope what she thinks about all this.

But Dr. Penelope is only interested in finding out if Clemence has experience writing audio scripts. "I can sense you have a flair for the dramatic," she says. Is that a compliment? She's going to be using transcripts of her clients' sessions for the podcast—with their permission, of course, but obtaining these will likely be simple. She's looking for a writer to change details for the sake of anonymity, to spice up the dialogue. She has clients, she admits, who are pretty insufferable, and it's asking a lot of listeners to submit to that.

Clemence fibs and tells her she's well versed in the area. *Wedding Belles* had made a podcast, a last-ditch effort to avoid sinking into media obsolescence, though Clemence was part of another department, but Dr. Penelope doesn't need to know that. Clemence tells her about her years at the magazine, about everything it taught her about the wedding-industrial complex.

"Now there's a scourge," she says, and Dr. Penelope agrees. Clemence tells her about her own wedding, and the trip to Tahiti. "I was so consumed by the idea of the wedding that it never occurred to me what a commitment we were making. Or supposed to be making."

"It's a huge commitment," says Dr. Penelope. "The rest of your life. But who's to say that a handful of years isn't also some kind of an achievement? It's hard work, marriage. Even one that doesn't last."

"But maybe I didn't work hard enough," Clemence admits. "I think I knew it was never going to work. We both wanted different things."

"Like what?"

"Well, I wanted to not be married to him. It's pretty irreconcilable."

"And you want me to absolve you," says Dr. Penelope.

Does she? Maybe. "I guess you get a lot of that from people, too."

"All the time. But the permission has to come from within yourself. It doesn't matter what anybody else thinks. I really do think any marriage can be saved if both parties are invested in making it happen, but the investment is what matters. Otherwise, you're just sleepwalking through your life."

"You're saying that love means having to say you're sorry..." Clemence is trying to make sense of it all, "but you actually have to mean it."

Dr. Penelope nods. "Your sister told me that you were in a tight spot."

"Did she?"

"It's hard out there for an indexer," she says. "Just like bank tellers, and grocery store clerks. Going the way of the dodo."

"I don't know if it's all as bad as that," says Clemence.

Dr. Penelope says, "The dodo didn't, either."

Twenty-Six

Clemence continues sorting in the bookstore. By the end of November, there's been enough progress that there's room to walk down the central aisle two abreast, which she and Toby do on their way to the closet under the stairs—the reason why the books aren't getting sorted any faster. She intends to spend the first hour of each shift on the shelves, but that hour keeps getting shorter. Toby has taken to appearing behind her, a hand on her shoulder, asking, "Clemence, can I see you about something?" She doesn't understand the subterfuge because there's no one else around.

In the darkness of the closet, reality falls away. Clemence doesn't have to think about the cauliflower, or the caterpillar, everything Toby had been willing to endure simply to preserve her dignity. Such willingness only making it easier for her to overlook his neuroticism, and propensity for rashes. The fact that he has never invited her over to his place, and that he doesn't intend to. "I don't really like other people interfering with my stuff," he says, and he's not crazy about coming back to her apartment, either, after what happened with the cat, no matter how carefully she's promised she's cleaned. "With an old house like that," he says, "it's impossible to eliminate allergens. All those crevices are practically impenetrable."

I'm not going to laugh, Clemence tells herself when he says this, and she doesn't even mind that he's refusing to let their relationship proceed in a standard fashion, in *any* standard fashion, because, well, let's just say that all the crevices are penetrable in the closet under the stairs. Their situation forcing them both to be creative, to find different ways to connect with each other. It's never boring, which Clemence knows it could easily be if she began turning up at his place for regular booty calls. Toby is straightforward about where he stands and who he is, and so although he's odd, he's never disappointing. And while Toby in the daylight can be middling, Toby in the dark delivers satisfaction like she's never known before, though it has been suggested by others that Clemence might be fooling herself.

"The closet is not a metaphor," says Clemence, arguing Naomi's assertions. "The closet is a closet, and this is my life. I am allowed to do things that feel good. Surely you, of all people, should understand that." A lecture about compartmentalization is more than a bit rich coming from someone who keeps her sex trapeze in a spare room drawer.

But even if the closet is a metaphor, what's wrong with that? A retreat of sorts, a space where what exists between her and Toby is natural and easy, and there's nothing for him to hit his head on. Where Clemence doesn't have to worry that her apartment is too small or unfashionable or tainted by cat hair, where she doesn't have to consider what her family is going to think, whether she's ever going to be ready to settle things with her ex-husband, or where her next paycheque is coming from. With Toby in the closet, Clemence doesn't even think about the jumble sale, which is a miracle, because these days she's even dreaming about the jumble sale. Jumble sale nightmares—a city made of jumble, towering cardboard boxes heaped with Royal Doulton china dolls, feather boas, and unlabelled VHS tapes, and in her dreams, there's always an earthquake, the jumble collapsing all around her, gaudy beads and baubles raining from the sky.

The reality itself is not so different from the dream, the church storage room overflowing out into the hall. They've stopped accepting donations officially, but boxes and bags keep arriving, anyway, late at night, after hours, discovered on the church steps in the morning. News has spread throughout the neighbourhood of the anti-jumble campaign, and so people have ransacked their basements and attics to show their support for St. Saviour's. The abusive posts on social media and defacement of the posters in the street have done more to spread the word than anything Clemence might have planned in her publicity campaign, and there was a week or so when she'd suspected that Reverend Michelle had orchestrated the entire controversy. She'd been a theatre major in a former life and no doubt she had it in her.

But in the end, it was Reverend Michelle who solved the mystery of who had it in for the jumble sale, who had been calling them FACIST SCUM. Church ministers have to be far more enterprising than in previous times, because there are fewer excellent women within the congregation to orchestrate everything. Clergy actually had to work now, undertaking investigations to get to the bottom of tracing the identities of online trolls, on top of writing sermons and whatnot. "It was simply a question of connecting the dots," Reverend Michelle explains when she calls Clemence into her office. "And in the end, it was obvious. I assume you know Mary-Ann Arbuckle, or that you've heard about her."

And Clemence says, "No." Her voice is unsteady. Where is this going?

"Well, consider yourself lucky," says Reverend Michelle. "She can be a lot to contend with." She invites Clemence to look over her shoulder as she enters Mary-Ann Arbuckle's name into the search bar, and the top result is the Sorauren Park Artisan Market, where Mary-Ann is listed as executive director. And then Reverend Michelle clicks on the market's social media page which is spammed with the same all-caps ranting about the St. Saviour's jumble sale. "I think she has strong feelings about fascism but doesn't know how to spell it. Apparently she's upset because we've been poaching her vendors." She looks at Clemence, her eyes narrowed. "*Have we* been poaching her vendors?"

"I don't know that I'd call it *poaching*," says Clemence.

She elucidates, "It's more that I was hoping to sprinkle a little artisanal dust on everything we do. This is hardly big-game hunting. All the vendors I talked to were happy to sign on. There's nothing untoward about this. Neither fascist, nor scummy."

"Mary-Ann is tempestuous," says Reverend Michelle. "She runs her market like a despot. I know her a bit, and I've done my research—they've had at least two schisms. She had a falling out with a lavender farmer that resulted in a restraining order. She bans vendors from her market on a whim—once because one woman's name was too long and wouldn't fit on the promotions."

"I heard about that one, " says Clemence. "So, what am I supposed to do?"

"We could arrange a meeting. Have it on neutral ground. Assure her that we're not a threat. We don't even pop up. We're only once a year. There's no reason why the jumble and the artisan market can't be good neighbours."

BUT JILLIAN AND NAOMI think that this is a terrible idea. "She's going to ambush you," says Naomi. "That woman is notorious. What about the time she attacked a woodturner with a walnut dildo?"

They're out for dinner at a restaurant close to Naomi's office, a holiday gathering for the three of them, and when the bill comes it will be as much as Clemence's rent, but Naomi has already said she's treating them. Clemence wonders if she's supposed to feel guilty for benefiting from her friend's generosity, but the gnocchi with truffle oil is far too delicious for her think about this long. Some things are meant to be, and it might the finest meal she's had in, perhaps, ever.

"But we have to give reconciliation a chance," says Clemence. "It's either that or cancel the jumble sale."

"Just watch your back, is all I'm saying," says Naomi.

"And look out for concealed weapons," Jillian adds.

"Because I'm not sure any church jumble sale is worth being bludgeoned with an artisanal dildo over," says Naomi. "No offence."

Clemence says, "I don't think it's going to come to that. Anyway, Mrs. Yeung is coming with us. It makes me feel protected."

"That woman's pretty hard to mess with," admits Jillian.

"And how's her son?" asks Naomi. "The lawn boy." She remembers him from the night they watched him cutting the grass.

"He's not a lawn boy—he teaches high school. And besides I told you, he's married."

"He didn't seem very married from what you said. Finagling his way into your apartment. Carrying boxes. Why is he always carrying boxes?"

"He's just very … helpful," says Clemence.

"Is that what they're calling it now?" asks Jillian.

"It is!" protests Clemence. "But I've hardly seen him since school started again. It's been a long time since September. He has a whole other life."

"And you've seen no sign of the wife," says Naomi.

"Except that his jumble donation was full of her clothes."

"What were they like?" asks Jillian.

"Very expensive and petite," says Clemence. "I think I hate her."

Naomi says, "Fair. Anyway, maybe you'll see her at the jumble sale."

"Trying to get her clothes back?"

"No! Supporting her mother-in-law. Like how we're going to be there for you."

"You are?" asks Clemence. Worlds colliding, and she's not sure how she feels about that.

"I like second-hand stuff," says Jillian. "I'm looking forward to it."

"And I'm willing to overlook the fascism," jokes Naomi. "Just this once." The server clearing their plates looks at them strangely as she overhears this, but Naomi doesn't notice, leaning across the table toward Clemence with her chin in her hands, a sly expression on her face. "And will your 'unsuitable attachment' be there?" she asks, her true jumble intentions revealed.

"I mean, probably not," says Clemence. Probably not now if everybody else is going to be. It's better if Toby remains theoretical for Clemence's friends and family. Toby in actuality might be too much to understand. They'd think he was rude and petulant, and they wouldn't be wrong, and also they wouldn't understand why it didn't matter.

"He hasn't come over again?" asks Naomi. Clemence had told them everything about that night, about the caterpillar, and the meh-standard intimate encounter.

It hadn't been an experience she was dying to repeat, and Clemence wondered if this was fate's way of diverting her from a more conventional arrangement. How easily she could have slipped into it all—the dinners with wine, the sex. Next thing, she would have been living in a starkly modern townhouse complex, seven years married, not a physical book in sight.

"I just want to know that he's good enough for you," says Jillian. "And to make sure that you're not fooling yourself."

"But it doesn't even matter, you know?" says Clemence. "That's the point. We're not committed, so it's inconsequential. The pressure's off. We're having fun. Maybe the whole thing is a bad idea, but who cares?" Jillian isn't buying it. Her judgment is written all over her face. "Come on," says Clemence. "Dr. Yelp?"

"That's different," Jillian insists.

"It always seems different when it's you," says Clemence.

"It's different because my thing is over now," says Jillian. "Finally. Something I had to get out of my system."

"You said it was over the last time," says Clemence. "Who's fooling who?"

"But I mean it *now*," says Jillian, sounding less than sure of herself than she usually did.

"You slept with him again?" asks Naomi, putting the pieces together. Looking at Clemence for confirmation. "Even after we posted our review?"

"Just once," says Jillian.

"Did he mention the review?" asks Clemence, carefully.

"He didn't," says Jillian.

"Maybe he doesn't monitor his Yelp," says Naomi. "After all, he's a very busy man."

"I think even if he does," says Jillian. "He wouldn't be able to tell who it's talking about. Have you seen what's happened since your review?" They hadn't. "There's been a pile-on. Apparently, I'm not the only one he's been involved with. Apparently, this is a standard part of his counselling practice. Apparently, none of us are special." And this, after everything, is what cracks Jillian's heart. Her eyes are wet, which is the Jillian-equivalent of lying on the floor sobbing. "I feel like a dumb-ass."

"You're not a dumb-ass," Naomi and Clemence say in chorus.

"He told me that this had never happened before. Like the two of us were in on it together, doing this wild, reckless thing. How come even my recklessness turns out to be underwhelmingly ordinary? And how come I didn't see through him? What's the point of being overeducated if you're not even savvy?"

"You're savvy," says Clemence. "You're the savviest. This was a one-time lapse in judgment. And didn't it feel good, in a way? To throw caution to the wind?" She imagines caution as a sarong with a jungle print, like the one Lisa was wearing the first time Clemence made her way over to their hot tub, remembering how afterward the fabric lay in a wild pile of itself on their deck, and how Clemence had felt as she noticed it, the fear, the dread, the *elation* of knowing that now her life was going to have to change. She says, "There is something interesting sometimes about being the author of bad choices."

"But that's the thing," says Jillian. "That's what I thought I was doing, but it turns out I was just playing a bit part in somebody else's script. It's humiliating."

"But now it's done," says Naomi. "You've learned some things."

"Like to get proper referrals for medical professionals," says Clemence.

"I liked his photo," says Jillian. "I thought he looked safe, and he was the only one listed whose profile didn't have inspirational quotes."

"I guess he helped you figure out what you wanted though. Using unorthodox means. I still think we should report him," says Naomi.

"I already did," says Jillian. "When I saw those posts, the way he'd treated all those other people. Those people were vulnerable and he took advantage of that."

"He took advantage of you," pointed out Clemence.

"I like to think that I was exercising free will," says Jillian, finishing her drink. "But now I'm not so sure. I think that's why Jeremy has been so forgiving."

"Well, good," says Naomi. "Plus, he loves you."

"He really does," agrees Jillian. "I don't know that I fully believed it before, or even that he really did. We'd had no cause to give our love any thought, and I wouldn't have predicted how far he'd be willing to go for me. I don't know if I would if the tables were turned."

"What if he'd been preyed upon by a therapist from Yelp, though?" asks Clemence.

"Even then," says Jillian. "I'd probably be furious that he'd been so stupid."

"I bet Jeremy's actually relieved that you've been stupid," says Clemence. "Your otherwise perfection can be intimidating. It's a lot to live up to. It's almost like you've done him a favour. Levelling the playing field, you know?"

"That's certainly one way to spin it," says Jillian.

"He won't admit it," says Clemence, "but deep in his heart he knows it's true."

"Plus, after years of all your friends thinking you're out of his league, Jeremy is finally getting a bit of sympathy," says Naomi. "The poor guy."

"I liked it better when you thought I was perfect," says Jillian.

"Oh, that was never us," says Clemence. "I mean, we know you. You're our friend."

"She's right," says Naomi. "If you were perfect, you'd be impossible to stomach. Plus, with the two of you turning into hard-core fuck-ups this year, I get to be the stable one in our friendship. I could get used to that."

Twenty-Seven

Although so much has softened between them, Toby still doesn't put his book down when Clemence enters the bookstore the following day.

"I don't need to," he tells her. "There are jingle bells on the door. And I know it's you. Who else would it be?" Crampton, beside him at the counter, is unruffled by Toby's attitude, because Crampton has never expected Toby to be anything other than exactly who he is.

But Clemence is feeling less generous. She's thinking of what her friends said, of what they'd think if they saw him now, even of what judgment could lie behind Crampton's neutral expression as she watches Clemence accept Toby's rudeness. Clemence has also come looking for reassurance, and this isn't it. "Don't you think you could still say hello?" she asks. "Isn't that just common courtesy to greet a fellow human being?"

"Arbitrary rules." He waves her off. "And anyway, I was

in the middle of a scene." He slouches back over the book.

"Don't you worry that he's putting off the customers?" Clemence asks Crampton.

"Well, he's certainly not putting you off. You're here, and this isn't even your shift."

"But it might be the last time you ever see me," says Clemence. "I've come to say goodbye. I have a meeting with someone called Mary-Ann Arbuckle today."

Crampton's brow furrows, but a different furrow from her usual furrow. Her entire face is rearranged. "Now why would you go and do that?" It's the most shaken Clemence has ever seen her.

"So you know Mary-Ann Arbuckle?"

"Does she ever," says Toby, speaking without being directly addressed, so this must be a special occasion.

"Mary-Ann Arbuckle is the only person in all of history to be impeached by the Business Improvement Association," explains Crampton. "A dark time in our history."

"Is she the one who's been calling you racist?" asks Toby.

"It was actually 'fascist,'" says Clemence.

"Well, of course it was," says Crampton. "Mary-Ann is passionate, but not very bright. She's the one who came after me about my cleaning my windows. You know, before you did." She's pointing at Clemence, who feels unfairly implicated. "She wanted online entrepreneurs to be able to join the BIA, which made no sense. She kept calling me a 'girlboss,' and wanted me to teach her how to—so she said—'build an empire.' And when I told her the key was inherited wealth, she didn't like that, and she started calling *me* a fascist, but really she was just angry that I wouldn't pay for her online course, something about funnels. She had it in for me after that, but I think she's also politically confused. She was using one of the storefronts as a gallery space, but she never paid the rent, and refused to resign from the BIA executive, so we had to take matters into our own hands. She started up the artisan market after that, and I guess the drama continues."

"She's accused us of trying to steal her vendors," says Clemence. "But it's borrowing, really. I thought it might help our profile to feature some artists beyond whoever it was who'd made all those toilet-paper covers with the doll heads that somebody donated three boxes of. Plus a couple of people selling succulents signed on."

"So more of an homage, then," says Crampton, "than outright thievery."

"Right?" says Clemence. Toby keeps on reading, and she envies him this obliviousness, and his knack for avoiding entanglement in the lives of other people—at least until she came along. But his oblivious makes her furious, too. "It's not unreasonable," she says.

"It's not unreasonable," Crampton agrees. "But Mary-Ann Arbuckle is far from a reasonable person. I hope you're not meeting her alone."

"I've got my landlady coming," says Clemence. Toby still hasn't looked up. "And the reverend."

"Well, good," says Crampton. "You'll have God on your side."

Toby moves to turn his page again, but Clemence stops

him. She snatches the book right out of his hand. "Toby, can you come here for a minute?" she calls over her shoulder, already halfway down the aisle toward the back of the store. "There's something I thought I saw ... under the stairs." She's hoping he'll follow, and he does, albeit falteringly, and maybe only because he wants his book back.

Crampton is calling out from behind them, "The bulb's burned out! I'm surprised you saw anything in there. Somebody needs to remind me ..."

Clemence pulls Toby inside with her and closes the door.

"We can't do this *now*," he whispers urgently, though Clemence suspects he'd go along if she insisted. The darkness, those confines, the smell of the books—something Pavlovian makes it seem like there is no other way to proceed. But that's not what Clemence is here for. Plus she's still got her coat on.

"Toby," she says. "I'm scared of this Mary-Ann Arbuckle person. And then I came in here hoping you and Crampton would tell me I was being ridiculous, but now I feel even worse."

"Oh," he says. They're standing the way they always stand, close together because there's no other option in such a small space, and now he puts his arms around her shoulders the way a normal boyfriend might. "Well," he says, buying time, still thinking. "She's a scary lady, it's true. But she's probably unlikely to murder you in broad daylight." Clemence sinks into him, the way she used to sink into her husband. Is this codependence? What would Dr. Penelope think?

"I'm sorry," she says against his shoulder. Wasn't the point of this new life she'd made that she wouldn't have to need anybody like this?

But Toby says, "It's fine," smoothing her hair, speaking in the most soothing tones he's capable of. He's missing so many essential emotional parts. And yet. "And I'd say you even have a good chance of coming out alive," he says. "You're going in there three against one, which makes it almost even."

"Almost?" It's hot in the closet. Clemence wants to be with Toby, but not like this. "Couldn't you come over tonight? The sheets are fresh. Just this once?" She's desperate, and she sounds it.

And he seems to know it, too, because he says, "I guess so," instead of refusing. And then he buries his face in her neck and starts kissing her. "I don't know what it is you do to me," he says. "You're the only person I can't say no to."

"And also the only person who ever asks you for anything."

"You really are," he says, beginning to unzip her coat. "I don't know what you're thinking."

"I'm thinking we have to get out of here before Crampton gets wise to us."

"I think she's wise already," he says, before running his tongue along the curve of her ear.

"Toby, no," she says. "I'm getting heatstroke. And I've got to get to this meeting. But come tonight, okay? There's a whole world outside of this closet," and, to prove it, she reaches to open the door, to let the light in, and there is Toby's face, white and earnest. Does she really want this? She takes a deep breath and walks out into that world. So what if she does?

But Toby doesn't move. She turns to him, "What?"

"My book," he says. "I need it back."

Clemence is still holding it. She passes it to him, before reaching back into the closet to grab another book out of the darkness. And as they walk back through the store, Clemence is speaking loudly, conspicuously, "Thanks for helping me find this," emphatically waving the paperback in her hand. She sees her luck could have been worse—a copy of *How to Win Friends and Influence People*, only mildly mildewed. She insists on buying the book to save face with Crampton, even though Crampton sees through her, that narrowed look. Crampton sees everything. But it will make a good enough donation to the jumble sale, Clemence thinks, as Crampton wraps it in brown paper, and then she and Toby wish her luck in the afternoon's endeavour.

"You'll be fine," Crampton tells her, but her voice is more tentative than Clemence has heard her sound before.

THEY ASSEMBLE AT THE church beforehand, and while Mrs. Yeung is the same as ever, Reverend Michelle is jittery, awkward, thinking up nonsensical reasons to stall their departure. She needs to water the plants in her office, she explains, and so Clemence and Mrs. Yeung wait in the hall, and it is a very bad sign indeed if Reverend Michelle is off her game. Usually her capacity to love and appreciate difficult people is her superpower, including any drunk man with no pants on wandering into the sanctuary, the woman who used to shoot up in the narthex, and the old guy with visions who screams during her sermons. Convicted murderers on parole had been welcomed into the congregation, so you would think that Reverend Michelle might have room in her heart for practically anyone, but Mary-Ann Arbuckle has brought her to the brink.

Not that Reverend Michelle will admit to being rattled. "Mary-Ann is harmless," she explains, as they make their way to the coffee shop by the fromagerie. "You've got to admire her really—the passion, that fire."

"Even if it's hellfire?" offers Mrs. Yeung.

Reverend Michelle ignores the comment. "She'd actually be a useful person to have on our side," she says finally, carefully, after taking a look up and down the street and around the corner to make sure Mary-Ann Arbuckle wasn't waiting to ambush them. "If only she were remotely tameable."

Reverend Michelle pauses once they reach the coffee shop entrance. "Are we ready?" she asks. The other women nod, and they go on in.

Mary-Ann Arbuckle resembles an operatic Viking, rising from her seat when she sees them. She's tall and broad-shouldered, the effect emphasized by the blond braids she wears wrapped around her head. She's acquainted with Reverend Michelle through the BIA, and they shake hands in a way that's almost civilized, Clemence considering that maybe everyone's blown this out of proportion and the meeting is going to go fine, especially once Mary-Ann Arbuckle has treated them all to a round of hot chocolate, made vegan with oat milk. But once they're seated with their drinks, she pulls a folder from her tote bag, slaps it on the table, and informs them that they're all being served with a lawsuit.

"What's all this?" asks Mrs. Yeung, flipping through the pages, which are bound with a hot pink bulldog clip. "You've hired a lawyer?"

"I *am* a lawyer," says Mary-Ann, sinking back into her seat. Her braids are as meticulous as her manicure, which Clemence notices as she folds her hands together like something has been settled.

But Reverend Michelle is undeterred. "You're not a lawyer, Mary-Ann," she says.

"I've been to law school."

"For one semester," she says, her voice soft and steady. Reverend Michelle is skilled at working with unreasonable people. "Which is long enough to know that this," she indicates the papers Mrs. Yeung is holding, "isn't legally binding." She says to Clemence and Mrs. Yeung, "She's trying to scare you."

Clemence says, "I think it worked?"

"I've been running this sale for fifteen years," Mrs. Yeung tells Mary-Ann. "We've never had a problem. There is room for our sale and your market. There's always been."

"Not when you're poaching my vendors," says Mary-Ann. "If you push, I'll push back."

"The pushing was all her," says Mrs. Yeung, throwing Clemence to the wolves.

"But it wasn't poaching," Clemence defends herself. "This is a one-off thing. It's for charity. I wanted to freshen things up. We admire what you do. You're a local icon." Now she was grovelling. "I never thought you'd see it as a threat."

"You're undermining my business," Mary-Ann replies. "You come along with your cheap table rates, and my vendors start wondering if they really want to work with me."

"But we have two sales a year," says Clemence. "Surely that's not enough to sustain their businesses. Isn't there room enough in this neighbourhood for the both of us?"

"And what if your vendors don't want to work with you because you're mean to them?" suggests Mrs. Yeung. "That's got nothing to do with the jumble sale."

"People are intimidated by confident women," Mary-Ann enunciates. She raps her manicured nails on the tabletop. "Because we refuse to let other people walk over us. I'd kindly ask you to read over the lawsuit." There is nothing kindly about her tone at all. "I may not be a law school grad, but I know what's legally binding."

"How about this," proposes Reverend Michelle. "We give out flyers for your market at the jumble sale. We'll put an ad—for free—in the church bulletins. We could consider offering you use of our community spaces for a much-reduced fee. Do you think that might be a start in putting all this right?"

"Perhaps a start," says Mary-Ann.

"If you could leave our Facebook and our posters alone."

Mary-Ann has a poker face. "I had nothing to do with that."

"I'm sure you didn't," offers Reverend Michelle. "But maybe could you call off your minions? Do you think you'd have control over that? I feel like we could find a solution for peaceful coexistence. You know we know that our jumble sale is worlds away from your enterprise. We never considered that you'd think we were stepping on your toes. You're operating on a whole other plane, Mary-Ann. Don't think we don't know it."

Mary-Ann appears subdued. Clemence is blown away by how Reverend Michelle has handled her. Mrs. Yeung, looking over Clemence's shoulder, says, "Hey, isn't that guy your boyfriend? That Italian?"

The table shifts their attention to where Toby is standing by the door huffing on his inhaler.

"He's—I mean, he's not Italian," says Clemence. "He isn't even my boyfriend. Not really."

But Mrs. Yeung and Reverend Michelle are waving, and now he's approaching, as if drawn by an irresistible force. From the expression on his face, Clemence can tell that he's in agony. Why is Toby here?

"I thought maybe I wanted a latte," he explains.

"And?" asks Mary-Ann. She gestures around the table as if to ask the others, *What's with this guy?* "I mean, listen, dude, don't keep us all in suspense here."

Toby blinks. "I don't know you," he says, and Mary-Ann shrugs. He says, "I thought maybe I wanted a latte, but I changed my mind. Hi, Clemence." His face is flushed. This is why he avoids most company, because there's too much explaining involved. Clemence is confused about what's going on, until he leans down toward her ear and whispers, or at least he probably *thinks* he's whispering, because Toby has a hard time gauging these things, and everybody can hear: "I've come to check on you. Are you okay?"

"We're having the meeting about the jumble sale," Clemence tells him, trying to sound offhand, like they hadn't just been talking about it an hour ago in a closet.

"I know," he says, refusing to follow her lead to tone down the weirdness so as not to further inflame Mary-Ann Arbuckle. "That's why I'm here. Crampton made me come." Although even Crampton, Clemence knows, isn't powerful enough to inspire Toby to do anything he doesn't want to do *really*.

"And because you wanted a latte," says Clemence, one last attempt at making this seem normal. "Maybe."

Toby says, "Nah."

"Reverend Michelle, this is Tony," Mrs. Yeung interjects. "Clemence, you really should be introducing your friend. And this is Mary-Ann. We were just finishing up. Tony, it's nice to see you again."

Toby ignores her. "Crampton was afraid you might be in trouble. So she sent me. To save you."

"How?" asks Mary-Ann. "By having an asthma attack?"

"*Toby*," Clemence corrects Mrs. Yeung. "His name is Toby." To Reverend Michelle, "Are we done here?" If they weren't, she had a feeling that she might be in trouble for real.

Reverend Michelle attempts to build a bridge. "I think we're not far from some kind of understanding."

"She served us with a lawsuit," Mrs. Yeung tells Toby.

"Well, not an *actual* lawsuit," says Clemence. What she thinks, but doesn't say, is that it was more of an artisanal lawsuit.

And as she's thinking this, she watches Mary-Ann's expression turn. "It's not like you even bothered to read it," Mary-Ann snarls. She turns to Reverend Michelle. "And if you think a mention in your church bulletin is any kind of peace offering, you're delusional. You deserve to have your roof fall in."

Reverend Michelle never stops smiling. "God bless you."

"What is wrong with you people?" Mary-Ann demands in disbelief. Back to Clemence: "And what are you even doing here? I googled you. You used to be a big deal. You used to write live dispatches from your honeymoon in Tahiti. So what happened? *Where's your husband?*"

Almost as if on cue, Clemence's phone starts buzzing.

"Here we go again," sighs Mrs. Yeung.

But Mary-Ann Arbuckle is still staring at Clemence, still demanding. In fact, everybody is watching her now, as her phone continues to vibrate, urgently, impossibly, like it has never buzzed before. A gadget possessed. Dancing across the table, flying off the edge—Clemence catches it in mid-air. "I've got to take this," she says. What else can she do?

"Sure, sure," murmurs Mrs. Yeung, but nobody else has moved, everybody with their eyes still on her. They've got her blocked in and there's nowhere to go, the bulk of Mary-Ann Arbuckle looming, her yellow braids gleaming, shiny and terrifying.

Clemence accepts the call, knowing precisely what she's getting into. "Hello." This is her only escape route.

Silence for a moment, and she wonders if he hung up too soon, then his voice on the line. "Clemence?" That nasal twang she'd gone so long without hearing that her name as he said it wasn't her name at all. Who was the person he was asking for?

"Hello?" she repeats.

"It's me."

"I know."

"I've been trying," he says. "Your mom gave me the number. I thought maybe it was wrong, and the lawyer was in touch—"

"I know," she says again. "I just couldn't—" And he's waiting for her, but she's got nothing now.

The only good thing about this situation is that it has made the tense scene before her in the café disappear, taking the rest of the world with it, the entire universe distilled into a single pinpoint that is the sound of the man she once tried and failed to love telling her again, "This is destroying me." The same words he'd used all those months before, weeping on the floor in their bedroom. So it wasn't news, merely confirmation, and she wasn't sure that hearing it again was any worse that those same words as an echo in her mind.

She tells him, "I'm sorry." And she is, even though love is about saying sorry, and she doesn't love him anymore, but she is sorry about that, too. She is so sorry about everything.

He says, "But can't we try—"

And she says, "No." She will never be sorry enough for that. She ends the call, and the world comes back, all those around her with no idea of how that seemingly innocuous exchange had made her so vulnerable, every bit of her armour disappeared.

Or maybe they do know. While Mary-Ann across the table seems as invincible as ever, her expression is less defiant. She looks confused. Like everyone else, she is trying to piece together what has transpired, who Clemence had been talking to, how so few words could hold so much weight.

"Are you okay?" asks Reverend Michelle, reaching for Clemence's hand to steady her, to help her return to the present. Her grip is soft and firm at once, and Clemence is surprised to find she's grateful for the contact, to realize she is shaking, and how glad she is to not be alone, for this company—Mary-Ann Arbuckle notwithstanding.

Is that Toby's hand on her shoulder? And even Mrs. Yeung has stopped rolling her eyes.

Fellowship, community—it's a disaster, but it's also everything, and Clemence has it in abundance, even after all her mistakes and misdeeds. It was what she'd come home for, and since she'd been back here it had only grown, no matter how motley the fashion.

Clemence suddenly thinks about how Mary-Ann seems impossibly alone, and she remembers. "Hey, I have a book for you."

"A book?" Mary-Ann looks almost disgusted as Clemence pulls the package from her bag and pushes it across the table.

"It's a very good book. Millions sold. An entrepreneurial bible. Plus, it's vintage."

Mary-Ann has unwrapped the paper and examines the cover. "*How to Win Friends and Influence People.*" She looks up at Clemence. "Seriously?" Clemence nods emphatically. "Okay," she says. "Thanks. And listen," she looks up at Reverend Michelle again. "I didn't mean what I said. About the roof."

"Can we have a truce?" asks Clemence. "Because I've been losing sleep over this, and I hate that. And we have other books, if you like that one. All kinds of them." Toby's hand is still her shoulder and it's helping her be brave.

"Um, I *actually* have a lot of friends already," says Mary-Ann, still examining the book. "I like vintage books though. I arrange mine by colour." She opens the cover, letting the pages unfurl like a wave. "Okay," she says. "I will cease and desist with the cease and desist."

"Oh, well, that *is* a relief," says Reverend Michelle, who is a good diplomat, but a very bad actor.

"WHAT DID YOU THINK," asks Toby later that night, "of me swooping in there like a hero?"

"Was that what you were doing?" asks Clemence.

"I'm not always the best judge of which people are unhinged," he says, "but that woman radiates it."

"And what would you have done," Clemence asks him, "if she'd proven a physical threat? If you'd been forced to place your body on the line?" Tracing her finger along the length of his body for emphasis, or at least as long as her arm can stretch. They're lying in her bed on their sides, which is the only way they both fit. She is pleased that they've managed to make love without Toby hurting himself. She has scoured the place to get rid of cat hair. This is the closest she's come with him to something that's almost comfortable.

Toby answers her question. "Easy. I would have pulled her hair. Those braids are just like rope. Like a tug-of-war. Didn't you just want to?" And she really had. Clemence knows what he means exactly, and it is at moments like this that their connection seems like a kind of miracle. Securing her heart to his, and she wonders if she really could love him. If she should.

Clemence had told him it had been her ex on the phone, that the call had rattled her so much that Mary-Ann seemed like an easy challenge in comparison. "There are things still unresolved, I guess," she'd said, "between me and my ex." But Toby hadn't asked her to delineate what those things were. Clemence tells him, "You know, you're braver than I'd given you credit for, daring to confront Mary-Ann Arbuckle like that."

"Well, you confronted her, too," says Toby. "You gave her a book."

"But that's different," says Clemence. "I always knew I was a little bit brave. What I didn't know is that you'd show up for me."

"I didn't either," he admits.

"So what you do you think it means?" she asks him. "If it means anything, I mean. Not to say that it does. But still."

"Does it have to mean something?" he asks.

"Toby, you're a reader," she tells him, rolling onto her back so he's squished against the wall. "Surely you know that meaning is the point."

"But meaning is not always definitive," he says, turning so he's on top of her. "Or stable."

She agrees. "Nothing is. Subject to interpretation. There's ambiguity. That's what makes it interesting."

He says, "What it means, though, I think, is that I care about you." He looks into her eyes. "Is that what you want to hear?"

"And is that really so hard to say?"

"Why do I have to say it when it's demonstrable?"

"Because sometimes," she says, "it's just good to know where we're at."

"We're right here," he tells her, and pulls her closer. He's kissing her neck, his lips drawing a line down to her chest, and then lower, until his point is really undeniable.

Twenty-Eight

Since time immemorial, the St. Saviour's winter jumble sale has taken place the first Saturday in December, and no attempted sabotage is going to change that. Even though Clemence rises from bed that morning stiff and sore from carrying all those heavy tables for set-up the previous evening. She rubs frost from her windowpane to reveal a fresh dusting of snow, putting her firmly in the mood for festive things. After months of planning, the jumble sale is here, and Clemence feels proud of what she's accomplished, helping to build something real and tangible that will make a difference in people's lives. Examining herself in the mirror as she fastens a butterfly brooch to her sweater, she wonders: *Is this, after all this time, what a person of substance might look like?* She steps back to admire how the amethysts gleam. The jumble sale had been overrun with brooch donations, and Mrs. Yeung encouraged her to help herself. These items which were decorative instead of valuable, and also weighty, passed down through families until there was no one left who wanted them, but Clemence does. Imagining the stories attached to the butterfly brooch, all the places it had been, an anchor and a connection to the past, and to so many women who'd come before her.

As the person charged with promotions, most of Clemence's job is finished by the day of the sale, and so she's an ancillary worker, directed by others, doing whatever needs doing. Plugging in coffee urns, arranging jumble in an organized and attractive formation. When the artisans arrive, and Clemence helps them to their tables, everyone apologizing about all the trouble with Mary-Ann Arbuckle, but no one says too much, because who knows where loyalties lie and, also, walls have ears.

By the time their city councillor arrives for the ribbon-cutting, the room is crowded, already uncomfortably hot. Clemence has spied her entire family across the room, and she's conscious of their attention as she takes her place in the ceremony, tasked with the official role of holding one of the ribbon's ends—Mrs. Yeung is holding the other. With her free hand, Clemence tries to subtly fan her face as the city councillor steps forth and does what she does, cutting the ceremonial ribbon with the ceremonial scissors that she must bring with her everywhere. Declaring the jumble sale officially open.

And then Clemence takes her place at the cash box, where she's signed up for the first shift, and it's a flurry of activity, professional collectors having shown up early, first in line, so they can get their hands on the vinyl records, comic books, and china figurines whose extraordinary value the sale committee has not picked up on and will be resold online for huge profits. And after things have settled down a bit, Roger and Bonnie roll up with Charles Yeung's juicer, marvelling at the price.

"You've done a great job here, honey," Roger says.

Bonnie admits, "This actually isn't weird at all." They've met Reverend Michelle, and they adore her, naturally, and Bonnie seems no longer worried about her daughter having joined a cult. Clemence knows her family has only shown up in order to check in on her, out of concern as much as support. Over the general din, she can hear Prudence shrieking, "Don't touch that!" as one child or another has discovered something sharp or heavy or fragile.

Clemence's parents move away to let the other buyers cash out their bundles of baby clothes or towers of vintage bakeware. One guy arrives and purchases an entire box of CDs. Across the room, Clemence can see that the artisans are also doing a decent business, and Min Jee, who directs the small church choir, has set up in the corner with her acoustic guitar and started to sing "In the Bleak Midwinter," but there is nothing at all bleak about this scene.

Naomi and Jillian arrive, and Bonnie is delighted to see them. Clemence has finished her shift at the cash by now, and so she joins them as they figure out that the last time they'd all been together had been ... at Clemence's wedding.

"Well, the wedding was good for something, then," says Clemence, shattering the awkwardness of the moment, and then she goes with her dad to get everybody a cup of coffee. Returning with her hands full, and her mother has made an acquaintance with Mrs. Yeung. They are trying to get to the bottom of what is wrong with Clemence: her insistence on being so strange.

"I thought she was a man," Mrs. Yeung recalls. "The only reason I let her have the place. I had no idea with a name like that."

"Well, that part is probably my fault," admits Bonnie. "With a name like mine, I wanted my daughters to walk around in the world with a little more heft. My parents named me after Scarlett O'Hara's daughter who fell off a horse."

"I wanted to name my son after Ashley Wilkes," says Mrs. Yeung, avidly. "But my husband wouldn't let me. Because it's a girl's name."

"Probably worked out for the best," says Clemence, as she inserts herself into the fold, fanning her face again; it's so uncomfortable. "Is Charles coming?" She tries to sound easygoing about him. She tries to *feel* easygoing about him, because she has Toby now. If she saw Charles, it might not be awkward, and perhaps they could be friends.

"He said he'll definitely try," says Mrs. Yeung. "Which means no." She turns to Clemence's mother. "My son is a very busy person. Very involved in his community."

"Like you?" Bonnie offers, and Mrs. Yeung concedes that this is true.

"And what about the Italian?" Mrs. Yeung asks. "Where's he?" Confusing Bonnie, because she thinks Mrs.

Yeung is talking about Sandro, and what's he done now?

But Clemence tells her, "Toby's actually not Italian. Strictly Northern European peasant stock." She explains to her mother, "The guy I told you about. The one I'm seeing. Kind of."

"But not polyamory."

"No." Poor Bonnie Lathbury, trying to find her bearings in this brave new world.

And all this is going over Mrs. Yeung's head, thankfully. She tells Bonnie, "He's sort of a strange kind of person. He doesn't even look Italian."

"Because he *isn't* Italian," says Clemence, for the thousandth time, still trying to hold it all together. Except for the bond between these two women, which she is desperate to pull apart. Why had she worn this sweater? The temperature in the church basement is boiling. She says, "Anyway, I don't think Toby's coming today. Jumble sales aren't really his thing."

"I wouldn't have thought they were my thing, either," says Bonnie, "but look!" She unfurls the chenille bedspread folded over her arm. "My mother had one just like this." She sticks her face in the bundle and inhales. "It even smells the same."

Clemence cringes. "Make sure you wash that."

Min Jee begins to play "Go Tell It on the Mountain," and Naomi and Jillian rejoin the little circle of people who love—and are intent on torturing—Clemence. The nieces and nephews are happy because they've been allowed to pick out any toys they want, and it might as well be Christmas.

When was the last time they'd all gathered in a church? Had they ever? Certainly not at Clemence's wedding, which took place in a barn at a winery.

And then Toby is there, waiting in the doorway, looking pained as he takes in the crowd.

"It's Harold and Maude," whispers Jillian, because indeed Toby is standing there with Crampton, who gives off a Ruth Gordon vibe, and who has somehow decided to set foot in St. Saviour's after her decades-long grudge. What's going on here?

Clemence tells Jillian, "No, it's Toby."

"*That's* Toby?" says Naomi. "*The* Toby? Your unsuitable attachment?"

"He looks like an undertaker," whispers Grace. "Or a corpse."

"Well," says Bonnie Lathbury, with a strange smile upon her face. "Let's meet him."

Clemence says, "Now?" Crampton and Toby are already approaching the group. "Are you sure?" But it doesn't matter, because here they are, Toby is here. Why is he here?

"We have come to support your endeavour," Crampton announces in an artificial tone, as though she's reading from a script, or maybe she's only reading Clemence's mind. "Hung *Back in thirty minutes* signs up in the windows, and here we are. You've got quite the turnout."

The room is even more crowded now, and maybe they were going to unload all the jumble after all. Clemence introduces Crampton her family, to her friends, Toby hanging back from the group. If Bonnie Lathbury tries to speak to him, the universe could possibly implode. But it doesn't.

"So, you're Toby!" Bonnie exclaims. "We've heard almost absolutely nothing about you. Beyond church and jumble sales, Clemence is not really forthcoming. You work in the bookshop, but that's all I know. I'm Bonnie, Clemence's mom."

And Toby just waits, with everybody's eyes upon him. Like he's frozen, until Crampton punches him hard in the arm, and he shouts in pain. "Why did you do that?" he asks, but Crampton shakes her head, gesturing to the people gathered around them, and he comes to his meagre senses: "Um, hi," he says, waving the hand attached to the arm that he's clutching.

"These are my people," Clemence tells them. Her mother, her father, her sisters and their kids, her friends. Jillian is holding an antique mirror, and Naomi is holding nothing, because she's sensible enough not to be swayed by a sweet deal and doesn't need anything more in her rich and fulfilling life. "And this is Toby." What to say about that? "Toby is my people, too." Does he need a sling?

"I think she really hurt him," Clemence hears Sandro whispering to Prudence behind her.

"Are you okay?" Clemence asks him.

"Oh, yeah," he says, but he's wincing. "She just." He pauses. "She caught me by surprise."

"You should have seen me in my prime," says Crampton. "I was a ladies boxing champion. Not that there was so much competition, but I really used to be able to throw a punch."

"Looks like you still can," says Roger Lathbury. This is the sort of thing that impresses him, and Clemence can't help but wish it were her boyfriend meeting with her father's approval instead of the elderly woman who'd just punched him.

"But Toby can take it," says Crampton, nudging him, and he flinches, as though she's about to punch him again. "No, don't worry," she tells him, *sotto voce*. "Just talk."

"You worked hard on this," he says to Clemence, locking eyes. "And everybody came."

"And some of them aren't even related to her," Prudence adds.

"It's the busiest sale we've ever had," says Reverend Michelle, who's just crossed the room like the answer to someone's prayer. Hooking her arms through Bonnie and Roger's both, leading them away. "Let me show you ..."

"So you're the one," says Jillian, now free to speak her mind.

"I guess," Toby says. He's looking around for Crampton—perhaps she'll punch him again; a diversion. But Crampton has disappeared.

"You guess?" says Naomi. "Because you either are or you aren't."

"You guys—" Clemence begins, but Jillian holds up a hand to stop her.

"I am the one," exclaims Toby too loudly, a bit strangely. But then he puts his arm around her like a normal boyfriend might. "I'm here, aren't I? I showed up at a church jumble sale?"

"Well, we all did," says Jillian.

Toby says, "Exactly. We're Clemence's people."

"And we're her sisters," says Grace, yanking Prudence into the circle, too. Toby is taken aback, Clemence sees, by these two more women, both with her face, or faces like hers, and one of them is very pregnant. If Toby can hold his own in this moment, there might be hope for him yet. Alternatively, this might be the last time she sees him. Would that be a bad thing? Clemence has decided that it would be.

But he is shaking their hands now, and he even laughs when Naomi mentions the caterpillar, how Toby, so squeamish, had been willing to brave it on his plate just to save Clemence from humiliation, and honestly, it's possible that no man has ever shown up so consistently before to put himself between Clemence and trouble. While the last thing she wants, in theory, is to need someone to save her, it's sure nice when he tries. Even now—he's only here to legitimize her choices, to assure everybody that she hasn't lost her mind. Which makes him almost suitable now, and Clemence considers how this might undermine her project.

But does it matter?

She pulls him away from the rest.

"You came," she says. "I never expected you would. I am sorry you got assaulted in the process." She rubs his arm where Crampton punched him.

"Your mom's nice," he says perfunctorily. "And this is actually pretty impressive. Busier than the bookstore even. I bet you don't have a box for Women's Fiction."

They're standing before the second-hand books now, most of them donated from Crampton's. The crate of paperbacks devoted to tarot and the occult is empty. Literary fiction is less picked over, and Clemence kneels down to sort through it, when she picks up a book that doesn't belong. *Minor Feelings*. It's not fiction. And maybe it's a coincidence, she supposes. She hopes. Flipping open the cover, but no—there it is. *C. Yeung*. "No," she says, a moan of despair. Like this is a tragedy. Because it is.

"What is it?" Toby asks.

"Mrs. Yeung," says Clemence, getting up again, clutching the book. "Where is she?" It's still crowded and impossible to see anyone, though she keeps getting glimpses of her nieces and nephews darting in and out of the hubbub. Clearly her family is still here, but where is her landlady? She had to be somewhere—this whole thing is her show. Turning over the empty occult crate to stand on it and get a better view, Clemence rises to her tiptoes, but she sees nothing. Min Jee has returned from a short break, starts playing, "Do You Hear What I Hear?" and it's all that Clemence can hear, because she's standing too close to the speaker and she has to get away from it; her head is starting to pound. Clemence makes her way through the crowd and finds Mrs. Yeung in the kitchen, putting squares on a tray.

"What is this?" she demands of Mrs. Yeung, whose tongs are dealing out marshmallow squares with the precision of a card dealer, and she doesn't stop for Clemence's question.

Barely looking up. "A book," she says.

"It's Charles's book," says Clemence. "You were supposed to give it back."

"He didn't want it," says Mrs. Yeung, using her tongs to wave Clemence away.

"But he loves this book," says Clemence, insisting. "I promised him that I would return it."

"Charles has too many books already," his mother says.

"He must think I'm such a jerk," says Clemence.

"He doesn't."

"But he'll think that I lost it, or that I kept it. That I'm just flaky."

"Charles doesn't think of you at all," says Mrs. Yeung. "Here." She places the tray of baking in Clemence's hands, and it's hard to balance with the book in her grip. "Go put these out. Happy tummies spend more money, and there's still mountains of jumble to move." She is pushing Clemence out the door, and where is Toby now? Perhaps he took his opportunity to escape, and she can't blame him. The scene is overwhelming, and it only gets worse as she approaches the baking table, the crowds thick around it. She's still got the book, got it stuck up under her arm, and she'll have to think of a way to get it back to Charles. Setting down the tray, she darts away from the hungry masses, and it's still so hot in here. Is it getting hotter? Her sweater is suffocating, and the brooch is weighing her down. How will she get the book back to Charles if his mother refuses to help? Clemence thinks of what else she's taken from him, the shiny knives, all his wife's clothing that she's rifled through, and perhaps he thinks she's a scavenger. The madwoman in the attic, indeed.

And then she hears her name and turns around, without even thinking, obviously, because if she'd stopped to think, she would not have turned. She would have taken off running, the way she's been ever since she'd left him in the spring, away, away, but the flight is over now, the jig is up, and she might as well have gone nowhere at all because Toad looks the same, hurt and sad, possibly wearing the very shirt he'd been wearing the last time she'd laid eyes on him, though it's hard to tell because Toad is the type of person who, if he likes something, buys fifteen of them. All of his clothes look the same. He is definitively not, however, the type of person who shows up at a jumble sale. He is also supposed to be on the other side of the continent.

"What are you doing here?" she asks.

"I needed to see you," he says, coming so close. He takes her hand, and there it is, his touch, once so familiar to her that his was an extension of her own body. Once it was her home. She'd once loved that face. Had she loved that face?

But then she realizes that he's not just holding her hand, he's holding her still. This has always been the problem, and she pulls away from his grip. "I'm working here," she tells him. "I'm busy. This isn't the place—"

"It's the only place where I knew I would find you," he says. "It's all over your Facebook. Clemence, what's happened? Have you lost your mind? A church jumble sale?" He's not holding her now, and but she's still stuck, because the room is packed, and the crowd has hemmed her in. "You won't talk to me. You've given me no other choice. This is *embarrassing*." He sounds pitiful. "We've got to work this out. I deserve that much. I do." His voice is wavering. He sounds like he's going to cry again.

She tells him, "No. I mean, you do. You really do. But I can't. I just can't." She doesn't see how he doesn't get it. She'd really thought that after doing what she'd done that there'd be no hope of salvage, that there'd be no pieces whole enough for any possibility of putting their world back together. She says, "You flew all the way here, though." He'd never been one for dramatic gestures.

And he still isn't, because he tells her, "Well, my dad's sick. Cancer's back." He'd had a mass on his lung four years ago. It had been scary and awful, and Clemence had been looped in to all that; part of the family. She'd helped coordinate the meal train during his treatment. Remotely then, but she is even further away from all that now. She'd had no idea.

She says, "I still can't, though." He's not going to guilt her into this just because of his dad. She feels sweat running down her brow.

He asks, "Can't what?" His eyes are locked on hers now, and he doesn't need a grip. There is nowhere to run.

"'Work this out,'" she says. "I can't do it, and I've tried to tell you. I've told you, in so many ways." She closes her eyes now, the only way she can find the courage to tell him straight. "It's over. We can't go back to how it was, and I don't want to. I don't even think you really want to either, if you're honest with yourself."

And he is silent in response. She dares to open her eyes, even though she's afraid she might have killed him with her brutal honesty, wondering if there is any way around this fact of having to hurt him like this over and over.

But Toad doesn't look hurt, instead confused. He says, "I don't."

"You don't what?"

"Want to go back to how it was."

"You don't?"

"Clem, we're done. I know we're done. And I want it *finished*. That's what I'm trying to tell you." He says, "I've met someone." *Minor Feelings* drops to the floor. Then the most cutting barb: "I think you might be overestimating just how hard you are to get over." His voice is fading, even though he's still right there in her face. "To be honest, you've made it easy for me. I should probably thank you."

Leaning down to pick the book up again, blood rushes to her head, and she begins to feel even more woozy. "Are you okay?" somebody's asking, and is it Toby or is it Toad? And why are her sisters here, and Jillian and Naomi? All of Clemence's people. Everybody's mouths are moving, but the sounds don't match, and why is the whole scene swimming? Toby looks uncomfortable, this is perhaps the sole aspect of the scene that makes any sense. And Mary-Ann Arbuckle is here, too, but she's the size of a mountain, moving in and out of focus: "I think you might be overestimating just how hard you are to get over," she is saying. And then all that Clemence can hear is the dull roar of the room in her ears, the sound of a seashell, or maybe it's the sea. How is it possible to hear the sea from here? Could somebody maybe crack open a window? It's so hot. And Mary-Ann Arbuckle is everywhere, growing like Alice in the rabbit's house, and the only thing that Clemence has to defend herself with is her brooch pin, and she's not afraid to use it. The world going black for a moment, and she's suddenly overwhelmed with the smell of books, that room beneath the stairs, everybody she's known in her whole life gathered around her, but then reality snaps back, and Mary-Ann Arbuckle is all of it. Perspective skewed, so that when Clemence holds out her pin, it's a sword after all, and so maybe she's not so defenceless, but then everything goes dark, and this time it stays that way.

Twenty-Nine

Are you ever really home unless you've finally come home again, after a holiday, a convalescence, or why not both? When Clemence was here last, snow was merely suggestion, a decorative powder, but now it's a blanket on the world, unrelenting, and so the scene is transformed. She barely knows this street, hardly recognizes the houses, all of it so much to take in after three weeks in her parents' spare room, recovering. It turned out she'd been desperately sick—bacterial pneumonia. Spending five days in the hospital before her father arrived to take her back home to her parents' place, and a part of her had wanted to fight it—she had her own home just a few blocks away. But she didn't have the strength, and besides, there were so many stairs, and she was struggling to breathe at all. She couldn't have managed. That she would ever feel better again seemed impossible, and how was it even supposed to happen with her simply lying there, waiting, but somehow it did, thanks to the wonders of antibiotics: Clemence started to recover. So that by Christmas, she was well enough to come downstairs and spend the day with her family, her sisters, and their partners, and their kids, but also had a convenient excuse to retreat from the chaos when the whole thing got to be too much.

And then by New Year's, she was almost herself again, ringing in the hour with her parents, which perhaps was not the most auspicious start, but it was better than the New Year's Eve the year before she'd spent fighting with Toad about the placement of the mirror in their downstairs bathroom. At least the home she had to return to now was her own, and she had missed it. She'd wondered if she would, if after the comforts of her parents' house, finally come to see its deficiencies. The drafts, the cheap old windows whose glass frosted up in the cold, and that lumpy bed she'd convinced herself she'd become accustomed to, but now she wasn't sure. What if the entire life she'd made had been a delusion, her perception of reality confused since her fever and subsequent hallucinations? She'd woken up in the hospital three days after the jumble sale, convinced that she'd stabbed Mary-Ann Arbuckle to death with a brooch pin, and everyone had had to tell her that Mary-Ann Arbuckle was completely fine.

But Clemence hasn't dreamed it—the house is real, albeit transformed by winter. And there is Tom the handyman shovelling the steps. She had forgotten about Tom, but she's grateful that he exists, because she'd been wary of slipping. She's still not steady, and everywhere is coated in ice, except where Tom has diligently chipped it away so Clemence can climb the steps safely. He greets her on the porch with the tip of his hat with the earflaps, and Clemence wonders is he's fixed the leak in the hall yet. If Mrs. Yeung has brought him in to do over the place from top to bottom, but no, she sees, once they've come inside. Everything is the same. After all, it's only been a few weeks, not even a month, but it seems like longer. So long that she is surprised to find it at all, the walls and door frames as solid as they ever were, albeit stained and haphazard. The mark from the leak unchanged, and the smell of the place—Mrs. Yeung's Korean cooking melded with whatever everybody else has been cooking on their hot plates.

"What a beautiful old home," says Bonnie Lathbury, who likes to see the good in things, and no doubt can even see that once upon a time, her statement had probably been true. Standing at the bottom of the stairs, she's examining the newel post, the sole remnant of any original woodwork, never mind the crummy carpet, the holes in the plaster. She's carrying bags of groceries, and Roger has more: fresh fruit and vegetables. They're convinced that Clemence wasn't taking care of herself, and Bonnie's concerned that the problem had been mould. Both of them uncertain about delivering her back here, reminding her over and over again that she is welcome to stay with them as long as she needs to. Forever. Bribing her with home-cooked meals and freshly changed linens, but they would tire of this eventually, Clemence knows. She would tire even sooner.

And believe it or not, Clemence actually wants to return here, to this strange house in the middle of the city, a house that seems, at first glance, thoroughly devoid of charm. She is happy to be climbing these two steep staircases, just as airless as they were in the heat of the summer, and she turns to tell her parents, "It's not much farther now." They're laden with the groceries, and haven't permitted her to carry a thing, which was probably wise, because she's more winded than usual on the way up.

It's remarkable how much this feels like a homecoming, unlocking that door with her very own key, even though most of the room's furnishings used to be someone else's. Everything exactly where she'd left it, right down to the plate by the sink from the toast she'd had the morning of the jumble sale, still scattered with crumbs. She doesn't even need to turn the lights on, because with all the leaves off the trees, her room is brighter than ever, the cushions on her daybed carefully arranged, which is the sole reminder that Jillian had been here, popping in while Clemence was in the hospital to gather clothes and personal items. Everyone had been concerned for Clemence that day, except for Clemence herself, whose mind was far away.

"It's actually kind of lovely," Bonnie is saying, as Clemence could have predicted, but there is surprise in her voice that she doesn't have to lie or embellish. The gingham curtain beneath the sink, behind which Clemence keeps her tea in a tin, and other canned goods.

She tells her parents, "I'll put the kettle on," and she is prouder of this, of having them here, than she'd ever been when showing them around the beautiful two-thousand-square-foot townhome that she'd shared with Toad, which had always seemed more like a step on the property ladder than an actual place for people to live.

Outside on the balcony, Clemence thinks she can see paw prints, and wonders about Bailey, if he's missed her. Where he goes when he's not here, and whether there are other people all over the neighbourhood imagining he belongs to them. She regrets having shut him out over those few weeks in order to make her apartment hospitable on the off chance of Toby who—unlike the cat, old reliable—rarely showed up at all.

Her parents are standing around awkwardly, hovering. Clemence realizes they're uncomfortable with sitting on her bed; they don't want to mess with the arrangement of pillows, plus no doubt they feel it's an intimate, personal space, so she pulls out the chairs from her small kitchen table, offering these instead. The table is crowded with her laptop, and Dr. Penelope's notes—Clemence is not yet behind on her deadline for the index, but she will be unless she quickly gets herself together. The idea of having to scramble and rush seems strange and foreign from where she's standing now, and she's not sure she remembers how to do it.

"And all your books," Bonnie is saying now, studying the spines that are lined up on the shelf, something else she can use to try to decode the mystery that is her daughter. "Mortimer, Farmer, Lively—how can there be so many authors called Penelope?"

"And over here, too," says Roger, perusing the pile on

the table, holding up Penelope Harkness's backlist—*Say Yes: The Secret to a Happier Marriage*; *Zap: How to Bring a Spark to Your Romantic Connection*; and *After You Stray: Putting Your Marriage Back on Track*. "Pen by name, pen by game?"

He laughs. Nobody else does. Bonnie is too interested in the titles in his hand. "Clemence, what is this?" she's asking. "What are you doing with these books?"

"They're for work," Clemence says, and she doesn't know how to read her mother's anxious questioning, if she'd be happier to know that the books were for personal research and Clemence was actually trying to rebuild her former life. Bonnie says she doesn't like to judge, but of course she judges. Everybody does. She just makes a special effort not to show it. What would it be liked if they talked to each other, instead of functioning as respective ciphers, but no, because then they would fight all the time. If she's being judged, Clemence doesn't want to know. "I'm doing the index for her latest book. She's friends with Grace. Did you know that?"

"Grace gave me an autographed copy of *Zap* for my birthday. Some of the ideas she suggested were very effective. You know the one, Roger?"

"Gross," says Clemence. The kettle is boiling, not a moment too soon. She picks up her yellow teapot and waits for Bonnie to admire it, because she wants her mother to know that Clemence too can have beautiful things. As she prepares the tea, she explains how she bought it from a potter at the artisan market in the summer, and there is a moment of silence as everybody thinks about Mary-Ann Arbuckle, and how Clemence had tried to stab her with a brooch. "In a fit of delusion," Clemence would add, if she were explaining the situation.

Clemence gets down three mismatched mugs that had come with her apartment, chipped and charmless, but at least they would not remind anyone of Clemence's very public breakdown. Although if anyone had mentioned it, Clemence could gently remind them that the sale made record profits, moving jumble like no committee had managed to in decades. She'd been a part of that, in spite of everything, and the negative attention inspired by Mary-Ann Arbuckle's campaign could hardly take all the credit.

"So you're going to be okay here," says Bonnie, as Clemence places the mugs on the table. She's talking about the cozy room and the pretty teapot, the books and papers that are piled on the table because Clemence is employed, if not altogether gainfully. She's talking about how Clemence's cough has subsided after weeks of her sounding like a barking seal, her chest still rattling audibly every time she inhaled, but now she breathes almost normally. Bonnie is still worried about mould, but the gingham curtain and the teapot have helped bring her around. She's exchanged numbers with Mrs. Yeung and they've been texting, and Bonnie admires her, trusts her to be looking out for her daughter.

"I don't need anybody looking out for me," Clemence tells her. "I'm a grown woman."

"A grown woman who is still convalescing after a very

scary illness," Roger corrects her. He worries as much as Bonnie does.

"Everybody needs someone," says Bonnie. "Though it does seem like you've got an awful lot of someones." The last month had demonstrated this, friends and family showing up. Crampton Goldberg had sent a floral wreath, and there had been great debate as to whether she thought that Clemence had died. Once Clemence regained capacity for speech, she'd phoned the grocery store—perhaps the last grocery store left on the planet where an actual human being answered the phone—to thank Crampton for the generous gesture, and also as proof of life.

But she hadn't heard from Toby. Perhaps he'd gone home for the holidays to see his mother, which was what he'd been planning, even though his stepfather's cologne aggravated his scent sensitivities, and he'd end up with brutal migraines. Toby had tried to talk to his mother about it once, but it turned out that his stepdad had a glandular disorder and the cologne was to disguise his body odour, and Toby's mom is stuck between a rock and hard place, and so Toby doesn't go home a lot.

Sitting with the tea in Clemence's apartment, no one mentions Toby now, a conspicuous omission. Because they'd met him, Clemence's unsuitable attachment, a face to match the idea, undeniably real, and so where had he been while his sometime girlfriend had been ill enough to be hospitalized and then even after? He'd been there when it happened, when the paramedics came. They'd all seen him there, as useless as the rest of them, mouth gaping, arms hanging. And then after, once Clemence's mom had gone in the ambulance, and the rest were figuring out what was what—touching base, making plans—he'd somehow disappeared and no one saw him again.

Clemence had been hoping for a message of some sort. But Toby was out of reach, their relationship existing in the realm of the physical. And they'd never had another conversation about the terms of their relationship besides its boundlessness. Had she missed him? Truthfully, not really. In the throes of her illness, everything was overwhelming enough that she hadn't had the latitude to think about anything else—except she must have been, because Toby kept appearing in her fever dreams. But then so did Mrs. Yeung, and Charles, and Crampton, and Clemence wondered if she'd dreamed it all, surreal and absurd. What if Toby was actually a figment of her imagination? When she googled him, she got no results. The only other person who could corroborate his existence was Crampton, and who's to say Clemence hadn't dreamed her up, too—but no, there was the wreath. Tangible evidence.

Clemence knows that getting rid of her parents will be a problem, that they would find every excuse to linger. To throw her back in the car and bring her home again where she could be under their watch, with no mould, and they can monitor her life choices. No more jumble sales, because those turned out to be stressful and dangerous—who knew?

Roger decides that he can fix the leaky pipe under her sink—he'd brought his tools specifically for the task—and stretches out underneath the gingham curtain to do so. Bonnie says that she might as well clean Clemence's tub while she's waiting for him to finish, and Clemence lets her mother do what she needs to do to feel useful, taking the opportunity they've offered for her to take it easy. She sits down on her bed, which will take some readjusting to. It's true, she's quick to tire, and she was only planning to sit, but now she's lying down, and she closes her eyes, listening to her mother's tuneless hum, the incessant sound she doesn't even know she's making, but to Clemence it sounds like home.

When she opens her eyes again, her parents are sitting on the edge of the bed watching her.

"What? Where? How long have I been lying here?" she asks them. Lately time has been a slipstream. Has it happened again? But no, just a few minutes, they tell her. The tub is scrubbed. The leak is fixed—for now. Roger doesn't have a good feeling about the hardware, but he's done the best he could.

"This place needs some overhauling," he says, looking around, but with the cost of an overhaul, the rent would no longer affordable. It was a fact. Shabbiness was built into the program, and you learned to live with it, leaky pipes and all. By now it's unfathomable to consider the convenience of the kitchen she'd once had—counters that wiped clean, a stove with four burners, a refrigerator that made ice cubes and could tell you when you were out of butter.

But this place has character. This was what Bonnie said, and she even sounded like she meant it, hugging

Clemence as they said goodbye, telling her no, she didn't have to walk them to the door. "All those stairs," and Clemence could hear in her mother's expression that the stairs had replaced mould as primary household threat.

"I'm going to be okay," Clemence promises them both, after they'd promised her that they would pull the front door firmly shut behind them, testing it too because sometimes the latch sticks and the door blows open again. "I'll take it easy on the stairs, get lots of rest, and not push myself too hard, and take lots of vitamins."

And finally they are gone, and Clemence is alone, really alone, for the first time in weeks, comfortable in her own space, and properly home. She's missed it, the way the wind makes the windows rattle, and how the little radiator chugs along, creating a warm oasis in such a cold world. Clemence had arrived with so little, and here she'd gone and built a universe. She'd missed her pillows, and her books, and that beautiful teapot. She likes this place. She doesn't mind the solitude.

Particularly because there's never very much of it—there's someone knocking on the door right now. "Come in!" Clemence shouts, looking around the room for whatever it is that her mother may have forgotten. But when the door opens, it's not her mother at all. Instead, it's Charles Yeung, a sight for sore eyes, and he's carrying a jar of—"Soup!" Clemence exclaims. Is it possible that Charles's pecs have become even more defined since the last time she'd seen him? "Aren't you supposed to be back to work?"

"Not until next week," he says. "My mom sent me up."

"Of course she did," says Clemence, who feels ridiculous

reclined on her daybed, but she's also too tired to sit up. Those stairs had been quite a climb.

But wait—there is something about Charles, something that's wrong, and Clemence can't seem to remember what it is.

"Are you okay?" Charles asks her, reading the bewilderment passing over her face.

"I am," says Clemence. "I mean—" And then she remembers. "Your book! *Minor Feelings*! Charles! Oh my god! I thought I gave it back to you. I gave it to your mother." She is sat up on her bed in a panic.

But Charles is laughing now. "I got it," he says. "Unbelievably. My mother is not the most reliable messenger. She's got her own priorities. Unless it's soup, she's just not that into it. But then she thought you might die, and that it was being upset about the book that had done it, and she took a taxi all the way up to my place, showed up at my front door. She's never done that before. She normally doesn't feel comfortable north of Highway 7. She says she gets vertigo. I think she made a deal with God—she returns the book to me, and you get better."

"I guess it worked," says Clemence. All these unseen forces beyond her knowledge. "How did your wife take it then?" Clemence asks him. "Your mother showing up there unannounced?"

"What do you mean?" says Charles.

"I don't know." Clemence mainly wants to demonstrate that she's in the know, that she's not interested in Charles in that way, and that she's not a fool after all, in spite of all her experience attesting otherwise. "I was just—" She was just trying to pass as someone normal. "How come she never comes downtown with you?"

Charles says, "We're separated. It's been ages. I don't even know how you know about her. I don't think I ever said—"

"Your mother," says Clemence.

Charles says, "Ahh." The light is dawning.

"She talked about her all the time. I guess they were close."

"My mother hates Claudia," says Charles. "She always has. I wouldn't say that was the whole problem, but she made it hard sometimes."

Clemence says, "I had no idea." Were other people's lives ever what they appeared to be from the outside? "She told me all about her. You have a wife, and she's a doctor."

"Well, she is a doctor," affirms Charles. "And I think my mother hates the idea of divorce even more than she hates Claudia, which is saying something. She says she was never good enough for me, but she also hopes we reconcile. She wants grandchildren. My mother contains multitudes."

"Walt Whitman."

"Just like him," Charles says. "Listen, I'm sorry all this is weird. I think she was nervous, too, about you and me. She's protective. She knows I'm not in the right headspace for a new relationship now. I think she could tell that I like you. But the timing's just—"

"I know," says Clemence, and she does.

"It's honestly just refreshing to meet somebody and be friends—that doesn't happen for me very often anymore. And besides, you've got a boyfriend. The Italian guy."

Clemence has given up arguing the Italian part. "He's not my boyfriend. I haven't heard from him in a month." And now here's Charles, and he's brought her soup. How has she managed to get all of this so wrong?

"But he left you those notes."

"What?"

"They're piled in the hall," says Charles. "Did you see them on the table on your way in?" But she hadn't bothered to look. The only mail she'd received was from Toad's lawyer, but now that's over. Charles says, "My mom says he was over here all the time."

"But your mom also told me you had a wife."

"The notes are there," says Charles. "The notes are irrefutable. Come on!" He gestures for her to follow him back downstairs, and there they are, a stack of envelopes. She picks them up, examining Toby's messy scrawl with bright blue pen, like the penmanship of a child who's writing with his eyes shut. Ugly, and yet strangely appealing, which sums up Toby himself quite perfectly, and Clemence feels that frisson again, the curious feeling that keeps her thoughts returning to him, in spite of so many reasons why they shouldn't.

Charles is waiting as she rips the envelope open—a piece of lined paper torn inside, torn from a three-ring binder. It's a drawing made with the same blue ink, a rough drawing of a woman's profile, a sparkle evident in her eye, something slyly amused within her smile.

"What is it?" asks Charles.

Clemence says, "It's me," surprised, and she shows him, because she's recognized herself at once in those few lines, more familiar even than her face in the mirror. Nothing else is written on the paper except Toby's name, scrawled in the right-hand corner.

"It's good," says Charles, surprised, and Clemence is surprised as well. Opening another envelope to find a different drawing, same pen, same face, Clemence laughing with her mouth open wide and her eyes shut.

The third envelope Clemence opened contains a drawing of Clemence with her chin in her hands, rolling her eyes, but she's smiling.

"They're really good," says Charles. It is hard to believe. That even Toby has a hidden side, hidden talents, and that he sees her, really sees her. She'd sensed it, but here was living proof, pages and pages of it.

"I think," says Charles, "that you've been on his mind."

"What day is it?" Clemence wonders. It's been so long since such details mattered. But it's Thursday, which means that Toby will be at the bookshop. "I need to get my coat—" she murmurs. All the way back upstairs, but it's freezing out.

"Here." Charles hands her his own coat, which he's slung over the banister. "He's been waiting for you." Indicating the envelopes, the drawings. "You should go."

So she does, even though the snow is falling again, and the sidewalks are still treacherous. Making her way back to the main street again, this neighbourhood she's been missing. All the way to the bookshop.

Because she needs to talk to Toby. Who looks up at the sound of the bells at the door.

Who sees her, and puts down his book.

Epilogue

Against all odds, this is a story that ends with a wedding, if not with a woman running around on the street in her underwear in pursuit of Colin Firth. No, here we find Clemence fully clothed, her hair in soft curls, her shoes a bit pinching, but her dress a vintage fairy-tale dream, all the tulle you could ever imagine. Clemence has never felt more like a ballerina, and she's tempted to twirl to prove it, to have her skirt encircling her like a cloud, but she doesn't. She has to be serious now, because Charles is nervous, his bow tie crooked, and it's mere seconds before it's their turn to link arms and begin their walk down the aisle.

She lays a finger on his chin to steady him, smiling up at his face. "It's going to be fine," she says, fixing the bow tie one more time, and securing the pin on his boutonniere. "You look fantastic," she says. A soft pink rose to match his tie, and her dress, and they hear the song on the organ change—their signal to enter the sanctuary and make their way to the altar.

And everybody is there, the pews are filled. Even Crampton has come, looking uncomfortable as ever, but this is important. And Clemence's parents, and Grace and Prudence, but not Sandro, who's stayed at home with the kids, save for new baby, currently guzzling at her mother's breast, just a few weeks old and already a fifteen-pounder.

Clemence is smiling as she takes in the scene, people she knows from the church, and from around the neighbourhood: Mila from the boulangerie, Peter from the payday loan place, and even agoraphobic Doug from downstairs, who's come out of his room, who said he wouldn't miss this for the world, even though—from the look on his face—it's also agonizing.

At the end of the aisle, Reverend Michelle is waiting, beaming. She says that weddings are the whole reason she got into this business in the first place, and she doesn't get to perform nearly enough of them. Not even just because weddings fill the church like nothing else does, and Clemence is taking in the scene as she makes her way past the pews, imagining what the church would have been like once upon a time back when it was full like this always.

Toby is sitting at the end of the first row, and he's left room for her to squeeze in beside him. He's smiling at her, looking less scruffy than usual, because he's just had his hair cut, and they delivered a hot shave while he was there, which means his face hasn't a single nick, and he's wearing his new suit, the one that fits so much better than anything Clemence has seen him in. There's even colour in his cheeks, or maybe the summer heat is getting to him. He's the only one who's looking at her now, because everyone else has turned to watch the bride and groom, walking arm and arm, Mrs. Yeung and Tom the handyman, who have found their happily ever after.

"My friends," Reverend Michelle begins, "we are gathered here today ..."

Acknowledgements

I began writing this book against the tragedy and uncertainty of the COVID-19 pandemic. I need to thank the healthcare workers who kept going through that terrible time, and the scientists whose innovations brought us to the other side. With everything that's happened since, it's easy to forget how most ordinary people kept their heads and did their best, even when things were hard. You are all my favourite part of the story.

The novels of Barbara Pym were inspiration for Clemence and her world (including the caterpillar), and I recommend these wholeheartedly. The notion of artfully refusing the question of how to be a woman comes from Rebecca Solnit's essay "The Mother of All Questions." Crampton's desire for the world to be a kinder place for strange people is an idea I never stopped thinking about after hearing it conveyed by Tracey Pegg, who was my children's first teacher at Huron Playschool and who taught my family most of the best things we know about community.

Thank you to my agent, Samantha Haywood, for being in my corner all these years, and to Eva Oakes, Megan Philipp, and everybody at the Transatlantic Agency for taking such good care of authors and our works.

As someone who has been wearing the same ratty House of Anansi T-shirt to bed since 2012, to have joined the incredible Anansi family feels like a perfect twist. Thank you to Shivaun Hearne and Karen Brochu for loving Clemence and her story as much as I do; Jenny McWha, Shannon Whibbs, and Alison Strobel for their attention to detail; Alysia Shewchuk and Melanie Lambrick for creating the perfect cover; and to Emma Rhodes, Melissa Shirley, Jessey Glibbery, Quinn Baker, Christina Valenzuela, Olivia Fellin, Emma Davis, and Leah Swalwell for all your hard work getting this book into the world.

Once again, I thank Joan Clare, Ken Clare, and Christy Massey for so many adventures and for supporting my writing aspirations, even when that seemed ill advised. To have Jennie Weller and Britt Leeking so present in my life after more than thirty years of friendship is the greatest gift. So is Erin Smith, who let me borrow her cat for my fiction. Thanks to all the friends who make my life a gorgeous tapestry, and to the particularly local ones who are part of the community I wrote this book in tribute to. To Suzy Krause, with whom I celebrated my book deal the day after we met. To Rebecca Rosenblum, Julia Zarankin, and Maria Meindl, writer friends since forever.

And Chantel Guertin, Kate Hilton, Elizabeth Renzetti, and Marissa Stapley, for being the real thing, in terms of literature and friendship both.

Biggest love to my children, Harriet and Iris—how lucky am I to share a world with you? And to Stuart, who, in the event of me bringing home a family of whale sharks, would start building an aquarium. You are my favourite person in the universe, and not even just because you're clever enough to know that the solution to too many books is taller bookshelves.

KERRY CLARE is the author of the novels *Asking for a Friend*, *Waiting for a Star to Fall*, and *Mitzi Bytes*, and editor of *The M Word: Conversations About Motherhood*. A National Magazine Award–nominated essayist, and editor of Canadian books website 49thShelf.com, she writes about books and reading at her longtime blog, *Pickle Me This*. She lives in Toronto with her family.